4

Praise for *Bitter I*

"A readable…story of generational tensions in America."

—*Kirkus Reviews*

"*Bitter Is the Wind* is…spiced with news events from the period that will bring back memories for anyone who grew up during the seventies."

—*Portland Book Review*

"I was struck by the clarity and simplicity of the prose—which reminded me of Hemingway's Nick Adams stories"

—Sami Moubayed, *The Huffington Post*

"Readers are treated to a story of working class experiences that especially excels in mentions of economic and social influence on character choices and evolution… As divergences appear much like cracks in the family structure, readers find themselves full circle in a winding story that follows family ties and ties to America itself."

—*Midwest Book Review*

"A pungent slice of working-class life in 1970s America, as well as a deeply-affecting father-son story. *Bitter Is the Wind* reminded me how hard it's always been to achieve success for those who weren't handed it on a silver platter."

—Stephen Fife, author of *The 13th Boy* and *Dreaming in the Maze of Love-Grief-Madness*

"A compelling tale of American aspiration and accomplishment told from the perspective of characters customarily deprived of opportunity, working folk whose lives and voices are rarely presented in first rate fiction."

—Frederic Hunter, author of *The Girl Ran Away*
and *A Year at the Edge of the Jungle*

"A fascinating character study and slice of life novel following two trapped men and how they attempt to cope with it. Honest and poignant, *Bitter Is the Wind* is a promising novel and points to McDermott as an author to watch."

—John Murray, *San Francisco Book Review*

"*Bitter Is the Wind* is a heartwarming story of the interactions between a father and son after they face horrible tragedy and get older. McDermott has done a fantastic job creating characters that are believable and easy to sympathize with. It is seldom that you come across a story about love, loss, and survival between a father and son that is not overly sappy and cliché."

—Amy Synoracki, *Manhattan Book Review*

"Jim McDermott brings us a great read in *Bitter Is the Wind.*"

—*Akshat Review*

Bitter Is the Wind

For Ted:
With gratitude
and much respect!

Thanks for your
support.

Jim McDermott
5.4.17

JIM MCDERMOTT

Bitter Is the Wind

a novel

A Genuine Vireo Book • *Rare Bird Books*
Los Angeles, Calif.

THIS IS A GENUINE VIREO BOOK

A Vireo Book | Rare Bird Books
453 South Spring Street, Suite 302
Los Angeles, CA 90013
rarebirdbooks.com

Set in Minion
Printed in the United States

Book design by Karl Lord
Cover photograph by Nancy Kennedy

10 9 8 7 6 5 4 3 2 1

Paperback ISBN: 978-1-945572-14-2

Publisher's Cataloging-in-Publication data

Names: McDermott, Jim, 1960-, author.
Title: Bitter is the wind : a novel / Jim McDermott.
Description: Hardcover edition | A Vireo Book | Los Angeles, CA:
Rare Bird Books, 2016.
Identifiers: ISBN 978-1-945572-15-9
Subjects: LCSH Bildungsroman. | Families—Fiction. | Father and
sons—Fiction. | Family-owned business enterprises—Fiction. | Working
class—Fiction. | Blue collar workers—Fiction. | American Dream—Fiction.
| New York (State)—Fiction. | New York (N.Y.)—Fiction. | BISAC FICTION
/ General.
Classification: LCC PS3613.C386886 B58 2016 | DDC 813.6—dc23.

For Pete Statelman

Who helped clarify this story,
Then vanished into his own.

And when rude death rides that wind of woes
To snatch a loved one from this living dance
Life becomes shadowed, empty, and unpinned,
Christ! bitter is the wind.

— George Johnson Jr.

CONTENTS

Trouble

DURING HIS FIRST SUSPENSION from Netherwood Junior High School in rural upstate New York for throwing ice cubes down a girl's shirt, George Johnson Jr. passed the time at home by himself. The thirteen-year-old boy played catch with a pitchback, an elastic net framed with aluminum poles. His Brittany spaniel, Buddy, watched the baseball rhythmically fly into the net and snap back into his waiting glove.

George remembered that, three years earlier, the 1969 New York Mets won thirty-eight of their final forty-eight games to capture the National League Eastern Division title. The Mets swept the Atlanta Braves in the playoffs and beat the Baltimore Orioles in five games to become world champions. George's mind focused on game three of the World Series. Tommie Agee made two spectacular catches in center field, robbing the Orioles of at least five runs.

Then he imagined himself, a scrawny baby-faced kid with predatory green eyes and long brown hair wearing a baggy uniform, stepping up to the plate. He belted a home run and was mugged by his teammates at home plate. Next he appeared on the mound, striking out batters with a blazing fastball and a sweeping curve. He made diving catches in the field, playing all nine positions.

George released the ball too early and it sailed over the pitchback. Buddy obediently returned it. George threw once more. The pitchback returned a hard grounder that he fielded in the webbing of his glove. He tried again to imagine the sold-out major league stadium, but couldn't. All that came to him was a dark, empty field. He took a deep breath and walked over to the well in the back of his house and filled his mug with water and sat on the cinderblocks bordering the well. Buddy meandered over and lay down. George drank half the water and let Buddy lap up the rest.

"Hey, Buddy," he said, patting the dog's head. "You think I'll ever get to the big leagues?"

The boy rose and walked into the house. Buddy followed behind him. George opened the upstairs hall closet. From a shoebox stuffed with baseball cards he pulled out a yellowed newspaper, *The Hudson Valley Watch*, and went into his bedroom, where he lay down on his bed before reading.

Mother and Daughter Killed in Car Wreck

Salt Point, NY, Feb 12, 1966—Mary Johnson and her two-year-old daughter, Susan, were killed yesterday by a tractor-trailer. They were pronounced dead at the scene. Mrs. Johnson was driving north on Creek Lane in her Volkswagen Beetle. An eighteen-wheeler driven by Gregory O. Dodson of the Bronx jackknifed and slid through the Salt Point Road intersection, crushing Mrs. Johnson's Beetle into a tree. Dodson was unharmed.

Mrs. Johnson is survived by her husband, George Johnson Sr., and a seven-year-old son, George Johnson Jr. A funeral will be held at 2:00 p.m. this Monday in Salt Point Cemetery.

GEORGE METICULOUSLY RE-FOLDED THE newspaper and pictured his mother's and sister's names carved into their gravestone. He rubbed his hands over his closed eyes, moving them downward past his thin nose and mouth. With both hands resting on his chin, he recalled a scene from six years earlier. In the morgue his father quietly kissed his mother's and sister's lifeless bodies. His father signed whatever papers needed signing. At home his father packed his mother's and sister's belongings into separate black garbage bags—clothes, shoes, Susan's toys.

George listened to the steady bursts of air leaving his dog's nostrils. Years of companionship remained with his Brittany spaniel, George told himself. Unless, of course, Buddy ended up in the way of a truck. George rolled off the bed and lay down on the rug next to Buddy, enveloping the dog in his arms and up against his chest. After a minute, he kissed the top of Buddy's head, rose, and returned the folded newspaper to the shoebox.

❖

BETWEEN HER CIGARETTE BREAKS, Miss Annette Mackey taught science. Three days into her first attempt to quit smoking, she observed George staring out the window. A family of squirrels was playing near the base of a maple tree. George smiled. It seemed as if the mother squirrel was playing tag with her kids.

"George," Miss Mackey called out, "recite for the class the first five elements of the periodic table."

George turned toward his teacher and stared at her red hair and freckles. "What's a periodic table?" he finally said.

Miss Mackey rolled her eyes. "You ought to pay attention to me," she instructed. "Those squirrels can't teach you science."

Laughter filled the classroom. George lowered his head, stared at the doodles that students of years past had etched into his desk, and resolved to get even with his science teacher.

He knew Miss Mackey cherished the workbooks her students used to record experiments, which accounted for half of a student's grade. She stored them alphabetically in a large cardboard box at the back of her classroom.

A week after being criticized, George sat in the front of class listening to Miss Mackey's lecture on the chemical components of pesticides used in crop dusting. When the bell rang, students began to file out of the classroom. George walked past the cardboard box and nonchalantly flipped a lighted match onto the workbooks, producing a magnificent fire. George slowed his gait to gauge Miss Mackey's reaction. He watched her running from the flames, flailing her arms like an octopus. She rushed to the front of the classroom, grabbed the fire extinguisher and put out the fire. All the books were covered with wet, gooey white foam.

At least one person could identify George as the arsonist. Jennifer Conlin was one of the tallest girls in the eighth grade, and the hairspray she plastered on her blonde hair made her appear even taller. She also had a developed bosom, which made her one of George's prime ice cube targets.

Miss Mackey conducted interviews to identify the guilty student. She quickly narrowed the universe of potential culprits to five students.

The interview process took half a day. George denied starting the fire. He reminded Miss Mackey of his perfect scores on the first two experiments. Why would he want to destroy his successful work?

Jennifer was interviewed last.

"Did you see who started the fire?" Miss Mackey asked.

"Uh, no," Jennifer replied.

"I don't believe you. Whoever set that fire was destroying your work. Whoever set that fire could have burned you or someone else. You can't protect such a person. He or she has to be punished. Now, Jennifer," Miss Mackey's voice lowered, "let me ask you one last time. Did you see who started the fire?"

Jennifer hesitated, "I'll only tell if you promise not to say who ratted on him."

"I promise. Now, tell me."

"It was…George Johnson."

"Are you sure?"

"Yeah. I saw him light a match as we were leaving class. I wondered what he was doing. I kept watching him. Then I saw him throw the match in the box."

"Thank you, Jennifer. I'll keep your confidence."

Miss Mackey spoke to Frank Taylor, the Netherwood Junior High School principal, who placed a telephone call to George's dad.

❖

THE JOHNSONS LIVED ON Fox Run Road, a dirt road on the outskirts of Salt Point. All the houses were built on the north side of the road; the south side bordered a swamp, which breathed its stench on all who ventured into it. The quagmire extended all the way to Netherwood Road, the only paved road connecting the town of Deer Creek with the unincorporated Village of Salt Point.

According to the 1970 census figures, 2,800 people lived in Deer Creek. Many of Deer Creek's residents worked at Woo Industrial Laboratories, which manufactured treated glass of assorted sizes and shapes for the burgeoning computer industry, anchored in the Hudson Valley by IBM. Salt Point had 150 residents and its own post office. A blinking traffic light stood at the heart of the Village, bordered by the post office, PJ's Salt Point Grocery, a Texaco station, and evergreen trees.

The Johnsons lived two miles from the Village in a nine hundred-square-foot white Cape Cod house with blue shutters. A dilapidated and windowless barn that had been boarded up sat on one end of their property. George and Mary Johnson bought the small house when they married in 1958. Both were fresh out of Deer Creek High. They began dating during the spring of their junior year. By then, George was a local baseball star who became an all-New York State shortstop for two consecutive years.

Mary Pierson and her friends always watched Deer Creek's home baseball games. Mary became smitten with the shortstop.

Soon Mary and George became inseparable. They stored books in each other's lockers. George walked Mary to her classes. In the middle of George's senior season, he visited the Pierson house.

"George, get in here!" Mr. Pierson exclaimed, opening the screen door.

"Hello, everyone," George said. He saw Mrs. Pierson and Mary, each sitting with their legs crossed in the two living room chairs. Mary appeared worried; her eyes left George's eyes and veered toward her father, who was pacing around the living room. George took a seat on the couch. A few moments later, Mr. Pierson sat down on the couch beside him.

"George, Mary and her mother have just come from Dr. Irving's office," Mr. Pierson said. He looked at his daughter. Mary averted her eyes.

"Are you all right?" George asked.

"I don't know how to say this." Mr. Pierson paused. "She's not okay. Mary's pregnant. She says you're the father."

Three sets of troubled eyes fixed on George. Even the German shepherd lying on the living room floor awakened with interest. George let out a deep breath. What to do? What to say? George wished he could talk to Mary alone. Should he admit it? Should he deny it? Should he hug Mary? Should he leave? Adrenaline surged through his body. His pulse quickened.

"It's me, sir," he began, coughing up the words. "I love Mary. Can I talk to her alone?"

"Okay."

Mary and George walked down the driveway, out of earshot from the house. George turned to face Mary and took hold of her shoulders. He stared into her eyes. "We shoulda used something."

Tears began dripping down Mary's cheeks. "Yeah. I thought we were safe. I'm sorry."

"We're both responsible."

"I know. It's awful. I know you've got designs on getting out of here. Going to college, playing baseball."

George stepped back from Mary and looked up at the crescent moon. "Listen, I'm with you on this. I'm not going anyplace."

"That's what my father wants to hear." Mary licked the tears away from her mouth. "And that's what I want to hear."

The next day, George consulted with the St. Stanislaus Parish priest. They spoke in the rectory.

"I'm sorry to learn of this, my son," Father Norman Dombrowski replied. "But the Lord moves in ways not always discernible to his worshipers."

"Father, what about an abortion? College coaches keep calling the house. I'm having a great year again. First in the league in hitting. I'm gonna get a scholarship. Probably even gonna get drafted."

The priest frowned. "You've been an altar boy in this parish for seven years, George. You've earned my respect and admiration. And the congregation's. You know the Church's teachings. You can't violate them. You have a responsibility to your maker. And to the girl."

That discussion ended George's search for an alternative to marriage and family. The Mets drafted him in the fourteenth round, but offered no signing bonus. The expenses of a wife and baby made the choice obvious. After graduation, George took a job on the chrome-plated glass line at Woo Labs.

In the summer of 1958, Father Dombrowski performed the marriage ceremony. The newlyweds honeymooned at Niagara Falls, then moved into the house on Fox Run Road.

Mary gave birth to George Johnson Jr. in the winter of 1959. Visitors remarked that he had large green eyes like his father's. In 1964, Mary gave birth to a second child, Susan Erica.

❖

AS PRINCIPAL TAYLOR EXPLAINED Miss Mackey's classroom fire over the telephone, George Sr. felt his heart rate quicken. Men were filing past him out of the company cafeteria, but he didn't notice. When the principal hung up, George held the pay phone receiver in his right hand, staring into it, replaying the description of his boy's latest escapade. The foreman tapped him on the shoulder. Racks of glass needed to be moved down the line.

Once George's shift ended, he raced toward his truck in the employee parking lot. George Jr. and Buddy were inside the barn when he pulled his pickup into the garage. George Sr. cut the engine, got out, slammed the truck's door, and walked out of the garage.

"Hey, Dad! Check this out!"

"I'm coming." He walked toward the barn, carrying his lunch pail. Once inside, he saw a slow-moving animal in one corner. George Jr. and Buddy seemed to be playing with it.

"What's goin' on?" the elder Johnson asked.

"Buddy caught a woodchuck. Maybe it's the critter that's been messin' with them rhubarb bushes."

"*The* bushes George. Not *them* bushes."

"I know, Dad. *The* bushes."

"How'd a woodchuck get in the barn?"

"Buddy chased it in here. He whacks it a few times, even sits on it some. Just when I think that bugger's gonna get away, Buddy corners it again. It's pretty slow now. But you shoulda seen it before."

"It's half dead, son. We should put it out of its misery. I'll be right back."

When the elder Johnson returned with a 12-gauge shotgun, George Jr. was on all fours on the dirt floor. Buddy barked, and the boy imitated Buddy's sounds. George Sr. loaded the shell into the chamber and removed the safety.

"Hey, Dad. Let me shoot 'em. Please?"

"You're too young to be shooting guns. Guns kill, as you're about to see."

"I've never even taken one shot. Other parents let their kids shoot guns. I asked Father Dombrowski if guns're okay. He says they are."

George Sr. let out a deep breath. The fast-paced, stream-of-consciousness argument was typical. The boy loaded all his thoughts into his lungs and then blurted them out.

"Father Dombrowski isn't raising you. I am. Father Dombrowski's a priest. He's never been a parent himself." George Sr. pointed toward the barn's wall. "Look, take Buddy and move over there. I'm gonna shoot the woodchuck. Then you and I need to talk."

George Sr. fired one shot. Buddy flinched, then walked over to sniff the dead rodent. George Sr. pushed Buddy out of the way, picked up the woodchuck with a garden shovel, and put it in a plastic trash bag, which he tossed into the metal trash can. Father and son walked into the house. Buddy stayed outside.

Something was bothering his father, and George Jr. knew that it involved him. He decided against prompting. Eventually it would come out. And it wasn't going to be good. Maybe the problem would disappear. Monday Night Football would be on, but not until 9:00 p.m.

George Jr. helped his father prepare spaghetti and tomato sauce for dinner. For the dinner greens, George Sr. boiled two servings of frozen beans, harvested from their garden the previous summer.

George Jr. ate a few beans and scattered the rest around his plate. When George Sr. rose to change the Loretta Lynn record— "Louisiana Woman, Mississippi Man"—George Jr. tilted his plate and slid most of the green beans into the napkin resting on his lap.

"Wadja put on?" he asked.

"Johnny Cash. His new one."

"I don't like that jailbird. I'm gonna start the dishes."

"What about the beans that're still on your plate?"

"I ate most of 'em."

George Sr. glared at his son.

"Alright. I'm eating 'em right now." George stuffed the three beans into his mouth. "See," he said as he swallowed.

He rose from his seat and slipped the napkin full of the uneaten beans under his plate. He picked up his silverware, walked into the kitchen, and buried the napkin in the trash bag. A few seconds later, George Sr. handed his plate to his son. They both finished cleaning up the kitchen.

As they walked into the living room, George Jr. headed straight for the black & white television set.

"Don't turn on the TV," the elder Johnson said. "We have to talk." George Jr. pivoted and walked to the blue reclining chair. He didn't want to sit next to his father on the couch.

"I got a call today from Principal Taylor." George Sr. paused and watched his son trying to prevent his body language from showing any tension. "A student started a fire in Miss Mackey's science class by throwing a lighted match into a box of workbooks. The principal says you did it."

George Jr. couldn't believe that anyone saw him throw the match. He was aware of his track record at school. And he couldn't decide whether to tell his father the truth. "Don't you see what they're doing, Dad? They can't find out who did it, so they're makin' me the fall guy. I'm the logical choice."

"Did you do it?"

George Jr. took a deep breath. "Yeah."

George Sr. rubbed his eyes with both hands. "Why? How come?"

"Miss Mackey made fun of me in class. She asked me a question. I didn't know the answer. I was watching a mother squirrel run after her babies. That made me think of Mom playing tag with me and Susan, right after Susan started walking."

"But, son—"

"Miss Mackey said I live in a fantasy world. The other kids started laughing. She made me look like an idiot."

"Do you really think that starting a *fire* is the way to get even? If Mom were here, what do you think she'd say?"

Young George squirmed in the recliner. "Ahh, Dad. I don't know. Mom hasn't been around for so long." He raised his hands to cover his eyes, and then began tapping them against his forehead. "Maybe she'd see this my way." He lowered his hands and folded his arms across his chest. "Or maybe she wouldn't. I miss having her around."

The elder Johnson bit his lower lip. "Yeah, me too. Me, too." He took a deep breath. "What're we gonna do about Miss Mackey?"

Young George glanced down at the carpet. "Aw, she's so boring. It's hard to pay attention. Besides, her stuff is so easy. She comes in and says the same things that're in the book. What's the point in that? I get all As! I daydream, so what! At least I go to class. I couldn't talk back to her. I'd definitely get in trouble for that. So I got even. But no one saw me do it."

George Sr. absorbed his son's outburst, unsure how to handle it. "Principal Taylor wants to meet with us. What do you think we should tell him?"

George leaned forward in the recliner. "Let's go see what he's got on me. If he's got something, then I'll have to own up. But if he's got nothing, why admit it?"

"I don't think it's gonna work. I'm really disturbed by this. Lighting fires is dangerous. You overreacted. She's the teacher. She makes the rules. Don't you see that?"

"I guess so," George Jr. forced himself to say. "But I just burned books. That's all. The box was on a formica counter. The walls are concrete. Plus, there's a fire extinguisher on the wall. It was safe."

"People could've gotten hurt."

"Okay," young George admitted. "I won't do it again. Promise."

"Hey, before we turn on the TV, there's something I wanna tell you. It's important."

"Okay."

"Look, I work on an assembly line. In a dead-end job. I work with people who only think of today. Paycheck to paycheck. That's how they live. Never for tomorrow. Only for today. They don't have an education. Neither do I, for that matter." George Sr. rose and faced his son. "But I've always thought about tomorrow. You gotta enjoy today, but you gotta think about tomorrow. I've managed to get a little something for myself. A house, some land, a job that pays a decent wage. But more important, I've got you. You're my pride and joy. I was a poor student in school, just playing baseball. But you've got a real brain in your head. You've got a chance to make something of yourself. Me, I only got a little. You can get a lot. But these outbursts worry me."

"Hey, Dad. It's—"

"Look, don't mess up, okay? Education is the key. Education is your ticket outta here."

The crack in his father's voice caused George's eyes to fill with tears. He tried to relieve the build-up by blinking. "Dad, I know you're looking out for me," he said. "But I'm okay. My schoolwork's fine. I'll keep my grades up. I promise."

"Okay. Stay on the right track. Don't lose sight of things."

"I won't."

"Alright, tomorrow I'll call Principal Taylor. I'll tell him it's a case of mistaken identity. We'll see what he says." George Sr. sat down. "Who's playing tonight?"

"The Jets and Bears. The game's at Shea."

"Who's favored?"

"Joe Willie Whiteshoes and the Jets by three. The Bears have too many injuries."

"I'll take the Bears and the three points."

"What're we betting?"

"The dishes tomorrow night. Wash and dry."

"You're on."

❖

ON HIS MORNING BREAK, George Sr. telephoned Netherwood Junior High School. He told Principal Taylor that his son denied starting the fire. Principal Taylor reiterated that George was the culprit, but that the Johnsons could appear for a hearing at three thirty that afternoon.

George Sr. hung up, realizing he wouldn't see his son until right before the hearing. He thought about calling the principal back and acknowledging George's guilt, but that would have meant breaking the promise he gave to his son. He shook his head and went back to the line. Five hours later, he drove to Netherwood.

Miss Mackey and the Johnsons sat in the anteroom of the principal's office, waiting to be summoned inside. The junior high principal waved them in, closed the door, and returned to the seat behind his desk. Frank Taylor was a robust, middle-aged man whose piercing eyes glared over the top of the bifocal glasses that rested on the tip of his nose. He carried a large gold watch appended to his vest by a gleaming gold chain. "This is a very, very serious matter," he finally said.

"Like I said on the phone, my son denies starting the fire," George Sr. replied. Surprised by the position his father staked out, George Jr. nodded and stared at the principal's watch. He felt warm inside listening to his father defending him, lying for him. A loved one standing up to a hated one.

"Our evidence shows otherwise. Miss Mackey, please summarize." The science teacher recounted her interviews, confirming that one student said George started the fire.

Young George's gaze wandered under Principal Taylor's desk. He could see that the principal's pants were too tight in the groin. He imagined the principal's scrotum littered with stray hairs sprouting in all directions. When Miss Mackey finished, George asked, "Who says they saw me throw a match?"

"I can't say which student saw you. I gave my word."

"That's it?" George exclaimed as he turned from Miss Mackey to Principal Taylor. "That's what means I did it? This is unbelievable!"

"Mr. Taylor, you did say that the evidence undoubtedly pointed to my son," George Sr. interjected. "There's room for doubt here, don't you think?"

"I don't think so, Mr. Johnson. Miss Mackey has an eyewitness account of your son throwing the match in the box. Nothing refutes that."

"I refute that!" George Jr. screamed. He jumped to his feet, pointing his right index finger at Taylor. "You're saying that I'm lying, aren't you?"

"Sit down, young man!" Principal Taylor snapped. He turned toward George Sr. "Can't you control him?" The principal turned back to George Jr. "I'm saying this. The overwhelming evidence points to you. You should end this charade and admit to starting the fire. You'll feel better."

"I feel fine! You're just lining up against me. But you're lining up against the wrong guy."

"Are you through?" the principal asked.

"Yeah," young George answered. He looked at his father. "Yeah."

"Alright. I'm going to rule," Principal Taylor announced. "This can't go unpunished. George is a repeat offender. I'm suspending him for three days, starting tomorrow."

George Jr. rose from his chair and stormed out. His father followed behind.

That night, young George went to his room right after dinner. He had an English paper due the following Monday. The assignment was to write an essay about an heroic act.

The Most Inspirational Four Points in
the History of Basketball

May 8, 1970 was a rare day in the life of most basketball fans. One particular New York Knicks fan will never forget that day.

The Knicks, led by their six-foot-nine-inch center, captain Willis Reed, were set to face the Los Angeles Lakers, led by the legendary seven-foot Wilt Chamberlain, in game seven of the National Basketball Association finals. New York's beloved Knicks had never won an NBA title in the franchise's history. But Willis Reed's leg injury cast a dark shadow over the Madison Square Garden crowd.

A deafening cheer exploded when the Knicks came onto the court from the locker room to begin warm-ups. DeBusschere, Bradley, Frazier, Barnett—those four starters were present—but where was the Knicks' center? Knowing Reed had torn a right thigh muscle in game five, and that his right knee must be feeling the strain of years of wear and tear, most Knicks fans thought Willis Reed would be unable to play in game seven. Reed's absence from the warm-ups confirmed the crowd's worst fears—he was too hurt to play. Chamberlain would be able to score at will, as he did in the Lakers' victory in game six.

Minutes later, after receiving a painkilling injection in his leg, a large black man wearing a Knicks uniform appeared at one end of the court. Could it be—was Willis Reed going to try to play? The crowd roared as Willis limped to the Knicks' end of the court. The grimace on his face told of the pain. All eyes were focused on him. Even the Lakers' players stopped to watch Willis take a few short warm-up shots.

Chamberlain won the opening tip. When the Knicks got the ball, Willis limped from the baseline to the foul line. A teammate passed him the ball. Chamberlain stayed back under the basket, looking to prevent a pass in the lane. Willis turned toward the basket and arched a left-handed jump shot. Swish! The crowd roared. The Knicks' players were patting Willis on the behind or back. My father looked at me with a big, wide grin on his face. "Yeah!" I shouted.

Minutes later, Willis made another jump shot near the foul line. Again, chaos.

Barely able to walk, Willis Reed played an incredible twenty-seven minutes that day. After beginning the game with four points, he never scored again. But the Lakers were never able to regain their momentum after those early minutes. When the final buzzer sounded, the Knicks' players mobbed Willis Reed. The Madison Square Garden crowd swarmed onto the court. My father and I stood up with our fists pumping in the air. Then we hugged. I can't remember the final score.

By George Johnson Jr.

GEORGE JR.'S ESSAY RECEIVED a note of commendation. George Sr. taped the note and the essay on the wall right over his position on the line. He enclosed them both in plastic, so the hydrochloric acid that sprayed off the glass plates wouldn't damage them.

❖

BETWEEN HIS EARLY TWENTIES and early thirties, George Sr.'s lean physique had become more defined. He gained twenty pounds within a few years after marrying Mary, and the added weight was evenly distributed. His protruding ribs no longer drew stares at the swimming hole. Physical exertion built up his muscles. Yet George's bright green eyes remained his most distinguishing feature. Over time, grooves began to appear on his forehead, along with crow's feet near his eyes. And his hair became dotted with gray.

George spent most nights at home with his son watching television. Once his son started doing homework, the elder Johnson began using some of the time to read. First, the newspaper, next magazines, then books. He bought *My Favorite Huddles* and *Baseball Needs Cheerleaders* at the Deer Creek book bazaar. He seemed bewildered in a bookstore, but not buying feed at Agway.

Occasionally, George wore his only three-piece suit, navy blue, with a peaked lapel and flared trousers. The fabric was 100 percent polyester. He hated putting on that suit, and his awkwardness in it was apparent. His speech and other mannerisms became more formal. He didn't know whether to hold open a door for a woman. He didn't know whether to let a woman enter a room ahead of him. He didn't know whether a greeting called for a handshake or a simple nod of the head. Mostly, he looked forward to getting home and changing out of the suit. He wore it to weddings, funerals, school events, and church.

One place George never wore the suit was to the Shop Rite, where he stopped after work on Fridays to buy groceries for the following week. One Friday afternoon, he ordered a pound of ground beef. Behind him in line was a woman dressed in a white nurse's uniform, with thick white stockings and white shoes.

She tapped George on the shoulder and waited for him to turn around. "Buy ground chuck instead. It has a lower fat content."

"Really?" George said.

"The extra cost is worth it."

George hesitated long enough for the butcher to begin weighing the ground beef. "Excuse me," George said. "Ah, change my order to ground chuck."

"Whadaya doin' to me, pal," the butcher replied. "I already got the beef weighed."

"Well, I want the ground chuck instead. Sorry."

"Alright."

"Thank you," George said to the nurse, who followed him from the meat counter to the frozen food aisle.

"I'm sorry if I got you in trouble with the butcher," she offered.

"No problem. And thanks for the tip. I appreciate it." He turned and faced the frozen food display, opened the glass door, and chose two Hungry Man TV dinners.

"You probably don't want a lecture on the preservatives in frozen foods," she said through a sheepish smile.

"Thank you for your interest, ma'am. But me and my boy, we do okay in the kitchen."

Still smiling, she said, "I'm Sarabeth Roth." She pointed to her badge. *LPN at Hudson River Psychiatric Hospital.* She extended her hand.

George shook it, unsure of whether to grasp it firmly or gingerly. He settled on a firm grasp.

"George Johnson," he said. "I work at Woo Labs."

"It's funny that you're raising a boy by yourself. I'm raising two little boys alone as well. They're at their father's house for the summer."

Before they reached the checkout counter, George accepted Sarabeth Roth's invitation for a preservative-free dinner at her home that Saturday. He arranged for his son to spend the night at a friend's house.

❖

GEORGE SR. KEPT ONLY two framed photos in the house. Both stood on the night table in his bedroom. The first showed father and son before George Jr.'s sixth grade graduation. The second was an eight-by-ten glossy of Mary holding Susan in her arms, taken at Deer Creek Studio a few months after their daughter's birth. George studied Mary's half-smile, pondering what she might be thinking of his behavior.

Mary's penetrating brown eyes led him to remember how she cupped her hands behind his back when they embraced. He remembered how Mary's hands latched together and nestled into the small of his back, pressing inward as if to tell him their embrace would never end.

The immediacy and intensity of George's recall had faded. But it hadn't disappeared. George continued peering into Mary's face. He again felt the tingling in his bones that crowded out other emotions. Instantly he returned to Mary's half-smile, and her spell lingered until his cheeks flushed with heat and became red. His eyes welled up with tears. George blinked. The blinking reminded him that his wife was dead and another woman was expecting him for dinner in half an hour.

George's thoughts turned to Sarabeth Roth, who exuded warmth and a certain authenticity. She had a down-home charm and a spotless uniform. He wanted to bring wine or flowers to dinner, but knew little about either. Figuring that a bottle of wine cost as much as fixing dinner himself, he ruled out wine for the first date. The prohibitive cost of flowers, and their inevitable early death, made them even less desirable than wine. He knew that women liked flowers, but they just stood there for a few days, then wilted and died.

On the way to dinner, George parked his pickup in front of Mrs. Nesbith's house on Malone Road. A widow in her early eighties, she was hospitalized, recovering from a stroke. Mrs. Nesbith had been an avid gardener who divided her garden between vegetables and the marigolds, daisies, and shrubs that surrounded her front porch.

George shunned the marigolds, which didn't look like they'd be sold by a florist. Using kitchen scissors, he clipped a few white and yellow daisies and placed them in a small glass vase he'd brought from his kitchen. He added a little water from Mrs. Nesbith's garden hose to the vase.

"They're beautiful! How thoughtful of you," Sarabeth Roth exclaimed when she greeted George in the vestibule of her apartment building. George's pangs of guilt subsided; a sense of accomplishment came over him.

Sarabeth wore a light green, short-sleeved blouse and light brown slacks that revealed a curvaceous figure, not lacking muscle tone. Through Sarabeth's silk blouse, George could see the lace of her bra.

As they walked upstairs to her second floor apartment, George could smell garlic.

"We're having baked chicken. Hope that's okay."

George smiled. "Smells healthy."

Over dinner, Sarabeth asked, "How come you and your wife had just one child?"

"Actually, we had two. Our daughter was also killed in the car accident."

"Oh, my. Sorry. I didn't know."

George bit his lower lip.

"I can't imagine having to outlive your child."

"You always carry it with you. You don't forget. You can't."

Sarabeth reached her hand across the table and grasped George's forearm.

He looked in her eyes. "Really made me feel helpless."

After dessert, he kissed her goodnight outside her apartment door.

On their second date, over an after-dinner coffee, George told Sarabeth about his twenty-second birthday when the unfairness of his life had scorched him with a rage so real and deep that he raised four racks of tightly packed glass over his head, glanced sideways, and made eye contact with the foreman. He should've graduated college or been playing professional baseball instead of being trapped inside a clean room. A few moments later he lowered the racks of glass back to their place on line three.

"Why didn't I smash the glass and leave? Why didn't I take a piece and slash my wrists?" he asked Sarabeth, staring into her eyes. "Because I had a wife and family to support. But that couldn't have been the only reason. Some force kept me walking that line without falling off. But what force?"

Sarabeth found herself inching away from George. She'd considered sleeping with him that night, but felt anxious. George stopped talking, but Sarabeth didn't know what to say. She offered George a half-smile and an awkward grunt.

"Well, who knows? After thinking about my life for the past thirteen years," George continued, "I know I missed out on getting an education. It all started with the pregnancy and quick marriage. I just didn't know any better. And I wonder how I could have."

Sarabeth folded her hands across her chest. "Hey, what's it like to work in a clean room?" she asked.

"Geez, guys at Woo start at the beginning of the line and work their way up toward the end. Promotions mean moving closer to the final product. Clean room regulations require everybody to wear a white jumpsuit, white booties, white hood, white gloves. The outfit makes me feel like the lunch lady in a high school cafeteria."

Sarabeth reached for George's hand. His eyes remained fixed on a spot on the floor underneath her coffee table.

"Why'd your marriage last ten years if your husband was such a jerk?" George asked.

"Well...I don't know where to begin. I..."

"Hey, you can share your secrets with me. It's okay." George turned his body sideways on the couch. He gently placed both hands on her shoulders in a way that couldn't be interpreted as a sexual advance. "Really, I'd like to know," he emphasized.

"Right after we were married, I got pregnant. The next year, I got pregnant again. I never thought our marriage was all that great." She shrugged at George. "We had food on the table and he never hit me."

"Where does he work?"

"He also works at Woo. In supplies."

"What's his name?"

"Byron—"

"Byron Roth. Never heard the name."

"No, not Byron Roth. Roth's my maiden name. Byron Adams."

"Oh, Adams! Yeah, I know the guy. He's our requisition clerk. Looks like a lumber yard worker, full beard, tattoos. Seems like a nice guy."

"Well, he's not so nice. He left me and the kids for some high school floozy."

George touched her knee. "I'm sorry," he said.

"Well don't be. I've been to counseling since then. And it's worthwhile. Very worthwhile. I've learned a lot about myself that I didn't know when I was married."

George took a sip of coffee. "Well, what's the most important thing you learned?" he asked.

"You're surprised that I see a psychologist, aren't you?"

"Yeah. I'm surprised, yeah."

"That's okay. At least you're honest about it."

"Well, what did he say?"

"It was a she. Basically, she said I have a low self-image. Byron used to put me down a lot. Told me I wasn't as exciting or as attractive as I used to be. I believed him. I thought I was doing everything wrong. But really, it was him. You know, we had a terrible sex life."

George gulped down the hot coffee in his mouth. "How bad could it have been?" he asked, wiping his mouth.

"You'd better not have anything in your mouth when I tell you this," she responded. George set his mug on the coffee table and looked back at Sarabeth. "My husband would only have sex with me at seven thirty on Friday nights. And only in the missionary position. It usually lasted less than a minute. If I was late to the bed, I'd have to wait until the following Friday."

George paused to digest what he had just heard. He seemed to be two words behind every word that came out of her mouth. "Why'd you put up with that for ten years?" he finally asked.

"Why do women put up with being beaten by their husbands?"

George shrugged.

"Because a lot of women don't know any better, that's why! You're Catholic. You can appreciate this. Catholic women are supposed to be virgins when they're married. So when we have sex for the first time, we don't know any better. We think it's *wonderful*, no matter how infrequent or dull it is. We're supposed to marry for life. To love, honor, and *obey* our husbands. When you combine those teachings with a lack of communication—we're *not* supposed to talk to our friends about our sex lives—what do you expect? We have no basis for comparison."

Most of what she said flowed right past George. He looked at her extra-long eyelashes, wondering if they were natural or phony, and contemplated what to do next. His penis twitched, announcing the impending arrival of an erection; his eyes settled on a lithograph behind the kitchen counter. A Mexican man, wearing a sombrero, walked alongside a pier toward a bait shop. Empty canoes were tied to the dock. George shook his head, steeped in the realization that baggage would go along with this encounter. Heavy baggage.

George lifted Sarabeth to her feet, angling her sobbing frame toward the bedroom.

The next evening, as George finished reciting his Sunday prayers on the side of his bed, an idea popped into his head. It was almost as if God had sent it down himself. *Get a vasectomy.* He walked out of the bedroom into the living room and took the dictionary off the book shelf. He fumbled through the "V"s. *Vasectomy—the surgical removal of all or part of the vas deferens. Not much help there—what's a vas deferens?* George's eyes wandered up the page. He found vas deferens—*the convoluted duct that conveys sperm from the testicle to the ejaculatory duct of the penis.* He could look up convoluted and duct, but he had a general idea of what would be involved.

George made an appointment with Dr. Irving, who made medicine understandable.

"I'll still be able to get it up, right?" George asked.

"Yes, that won't be affected."

"You're sure now."

"Yes, I'm sure."

"Well, schedule me for the operation then."

At his biweekly confession, George told Father Dombrowski about his vasectomy appointment. The priest stepped out of the confessional booth and opened the door to George's side. "Come with me," he said. George followed Father Dombrowski into the rectory, taking a seat in the chair across from the priest's desk.

"Having this operation would be sacrilegious."

"I'm not doing it for me," George said, arching his back so that his eyes met Father Dombrowski's. "I'm raising a son by myself. I'm making a vow not to have children with another woman. It's a way to remember Mary. To honor our family. What's wrong with that?"

"George, it violates the Church's teachings. Vasectomy is a method of preventing conception."

"What happens if I go through with it?"

"You will be committing a grave sin. You'll not be able to receive the sacraments. You'll no longer be in the state of grace. You'll no longer be involved in collections during mass." He looked sympathetically at George. "The Catholic church isn't flexible on this."

George looked at the hardwood floor for a few seconds. "I'm sorry, Father. But I'm going through with it. I don't think I'm violating God's will."

He had the operation a few weeks later. Father Dombrowski barred him from taking up collections and receiving communion at mass. Members of the St. Stanislaus Parish speculated that George Johnson Sr. must have been one helluva sinner.

George hated sitting in the pews while others received the body and blood of Christ. Parishioners made signs of the cross when they passed by him on the way back to their seats after communion. George sat as far back in the pews as he could. Soon he stopped going to mass altogether.

Young George pressed his father on the subject.

"That's between the Church and me," the elder Johnson said.

Most Sundays, George Sr. arranged for neighbors to take his son to church. Other neighbors brought George Jr. home on Sunday afternoons. When rides were unavailable, his father dropped him off and picked him up at St. Stanislaus. George Sr. parked his truck on the street outside the church, but never went inside. Instead, he prayed by himself, turning his body sideways in the truck to face the church's entrance.

❖

WINTER CAME EARLY TO Salt Point in 1972. The first snow fell in mid-November, and the Village got hit with fourteen inches. Woo Labs remained open. The plows cleared the main roads on the second afternoon, and George Jr. telephoned his father to tell him he was biking into the Village. The elder Johnson told him to watch for patches of ice and to call when he reached the pay phone next to the blinking light.

George took an extra dime with him and lugged his bike through the unplowed snow covering Fox Run Road. Buddy followed, gallivanting in the snow. When they reached Netherwood Road, George sent Buddy home. With his father's instructions echoing in his head, George peddled around the ice patches, especially those visible as he descended the steep hill that joined Netherwood Road with Salt Point Turnpike. A few cars passed him on their journey into the Village. A UPS truck approached from the opposite direction, spewing reddish-brown snow and fresh sand onto George's blue jeans.

Fifteen minutes after saying good-bye to Buddy, he arrived at the front gate that led to Ursula Brombecker's four-bedroom Victorian house. Ursula lived on Salt Point Turnpike, next to the cemetery. George walked his bike down the driveway and saw the naked light bulb that lit up the basement. He brushed the snow off his jeans, kicked his boots against the concrete steps, and pounded on her back door.

"Alright! Hang on! I'm coming." Ursula Brombecker, long-time Village matriarch and self-proclaimed repository of Salt Point's oral history, smiled at George through the storm window on her back door. George saw her bugged-out eyes, which rose to prominence after her thyroid died, staring down at him.

"Hey, Mrs. B? You gonna open the door? Or are you just gonna let me freeze out here?"

Ursula opened the door. "George Johnson Jr.! What're you doing here on a day like this? Probably came to mooch a bowl of soup and crackers off an ol' lady. Well, get in here before all the heat goes outside."

Ursula closed the door behind George. They embraced, just like they'd done ever since George's mother and sister had died, when he'd first joined her Cub Scout pack. Most people dismissed Ursula as difficult and bossy, but George saw her differently. She'd always radiated comfort. And in Ursula's thirty years as a den mother, George was her all-time favorite Cub Scout.

"Leave your boots next to the door," she ordered. "I'll get you a pair of old socks to wear from the basement."

"Before I forget, I've got to call my ol' man and tell him I made it here safe."

"Okay. You know where the phone is."

George dialed his father's work number and asked the foreman to put his father on the phone.

"Hey, son."

"Hey. I'm at Mrs. Brombecker's." George Jr. smiled at Ursula. "She's making me soup 'n' crackers." Ursula shook her head in mock indignation. "How about pickin' me up at six?"

"Sure. Let me say a quick hello to Mrs. B."

"Hey, Mrs. B!" George Jr. yelled. "My ol' man wants to say hello to you."

Ursula Brombecker made her way over to the kitchen telephone. She took the phone. "Hello, Mr. Johnson."

"Hi, Mrs. B. Hope all's well with you."

"Things are fine. Same as always," she said. "But I'm getting tired of dealing with that male-dominated Deer Creek Town Council. It's gettin' harder to get them to set aside money for Salt Point. Basic things, like paving roads out here."

For twenty-seven years, Ursula Brombecker served as Salt Point's lone representative on the Deer Creek Town Council. She received a fair amount of latitude from the men, partly because of her status as the widow of a veteran, but mostly because of her intimidating physical appearance.

"There's no one better than you at getting things done," George Sr. maintained.

"I'll try to instill some discipline and manners in your boy. I hear he's picked up some bad habits since graduating my Cub Scout pack. Don't any men supervise the Boy Scouts?"

Foreman Henry Pepper, with an unlit stogie hanging from his lips, began motioning George back to line three. George saw the racks of glass stacking up in his position. "I gotta run, Mrs. B. Thanks."

Ursula hung up the phone and turned to young George. "You're awfully lucky to have one parent who's worth more than the two most kids have." ·

George sat down at the kitchen table. "I know he loves me. And I love him, too," he said sheepishly, wondering how she got him to use that word twice.

"Loves you! He lives for you. Tries to give you every advantage so you can amount to something. And I hear mixed reports on your progress. Doing well in school, but getting into trouble. You've got to behave yourself, or you'll wash away everything else."

George winced, staring at the kitchen cabinet he knew was stocked with a selection of soups. Cream of mushroom, that's what he'd decided on. He shut down, closing up like a green turtle that had been in the sun too long. He wanted to leave, but resigned himself to the fact that she wouldn't let him.

Ursula tapped her fingers on the kitchen counter. "What gives with the two suspensions?"

George's thoughts became jumbled. Anger at his father for telling Mrs. B about the suspensions soon gave way to an image of his Catholic church. He saw himself sitting in the back pew. He'd gone to Sunday Mass believing in God and left with the same belief. But what happened while he was there? He'd knelt down, stood up and knelt down some more, nodded to familiar faces, and curtsied when leaving the pew. Then he was hungry and it took thirty minutes to drive home.

"I just got caught doing some things." George shrugged. "That's all."

"What do you mean, some things? Throwing ice cubes down a girl's shirt? Starting a fire? Are those the things I taught you in Cub Scouts?"

"Ahh, Mrs. B. They were picking on me." George grabbed onto the kitchen table with both hands. "Then I got mad. When I get mad, things sorta happen."

"You mad because your mother's not around?"

"I don't know. I sure wish she'd come back. You know, she used to read to me most nights. Stories about people who're happy. Stories about big-time sports heroes."

"You think your mother would like these suspensions?"

George looked away, noticing that the white paint on the wall was beginning to peel. "I guess she wouldn't."

"You think she'd feel like you let her down?"

"Yeah, probably. C'mon. Can I have some soup?"

Ursula shrugged. "Cream of mushroom?"

"Yes please."

"Tell me how long it'll be until you're an Eagle Scout?"

"The Boy Scouts don't let you get Eagle before you're seventeen," George answered. "I'm a patrol leader now. That's pretty good for being in the eighth grade."

"How many patrols does Troop eighty have?"

"Five. I got to be a patrol leader after I took down the flag at Netherwood the day after Nixon was reelected. I took it off the pole 'n' folded it up in a triangle. Just like you taught us in Cub Scouts. Then I gave it to Mr. Brickle right before his first period history class: He asked why I did it and I said, 'Because this one's dirty.'"

"And old scoutmaster Brickle made you a patrol leader early for that. He's got more backbone than I thought."

Ursula watched as George devoured the bowl of soup and half a pack of saltines. She was only twenty-six when her husband of five years collapsed in their driveway. The CPR unit revived him temporarily, but he died in Saint Francis Hospital's emergency room. "A congenital heart defect," the county coroner had said. "They're like a silent time bomb waitin' to go off."

Ursula gained sixty-five pounds in six months and never remarried. She used a portion of the life insurance proceeds to pay off the mortgage. The balance, combined with military and Social Security benefits, allowed her the luxury of not having to earn a paycheck. She stared at George and wondered if she'd feel differently if her own son were sitting there. Ursula regretted never having had the chance to be someone's mother. Scouting filled a void and provided a benefit to the boys. But it couldn't heal the real wounds. A decade ago, she'd investigated adoption, but the agencies weren't allowing single women to adopt.

Ursula and George spent forty-five minutes in the basement exploring recent innovations in handmade bird feeders. Ursula tinkered with different designs, and she rotated newer models into her backyard collection. George kissed her good-bye at the back door and lugged his bike through the unshoveled snow to meet his father in the idling pickup truck on Salt Point Turnpike. Ursula waved to him from the picture window in the living room, then moped through the foyer to the bathroom in search of a Kleenex.

❖

ON HIS FIRST QUARTERLY report card, George received an A+ in Science. As much as she didn't want to, Miss Mackey awarded that grade. He performed flawlessly on every exam and experiment. Miss Mackey's grading guidelines were strictly quantitative.

Young George became quieter as winter settled over the Hudson Valley. With the days growing shorter, less sunlight led to less conversation, to less energy. He spent more time indoors, slouched in front of the TV. Nixon had won reelection and continued to bomb North Vietnam. Plane crash survivors stayed alive in the Andes by eating their dead friends.

George Sr. decorated the Christmas tree that year without any help from his son. On Christmas day, they had a midday turkey dinner with Mary's parents. This was the last holiday dinner before the Piersons moved to Tucson, where Woo Labs had transferred Mr. Pierson. George Sr. wondered if seeing their grandson was too emotional of a burden for the Piersons to bear because George Jr. reminded them of the daughter they'd lost. George Sr.'s parents had retired to Florida, pledging never to spend another winter in New York. It seemed like the family was scattering, as if fleeing some sort of storm.

After the Johnsons returned home Christmas evening, Sarabeth Roth came by for a visit. She brought young George a package wrapped in bright red paper and decorated with green Christmas trees. Inside the package, he found a genuine, all-leather NBA basketball.

"Alright!" he yelled. "Alright!"

A sleeping Buddy found George's exclamations unnecessarily loud. The Brittany's high-pitched whining showed his displeasure. George thanked Miss Roth, while his father and her swapped smiles.

By mid-January, Miss Mackey had berated George a few more times in class, again for daydreaming. He responded to her last criticism by saying that if her class weren't so easy, he might pay attention. It was not a remark that endeared him to other students. He also considered throwing ice cubes down the science teacher's shirt, but decided she was unworthy of such attention.

Instead, while Miss Mackey was grading an exam, George emptied two containers of alcohol in a semi-circle around her desk. Next he threw a lighted match onto the alcohol. The combination momentarily brought flames as high as three feet into the classroom. Miss Mackey shrieked in horror, but the flames died out almost as fast as they had started.

Three students saw George throw the match this time; none were shy about coming forward to implicate him. The hearing was held the next morning in Principal Taylor's office. The principal, Miss Mackey, George Sr., and George Jr. all attended. There was some discussion of expulsion, but the principal settled on a five-day suspension with the requirement that George see the school district's psychologist once a week for the remainder of the year. He didn't say anything in his defense, ignoring repeated questions from the adults.

George Sr. was so upset that he sent his son to bed with no dinner and without a word about the latest incident. "We'll talk tomorrow," he announced, hoping a night of reflection would serve them both well.

When young George fell asleep, George Sr., placed a phone call.

"Hello," a voice announced on the first ring.

"Hi, Mrs. B. It's George."

"Aren't you supposed to be on a date?"

"Yeah, well. I've got a problem. You heard?"

Ursula let out a long, sorrowful breath. "Yeah. I heard. It's around the Village. People are talking. Pretty bad stuff."

"I don't know what to do. You have any ideas?"

"Well, I think he's an angry kid. He's acting out. It's got something to do with his mother being gone. He's not sure why it happened."

"Mrs. B. C'mon. Who the hell *is* sure why stuff like that happens? But I'm not starting fires. Or beating up my boss."

"You're not a teenager. If I remember, you didn't do everything so perfectly when you were younger."

"Alright. Any ideas on how to deal with this?"

"You know me. I always have ideas. You need something to bring you two together. So you can watch over him. He needs more companionship. He doesn't really have any friends."

"You saying we should do some kinda project?"

"Well, you're not the type who goes in for the Boy Scouts. But there must be something you guys could do together."

George grunted. "Okay. Okay." He grunted again. "Hey, Mrs. B."

"Yeah."

"Thanks. Thanks a lot."

"Don't forget to come over and see me when you're in the Village, okay?"

"Absolutely."

Early the next morning, George called into work sick.

"I've been awfully patient with you," he remarked as George Jr. descended the stairs on his way to breakfast. Young George said nothing. Head down and eyes averted, he crossed the living room, passed the blue reclining chair in which his father sat, entered the kitchen, and opened the refrigerator door. George Sr. decided to let him fix breakfast before they talked.

George Sr.'s eyes returned to the reading material draped across his lap. "There's money in raising rabbits for breeding stock and meat," it began. He turned to the second page of the pamphlet. "There is pleasure and profit in raising purebred New Zealand white rabbits. If you are looking for a part-time money making project, the rabbit business is for you. It costs little to start and is one of the best home money-making projects around. All you need is the space. We will provide the rabbits. You will watch them multiply right before your eyes."

George stared at the ceiling, reflecting on the extra space available in his barn. He continued reading. "The multi-million dollar rabbit industry is fun. We hope you will come to New Hampshire and visit Earl and Josephine's Rabbit and Worm Farm and join us in this wonderful enterprise. We stock everything you will need to get started, including your choice of over 10,000 rabbits."

Carrying the bowl of cereal and a glass of orange juice, George walked into the living room and sat down on the couch, knowing he should be the first to speak. No words came.

George Sr. closed his pamphlet and looked at the ceiling. "I've tried to be patient with you, son. I'm at the end of my rope. I just can't understand how you can get the report cards you get and at the same time get into such trouble. If you did this stuff outside of school, you'd be in jail by now."

"Are you through?"

"Through! Am I through?" George Sr. rose from his chair and walked over to the couch, hovering over his son. "No, I'm not through! What's your problem?! I oughta take you out to the barn and whip you."

George Jr. shuddered.

"Don't worry, I'm not gonna hit you. I don't believe in it. Count your blessings."

The elder Johnson glared at his son. George Jr. averted his eyes. Father and son looked at the carpet, not knowing what to say, each hamstrung by their feelings. George Sr. glanced at his watch.

"Go get dressed," he demanded. "We're going for a ride. I'll wait in the truck."

George Jr. climbed the stairs leading to his bedroom. Five minutes later he slithered into the truck. "Where are we going?"

George Sr. turned right onto Fox Run Road. "You're going to confession."

"Confession? I haven't been there since first communion."

"Then it's long overdue. They've been reminding you of the drill in Sunday school. I know you haven't forgotten."

"But, Dad—"

"No buts about it. Maybe your problems come from me pulling you out of Catholic school. At least there's some discipline in a bunch of Catholic rules. It seems Sunday school classes don't hardly teach the fundamental beliefs of Catholics anymore. Education has gotten touchy-feely. That school you're in can't even do a good job babysitting."

Young George knew better than to protest. He still remembered the confession litany, enough to get by, anyway.

The elder Johnson parked his pickup truck in front of St. Stanislaus. "Go cleanse your soul."

"It's ten in the morning. Is anybody gonna be there?"

"The priest will be in the confessional. Go on."

It was dark inside the church. The morning sun reflecting through the stained glass windows provided the only light. Church confused George Jr. He knew little about the symbols. He couldn't understand the prayers or hymns. His mind drifted during the homilies. But he knew the confessional booth was in the back right-hand corner of the church. He entered and slid the wooden panel to the right, exposing the dark mesh screen. The silhouette of a head became visible. George made the sign of the cross. "In the name of the Father, and of the Son, and of the Holy Spirit. Bless me Father, for I have sinned. It has been...hmm, oh...about six years since my last confession."

"What was the occasion of your confession?"

George recognized Father Dombrowski's voice. He was unsure if the head priest knew the sinner's identity. "It was right before my first communion."

"I see. Please continue."

"Well, I've...er, sinned." George wondered what officially counted as a sin. He wanted this to be an ordinary confession.

"Tell me your sins. Go ahead."

"I've had some trouble at school." George recounted the events leading up to the three suspensions. As he spoke, Father Dombrowski sighed, almost in relief. He knew this sinner was the son of his former altar boy, usher, and parishioner. Father Dombrowski hoped that George Sr. would rejoin the parish, even if he couldn't take communion. Reflecting on George Sr. took the priest's mind away from young George's confession, but Father Dombrowski was well versed on the sinner's exploits. Other churchgoers had kept him informed. Father Dombrowski sometimes thought of calling young George aside after mass, into his rectory, for counseling. Instead, relying on the non-intervention instincts of the priests of his generation, he asked for George's blessing in his solitary prayers.

George finished confessing to the antics that led to the suspensions. He also confessed to taking the name of the Lord in vain, figuring that was one of the Ten Commandments most everybody broke and to not confess it would have cast unwanted suspicion on himself.

"Do you have anything else to confess?"

George pictured himself sitting on his mother's lap in tears after his first day of elementary school. She kissed the top of his head. He hadn't remembered her enough in his prayers. "No, Father," he said.

"I absolve you of your sins in the name of the Father, and of the Son, and of the Holy Spirit. Amen. Now, for your penance, I direct you to say five Hail Marys and five Our Fathers. I will now hear your Act of Contrition."

George knew that one by heart. "Oh, my God, I am heartily sorry for having offended You, and I detest all my sins, because of Your just punishments, but most of all because they offend You, my God, who are all good and deserving of all my love. I firmly resolve, with the help of Your grace, to sin no more and to avoid the new occasions of sin."

At once anxious and claustrophobic, George thanked the priest, exited the booth, gathered his bearings and made a beeline for the last pew. Kneeling down, he mumbled to himself, "Hail Mary, full of grace, the Lord is with thee. Blessed art thou among women, and blessed is the fruit of thy womb, Jesus. Holy Mary, mother of God, pray for us sinners, now and at the hour of our death. Amen." He also said, a little louder, "Hail Mary times five. I'll get to the Our Fathers on Sunday." By the time George finished praying, more sunlight filled the church. The large clock above the holy water read 11:30 a.m.

Father Dombrowski stopped George before he left the church. "May I speak with you?" he asked.

"Not now, Father, please. My dad's been waiting in the truck for me. Can I catch you some other time? Maybe after church?"

"Your father is outside, right now?"

"Yeah, he's been parked outside waiting for me to confess and all. I didn't think it would take this long."

"You'd better run along then."

"See you, Father." With the door already open, George Jr. waved good-bye.

❖

AFTER THE THIRD SUSPENSION, George Jr. went out of his way to help with the chores at home, even the cleaning. His father had no idea that he knew how to operate a vacuum cleaner, let alone wind the cord and return the vacuum to the hall closet.

Always a voracious eater, young George detested cleaning the dishes, especially his own plates. It wasn't long before his appetite for housework subsided. George Sr. wished that the short-lived transformation had taken place during the summer, when free, semi-skilled labor could have been put to better use.

Driving home from work in light snow, the elder Johnson decided to drop by Ursula's house. He parked the pickup next to the porch. When she appeared at the door, he said, "I hear you make some mean soup."

"Jesus Christ! Another mooch? All right, get in here." She opened the door and George walked into the kitchen.

"Hey, c'mon now. How about a kiss for an ol' lady?"

"All women should be this easy," George mumbled, kissing her on the cheek and grasping her shoulders.

"You don't look so hot."

George took a seat at the kitchen table. "I don't know what to do about my kid. I'm still worried about him."

"Yeah, I bet. Has he been any better lately?"

"I'm not sure. He still seems mad at the world. Not all the time. Just now an' then."

"Has the school shrink helped any?"

"I don't think so. He doesn't talk much about the sessions. I bet he's just toying with the guy. Probably thinks it's a challenge to face off against some doctor. You know, to see if he can throw him off."

"Yeah, I can see him doing that. Did you think of a project for the two of you?"

"I've got an idea. A business thing. I'll let you know if he goes for it. I don't think I can force anything on him."

"You'll see. He'll wanna do something with you."

"He's a smart kid, Ursula. It's hard for me to square some of his antics with his report cards."

"Maybe it's one of those teenage phases. Be proud of the good."

"My problem is I got different levels of pride. I got the normal, low-level sorta pride. The kind that's there when my boy walks in the door and says '*Hi, Dad.*' I helped make him, taught him basic things like going to the bathroom. Things that're required for everyday living. I'm fine on that level, as long as he doesn't become a major league delinquent. But it's no great accomplishment to raise a kid who doesn't commit felonies."

Ursula smiled.

George returned the smile. "With my kid, it's harder. He's good in school. He also plays baseball. He's not the best player on the team. But he's not the kid who gets stuck in right field. Or the kid who gets just one at-bat when the coach can most afford a sure out. When I was growin' up, the kids who didn't have much athletic ability ended up tradin' in their gloves and cleats for library books. Or musical instruments."

Ursula nodded. "I know the ones you're talking about."

"Then they join the debate team. They go to the library when most everyone else goofs off. I guess those're the ones that grow up to be doctors or lawyers or plant managers. Those're the big shots at the high school reunions. George could be a big shot."

"If he doesn't mess up," Ursula said.

"I don't want him to waste the gifts he's been blessed with. I don't want this anger to get so out of control that he ends up in the state pen. I've seen it happen to guys on the line. If you raise too much hell you get caged-in like some wild animal, trapped with other animals much wilder than you ever were. Then you get their habits. Why's it so hard to follow a few simple rules for everybody's benefit?"

Ursula patted George on the shoulder. "At least he's not like the kids who've already been held back a year. You know, those foul-mouthed boys hanging around smoking cigarettes. Picking pockets and shoplifting. Using drugs. And talking in a dialect that the public can't understand."

"I know, it's not like that. But I wanna see my son achieve big things, important things, make real contributions. Dammit, I know he can. He's got a lotta promise. But promise ain't nothing unless it's realized."

The soup was boiling. Ursula got up and poured two bowls. "Put your coat on," she said. "Let's sit out on the porch."

George and Ursula sat side by side on the swinging bench. "I don't know whether to get in his face or get out of his way," George said, squinting to see the moon through the snow.

❖

AT BREAKFAST ON A Saturday in February, young George, dressed in a solid red wool sweater with a tag inside that announced "Hand Knit by Grandma Pierson," read *The Hudson Valley Watch*. The daily paper did little in-house reporting, devoting most of its attention to the editorial page and generating advertising revenue. Most stories were reruns from the major wires or *The New York Times*. The Watergate scandal fascinated George. Several Nixon aides pled guilty. Top aides resigned.

"Son, we haven't talked that much since you almost set Miss Mackey on fire—"

"I didn't try to torch her," he said. "I just scared her, that's all."

"Alright, put that paper away." George Jr. complied. "I've noticed you moping around the house. You need something to direct your energy toward. I've got just the thing. I wanna start a business on the side, and you can be my partner in it. We can make some money. What do you think?"

"I like the money part. What kind of business?"

"A rabbit business."

"Rabbits? What're we gonna do with them?"

"Breed them. Mate the bucks with the does. When the does have their litters, we're gonna keep the females for breeding stock. We'll sell the males to butcher shops or laboratories. A butcher across the Hudson is gonna pay a dollar a pound, live weight."

"Where are you gonna put them?"

"In cages in the barn. There's lots of extra space. I know a place where we can get cages real cheap. Whaddaya say?"

"Sounds like lotsa work. I'm not sure it'll be fun."

"You know, I didn't punish you for the fire—"

"So what're you saying? That my punishment is to shovel rabbit crap 'til I turn eighteen?"

"Nope. I'm not ordering you to be my partner. I'm just asking. The decision's up to you. If you want in on the action, let me know."

George Sr. returned to the financial projections he'd spread out on the reclining chair. He planned to buy two bucks and fifteen does of breeding age. After a gestation period of thirty days, each doe would produce litters of eight to twelve bunnies. Each doe would raise her litter for eight weeks. The bunnies would then be weaned. The mothers would get thirty days to recuperate before the process began anew. Each doe would produce three litters a year.

Three months after starting, he'd have one hundred and twenty to one hundred and fifty new rabbits. The males would be sent to the butcher while they were still lean. The butcher would buy them for meat and resell the pelts. The remaining sixty to seventy-five does would either be sold as breeding stock to other rabbit farmers or as pets. Some also would be sold to wholesalers or become additions to George's breeding stock. Two months after the female babies were weaned, they'd be impregnated. By the end of the first year, The Johnson Rabbitry would have over one thousand working rabbits.

"Hey, Dad?" George called out from the kitchen after he finished drying the last breakfast dish. "Tell me more about this rabbit thing."

"I'm going to buy some cages in the Village. Come along? We can talk on the way."

"Yeah, okay." On the ride past the schoolhouse and near where the road met the Taconic Parkway, young George asked, "Are we really gonna fill up the bed of this old pickup and the flatbed trailer with cages?"

"Yep, I'm picking up three hundred cages today from an abandoned mink farm. We'll have to make a few trips." He turned to his son, cupped his left hand over his mouth and said in a loud whisper, "I got the cages for only a buck a piece!"

"I'm in for a full day's work," young George said, sighing.

Twenty minutes later, George Sr. turned off the road into a narrow dirt driveway. A gray house in need of fresh paint came into view. He could see a decrepit wood shed beyond the house, extending into the overgrown fields behind it.

They loaded and unloaded three hundred rusted cages. For a nickel a piece, they bought ceramic crocks to hold food and water. George Sr. wrote a check for three hundred and fifteen dollars at the end of the day. Father and son began building shelves in the barn to house the cages. They stacked them four high, leaving enough room to insert dropping trays below each level of cages. Each cage was eighteen inches wide by fourteen inches high by four feet deep, including a one-foot square silver box positioned at the rear. The does would give birth and raise their litters in the silver box until the bunnies grew big enough to make their way into the wire portion of the cages.

By mid-March, The Johnson Rabbitry was ready to buy its foundation stock. Early on a crisp Saturday morning, George Sr. connected the flatbed trailer to his four-by-four. Father and son turned onto Fox Run Road and embarked on their four-hour journey to Earl and Josephine's.

"Why are we buying New Zealand white rabbits, not black or brown ones?" George Jr. asked.

"Because New Zealand whites produce the largest litters." George Sr. raised his left index finger and tapped the dashboard. "Also, they achieve optimum weight in the shortest amount of time. That means more rabbits producing more litters."

"So they multiply faster?"

"Yep. And their white coats are dyeable as pelts."

They drove for another hour, talking about the upcoming major league baseball season. "How exactly is this partnership gonna work?" George Jr. asked suddenly.

"Well, you're gonna be the junior partner."

"This ain't gonna be a fifty-fifty deal?"

"Fifty-fifty! Are you outta your mind, boy! Geez, fifty-fifty," he repeated, removing his blue Mets cap and scratching his head. "At least I'm raisin' a kid with balls."

George Jr. said nothing. He didn't envision himself being less than a full partner. "Tell me how you're thinking about dividin' up the work," he finally said.

"I figure we can do a lot of it together. The first thing we do is breed the rabbits. Each buck can handle three, maybe four does a night. We'll need to keep detailed records of the dates of breeding, litter size, who's been bred, what we sell, how much, all that stuff. I thought you'd do most of the recordkeeping, since you're so handy with numbers." George Sr. paused. "But you've got to promise me one thing."

"What's that, Dad?"

"If you get mad at me, you won't set the records on fire."

Young George laughed. "Deal," he said, softly punching his father's shoulder.

"Then how about an eighty-twenty split of the profits?"

"Eighty-twenty! Sounds like a lot of recordkeeping for twenty percent. How often do we gotta feed 'em?"

"Once a day. And water 'em at least once a day, probably twice in the winter 'cause it'll freeze up."

"I suppose I'll be doing some of that, too?"

"Of course."

"Sounds like I'll be doing at least half the work."

"You will be."

"And eighty-twenty's fair for that?"

"Yeah. Actually, you're gettin' a sweet deal because you're my son. Here's how capitalism works. Those who have the ideas and the seed money, they get all the spoils. It's like a pyramid. You get to the top because of ideas or money. Look at the people who go to college. That's the only way to get ahead these days. Only one in five kids actually gets to go. And the rich people, they're gonna try their damnedest to get their own kids in. So that leaves less room for everybody else. Plus, college costs lotsa money, which the people at the top have more of. Lotsa smart kids don't get to go because it's too expensive. So everybody at the bottom of the pyramid, they become the workers. Since there are so many people who have to work, that drives the price of labor down, because everybody needs jobs to support themselves."

George Sr. took a deep breath. "See, I've got the idea here. I found the rabbits and cages to get us started. I own the barn where we're gonna keep them. And I've got the initial capital outlay. Do you have any money to invest?"

George Jr. didn't answer.

The elder Johnson reached across the cab and squeezed his son's left leg. "I want more than anything for you to go to college. You have the smarts. I'm gonna do my damnedest to make sure I have enough money to send you."

George Jr. rolled his eyes. "You got a deal at eighty-twenty," he said.

❖

BY SUNDAY, THE JOHNSONS' foundation stock was in place. They were ready to breed the bucks and does. George Sr. named the two foundation bucks Larry and Hugh, after the publishers of *Hustler* and *Playboy*.

"Let's pick out the two feistiest bucks we can," George Sr. told his son the previous day at Earl and Josephine's. "We'll want them to hump even the most reluctant of does."

On the spot, George Jr. had developed a redness quotient scale, making notes of which of the hundreds of does were in heat so that he could select the best prospects for The Johnson Rabbitry. On the ride home, father and son agreed to breed as many does as they could.

The next night, George Sr. carried Larry over to a doe's cage. George Jr. opened the cage. "Come on, Larry, go to it!"

Father and son watched as Larry circled the doe. He approached from behind, sniffed under her tail, and mounted her without resistance. Larry's back legs shook, vibrating the cage. The Johnsons heard a squirting sound as the buck fell off the doe onto his back. Larry jumped up on all fours.

"Ready for more!" George Sr. shouted to Larry. The buck repeated the event with another doe in the next cage, then a third. The fourth doe resisted, circling around to keep her backside away from Larry. He soon gave up.

"Okay! Seems three's his limit. I guess you can't blame the bugger for not chasing number four." Hugh conquered four does, though, establishing himself as the evening's top performer. Number five proved difficult, backing herself into a corner of the cage. Hugh clawed and grunted at her, but George Sr. yanked him out of her cage before a fight started. "Looks like we got ourselves a real winner in Hugh," he said, returning the buck to his cage.

George Sr. walked back to doe number five's cage, picked her up, turned her over and checked her crotch. "How about that?" he said, extending the doe upside down, legs spread apart, over to his son for observation. "Her crotch was beet red yesterday. Now it's white, not even pink."

One week before George Jr.'s junior high school graduation, The Johnson Rabbitry weaned one hundred and twenty-six bunnies from their mothers. Fifty-nine females remained, each graduating to her own cage. Sixty-six males were sold to a butcher across the Hudson River. One buck sold for twelve dollars to an Indian woman dressed in a sari, who stopped by after seeing the "Rabbits for Sale" sign on the edge of the Johnsons' driveway. She only wanted its blood for use in baking blood pies, but young George told her she'd have to buy the whole rabbit and extract the blood herself. She paid him the twelve dollars.

Hope

I N THE SUMMER OF 1973, George Sr. only turned on the TV to watch the evening news. As a new businessman, he tried to understand the wage and price controls imposed earlier that year by the Nixon administration.

"If wages and prices really are controlled, then how come prices go up after the control period ends but wages stay the same?" George asked his foreman.

Henry Pepper shrugged. "Just move your line, Johnson," he said.

The Johnson Rabbitry was primarily a cash business, so George Sr's rabbit money had more purchasing power than his salary. "The IRS can't police the small businesses in America," he told his son. "So I don't have to pay taxes on cash sales. All businesses skim like that."

"They just report the checks? Not the cash?"

"Yep. The IRS can't track the cash. That's why small businesses keep two sets of books. One for the owners. And one for the IRS. Having a side business makes it easier to climb higher up in the pyramid."

The black rotary telephone in the kitchen started ringing. Young George grabbed the receiver after the third ring. The female caller asked for his father.

George Sr. took the receiver. "Hello."

"Am I ever going to see you again?"

"Uhh, Sarabeth. Sorry I haven't called."

"I feel forgotten."

George sighed. "I've got a lot going on with this rabbit business. And my son."

"I have kids, too. What about my feelings?"

"I have enough feelings to worry about here."

"What're you saying?"

"I guess I'm saying I need my space."

Sarabeth hung up.

The Ervin committee hearings dominated the TV that summer. Young George summarized the events for his father over dinner. "Do ya think Nixon'll get away with it?" he asked his father in a sly tone of voice.

"In politics, that stuff goes on all the time."

"What makes a guy like Nixon do that stuff? Breaking into the Democratic headquarters. Then lying about it."

George Sr. shrugged his shoulders. "What made you lie to that principal? Some guys, they just think they'll never get caught."

"Yeah, but I'm way down life's pyramid. What makes Nixon, a guy who's got more power than anybody, break the law? He's the president. He's got no boss. Everybody reports to him."

George Sr. rubbed his forehead. "The American people are his boss. We all elected him. Nixon works for us."

"What a bummer. Even if you get to be president, you still have a boss. Is there a job where nobody is your boss?"

"Yeah, God. He doesn't have a boss. Even the Pope reports to him."

"What about owning something?" Young George took off his baseball cap and pointed toward the logo on it. "Like the Mets. Everybody works for the owner. The players, the manager."

"Yeah, but he only runs the Mets. The baseball commissioner, Bowie Kuhn, he runs all of baseball."

Young George sighed. "At least we're the boss of the rabbits."

George Sr. walked over and placed his right arm around his son's shoulder and tugged on his baseball cap. "Just remember. I'm the boss of you."

Young George squirmed away. "Hey, only for a little while! Only for a few more years. Then nobody'll be boss of me!"

As business partners, father and son bred and weaned the New Zealand whites, bought hay and pellets, and cleaned the dropping trays. They decided to sell Larry when his sub-par performance began to slip even more. "There aren't any better jobs in the rabbit world," George Jr. said. "Larry's just not willing to try hard after he's done it once." The elder Johnson agreed that Larry's job should go to a younger buck.

George Jr. surveyed the existing litters for a replacement buck. "Which one of you wants to trade getting your head chopped off for a life of does?" he asked the young bunnies, poking his fingers inside the cages in an effort to smoke out Larry's successor. He finally settled on an eight-week-old buck he named Joe, after Joe Namath. He picked up Joe by the scruff of his neck and set him in his own cage. He'd chosen the buck all on his own. "Don't let me down," he said, pointing at Joe.

George Sr. watched his son deal with customers. He showed them how to handle the rabbits. He helped load the merchandise. He waved good-bye. He'd bring the money to his father. "A measly twenty percent of this is mine. You must be packing it away."

"Don't forget twenty percent of the costs are yours too," George Sr. responded. "Which I'm fronting."

George Sr. paid his son in cash, hoping that managing money would be a valuable learning experience. Besides, there wasn't much to spend it on in Salt Point. Right before Labor Day, George Jr. persuaded his father to drive him to the Hudson Savings Bank, where he opened his first savings account. "I'm saving up to buy a car when I turn sixteen," young George told an assistant vice president while handing over the cash. The executive assured him that interest would continue to accrue even if he didn't travel to the bank each month to have it posted in his passbook.

A satisfied George Sr. sat up in bed that night, bathing in the limelight of parental accomplishment. His kid would soon be starting high school. But the two child-rearing books he'd just read warned that troublesome teenage years lay ahead. George got down on his knees and prayed that his son's lawful behavior would continue. He had little trouble falling asleep. Things seemed to be aligned, and the world's demons seemed far away.

❖

ONE OF THE BELLS marking the beginning and end of classes at Deer Creek High was located outside the northeast bathroom. The noise was inordinately loud for those relieving themselves. As the sound resonated off the concrete walls, the three boys inside covered their ears.

"Man-o-man, freakin' loud," one boy said, speaking through a haze of cigarette smoke. A half-consumed pack rested on the sink next to the spigot. "Any of you guys gonna go to class?" he asked, turning to the other two boys.

"Naw, I got study hall," the shortest boy responded.

"Runtman, ya had study hall last period," the boy in the denim vest quipped.

"I just got me a real difficult schedule, don't I?" Runtman acknowledged.

"What about you, Destructo?"

Lester Devonshire earned his nickname when he dislodged one of the bathroom sinks from the wall. On a dare, while Runtman held the stall door open, Lester stood on the sink and tried to urinate across the floor into the toilet. Seeing that his stream at its peak was falling short of the toilet and spraying onto Runtman's pants, Lester rocked with laughter. That movement unseated the hinges fastened to the wall; the sink shot out and hurled Lester toward the toilet. "I got a Spanish class next period," Destructo answered. "But I haven't learned nothin' so far, so I won't be missin' nothin'."

The boy in the denim vest sprung up from the floor. "Guys," he began, "I know a place across the river where we can score some weed. Whaddaya say?"

"How much?" Runtman asked.

"A dime bag. Enough to get us buzzed."

Runtman and Destructo shrugged. "Alright, man," Runtman said. As the three boys walked toward the bathroom door, it swung open, nearly hitting Destructo in the face.

The clouds hanging in the air like smog, the stench of unvented cigarette smoke, the odor of stale urine, and the lingering disinfectant all combined to overload George's senses as soon as he pushed the door open.

The boys let the door swing shut. With their heads half-cocked and legs spread apart, they turned to face George's urinating profile. "Shithead, you got any dough?" Destructo asked.

George zipped up his trousers and pulled down the flush handle. Head down, he tried to leave.

Destructo and Runtman each grabbed an arm and moved George backwards. "I was talkin' to you, man. There ain't no other shithead in here," Destructo said.

George focused on Destructo's face, zeroing in on the soft, loosely scattered peach fuzz on his upper lip.

"Give us some dough and we won't hurt ya," Runtman offered.

"Dough?"

"Yeah, dough, asshole!" Destructo said. "Bread, moolah, green stuff, bucks. Fork it over."

"I don't have any." George tried to wriggle his arms out of the boys' grip.

"What about your lunch money?" Runtman asked.

"It's in my locker."

"Empty his pockets!" the boy in the denim vest ordered. He was leaning on the bathroom door, poised to block it from swinging open if anyone tried to enter.

Runtman and Destructo each opened a pocket. "Nothin' here," Destructo said. The bell sounded. When the boys' hands instinctively reached for their ears, George sprinted toward the exit. He managed to half-open the door before two bodies crashed against it. Destructo and Runtman grabbed George by the shoulders and backed him into the corner behind the door. George raised his forearms to protect his face.

"You leave when we say you can leave!" Destructo screamed.

"Toilet," the boy in the denim vest said. "Toilet!" He sounded like a drill sergeant.

"Toilet!" Destructo shouted. "Toilet! Toilet! Toilet!" all three boys screamed in unison.

George tried to resist, but his body soon went limp. Runtman and Destructo positioned him on his knees in front of the toilet, while the denim-vested boy guarded the door.

Runtman lifted the seat. Destructo grabbed George's shaggy hair and pushed his face into the toilet water. George closed his eyes and held his breath. Destructo didn't keep him submerged for more than three to four seconds and permitted him to catch his breath between dunkings. Runtman took his turn, forcing George's face down until his nose smashed against the bottom of the bowl. Destructo flushed, but George was able to gasp a breath of air when the water escaped to its lowest point, before it came rushing back.

"Let's move out!" the boy in the denim vest commanded.

Destructo pointed his finger at George. "Don't move until we're long gone, okay, shithead?" The three boys departed.

Fighting back tears, George sat on the floor in the stall, his water-logged hair dripping on his shirt and pants. His books were scattered on the floor. He opened the bathroom door and walked toward the front of the school, conscious of the gawking faces he passed.

George marched to the main desk. "Where's the principal?" he demanded. Speechless at the sight of a dripping wet, one hundred-pound boy, the woman at the desk sat motionless. George walked toward the row of offices in the back, evading the gray-haired woman who tried to block his path. She followed closely behind, shouting, "Mr. Shostankovich. Oh, Mr. Shostankovich, you have a visitor."

George found the principal's office at the end of the hallway. He stood over the principal's desk. "You see this?" George screamed, pointing to his head.

"I certainly do. It's dripping all over my desk, young man."

"Look, sir!" he began, raising his head. "I was attacked in the bathroom by three greasers. They shoved my head down the toilet!"

"Oh my. What bathroom?"

"The one by room 11E. I was coming out of my third period wood shop class."

"The northeast bathroom. What were you doing in there?"

"I was pissing. What else would I be doing in a bathroom?"

"Young man, we'll investigate. But that bathroom is, well, an informal smoking room. You shouldn't have gone in there alone."

George shook his matted mane like a dog, showering water on the principal. Mr. Shostankovich stood. "Stop it. Stop it!"

George stopped, but only to speak. "Is this how you run a high school? Kids can't go to the damn bathroom. How about the next time I come in here and piss in your private bathroom!"

Mr. Shostankovich raised his right hand, but stopped at the sight of four women hovering near the entrance to his office. "What are you all doing?" he asked. "Get this boy over to the nurse."

Two women walked George a short distance to the next office. Nurse Potter spent half an hour cleaning George before allowing him to take a shower. She placed a band-aid on the bridge of his nose.

When Nurse Potter took a phone call in the back room, George left. Rushing to his locker, he grabbed his lunch money and a windbreaker and ran out the side door into the school's parking lot.

It was a sunny, cool October morning. George could see a cloud cover moving in from the north. He slowed his gait and walked past the football field, squinting as the sun reflected off the metal seats of the empty bleachers.

An overwhelming need to run into his mother's arms overcame him until he began to shake. Tears dropped from his eyes onto his sneakers. He rubbed his hands across his face. Soon he began running as fast as he could, until he reached the entrance to the woods behind the school. He veered off the foot trail, not wanting to see where it led.

Conscious of the crisp leaves crunching below his feet, George came upon a small pool of water. Beavers had dammed off a stream of clear water to create the listless pond. Green and gold scum covered much of its surface. All the water wanted to do was keep flowing but the beavers had dammed it off, forcing it to stagnate. George could tear down the dam, but what would be the point? The beavers would just rebuild it.

"Damn those greasers!" he shouted at the trees.

George found his way back to the football field, then to the baseball diamond. He fantasized about the 1972 World Series. George became Rollie Fingers. He kicked the dirt with his spikes. He grew a dark mustache curled up at the ends and prepared to pitch to Cincinnati Reds catcher Johnny Bench. The count was three and two. The Oakland A's catcher extended his right arm in the classic intentional walk pose. Rollie Johnson instead unleashed a quick slider into Bench's strike zone. "Strike three!" the umpire shouted. A disgusted Bench made his way back to the dugout. What a ruse!

The distant cracking of thunder awakened George from his trance, and he ran for shelter where he waited out the storm. After the rain subsided, he hitchhiked home. Buddy greeted him in front of the barn. George found his baseball, set up the pitchback, and practiced ball handling drills in the wet grass.

❖

THE PRINCIPAL'S SECRETARY TELEPHONED George Sr. to report the bathroom incident and his son's escape from school. "We'll come see Mr. Shostankovich tomorrow morning," George Sr. said to her.

Neither father nor son spoke on the ride to school the next morning. The air was cold, almost frigid, and the pickup truck's heating system took awhile to begin pumping out hot air. Young George alternated between placing his hands in his coat pockets and rubbing them together.

"Go right in, Mr. Johnson. It's the last door on the left," the principal's secretary said, smiling at young George when her eyes met his.

The principal was on the telephone, but he motioned the Johnsons to a round table in the corner. Mr. Shostankovich hung up and greeted them. "Ah, the legendary George Johnson," he said, extending his hand to George Sr. The elder Johnson grabbed it. "I hear you were some ball player in your day. We still keep your MVP trophy on display in the lobby."

"That was a long time ago," George Sr. muttered through a forced smile.

Mr. Shostankovich offered the Johnsons an apology. He again advised George Jr. not to use the northeast bathroom. "All the other restrooms are completely safe," the principal said.

"You have bathrooms in the school that kids can't use?" George Sr. asked. "That wasn't the case in my day."

"That bathroom's near the woodshop and auto mechanics room."

"So what're you saying?" The elder Johnson's hands were fumbling around his suit pockets. The flaps were still sewn shut.

"I'm saying that there's a rougher element up there. Students avoid that part of the school. Nobody must've told your son. Now you know. The school's laid out so those kids don't pollute the rest."

"It wasn't like that when I was here," George Sr. mumbled.

"Things change. By the way, I pulled your son's file. He's already taking five courses. Why's he taking woodshop?"

"To learn woodworking skills. To learn how to use his hands. But it sounds like you should also teach boxing."

"Mr. Johnson, those kids are barely literate, hard-to-control imbeciles. We're a public institution. We're obligated to look after them. We let them smoke in the northeast bathroom so they'll leave the other bathrooms for the rest of the students. Just keep your boy out of that bathroom and he'll be fine."

"To look after them?" George Sr. said. "For crying out loud, why don't you try teaching them?"

"Why don't you do your job and let a trained educator decide how best to run this school, okay?"

"Now you listen to me," George Sr. said, rising from his chair. "I'm gonna hold you responsible for my son's safety. If there's another incident like yesterday's, he's gonna make your life miserable. Got it?"

"It sounds like you need an upbraiding, just like your son!" the principal said. The Johnsons stormed down the hallway.

Pride filled young George's heart. "Wow, you really kicked some butt in there," he said, patting his father on the back. "Awesome."

George Sr. took a deep breath. "Be cool today, okay? For me."

"Sure. You coming to the game today?"

"Yep, I'll be there after work."

Ten hours later, George Sr. walked his son to the truck after the freshman soccer game. "No incidents today, I assume," he said.

"Nope."

"You played a good game today. I'm starting to figure out the rules of soccer."

"It's pretty easy. You just kick a ball into a net before anybody stops it."

They ate a spaghetti dinner and watched the news. "Good evening," Walter Cronkite said. "Today, the country is reeling from Spiro T. Agnew's sudden resignation from the Vice Presidency. Mr. Agnew has been plagued by an ongoing federal grand jury investigation into kickbacks that allegedly occurred when he was governor of Maryland. Facing a probable indictment, the Nixon administration's most outspoken law and order champion has pleaded no contest to one count of income tax evasion. For more on this story we go..."

"Unbelievable," George Sr. said. "Just unbelievable. Everybody 'cept for good ol' Walter must be crooked. Nixon's got Watergate problems. Now the vice president resigns. The country's going to hell."

"Dad? What does no contest mean?"

"It means that he's really guilty. But it's a face-saving way of saying it. Just a loophole."

"Can he still go to prison?"

"A vice president? He's one of the rulers. No way."

Young George contemplated Agnew's crimes. Is everybody on the take? Does everybody have secrets they're hiding? Is everybody just a few steps from humiliation?

George Sr. went to water the rabbits again; the temperature had dropped. He went alone to the barn. A car turned into the driveway. The door opened and shut.

In a few seconds a large, bundled-up frame appeared in the doorway with a package. "Hey, it's freezing out here," said Ursula Brombecker. "What the hell are you doing?"

"Trying to support my family," George answered. "How come you're not out campaigning?"

"I just came from a town council meeting."

"What, you didn't give those guys a hard enough time, so you figured you'd come over here?"

Ursula laughed. "Hey, is that any way to treat a friend? I've brought you a gift."

"Whaddaya got there?"

Ursula removed a brown grocery bag. "I made this bird feeder just for you."

George kissed her on the cheek. "Thanks. It's huge. Looks like a dollhouse."

"That way, the pretty big birds will spend the winter in your backyard. How's the rabbit business going?"

"These rabbits sure have it good. They eat, drink, shit, and screw. They don't have to do anything else. No time clock running their lives."

"But you don't live in a cage."

"But at work I got a buzzer regulating me. That buzzer cages me in just like these rabbits."

"C'mon," Ursula urged. "It's different."

"Not really. You know what's going on at these plants. You've seen how the guys change. How they become robots."

Ursula patted George on his shoulder. "C'mon. Stop exaggerating."

"I'm not. Once these guys've been in the clean room for a few years, they don't buck the system like they did in their youths. At first they resist, but eventually they fall in line."

"Oh, yeah. What're they falling in line for?"

George grunted. "Money. After awhile, they get families, mortgages, medical benefits, salary increases tied to productivity, bonuses tied to output. Money is the great conqueror of the human spirit."

"Well," Ursula said. "At least you're not out on the streets turning tricks."

George shook his head. "That's no different, either. We all have a price. People say prostitution is immoral. But money makes them do it. So they can survive. Think about it from the opposite side. Most guys wouldn't have sex with Bella Abzug for free. But would they for fifty thousand dollars? ten thousand dollars? Less?"

"This cold spell must be getting to you. I'm going inside to say hello to George."

The elder Johnson finished watering the rabbits.

❖

THE REMAINING FALL AND winter months brought more rabbits into the barn. More births, and more cash sales to the butcher. The TV brought news of more Watergate indictments. Yet President Nixon declared from Disney World that he wasn't a crook.

The arrival of baseball season signaled an end to the Hudson Valley winter. Seven Deer Creek High freshmen competed for the shortstop position during spring tryouts. Whoever won the job as a freshman would likely play the position on the junior varsity and varsity teams. George played shortstop for Salt Point's Babe Ruth League Team, but it was less competitive than Deer Creek's senior league, where the other six boys played. Still, George won the starting

job in practice and kept it through the entire season. He even batted
.354 as the number two hitter in the lineup. The team went twelve
and three. And the girls were beginning to notice the long-haired,
skinny kid who combined a freewheeling attitude with high-strung
intensity. George also knew many of the answers in class.

Most rising sophomores in Deer Creek High were too young
to have summer jobs, so they loitered around their neighborhoods
playing among themselves. The better-off or talented few spent
part of their summers at camps, but most stayed around town.
Kids living in Salt Point were more isolated because the distance to
Deer Creek prevented them from visiting their school friends in the
summer. They could talk on the telephone, but they couldn't count
on catching a ride to town. Most of them hung around the Clinton
Rec Park or the Village.

Rabbit chores occupied much of young George's time. The
number of New Zealand whites reached two thousand, the
maximum capacity of the windowless barn. He worked in the barn
alone amidst a sea of white pelts. The upstate New York humidity
hovered constantly. On particularly humid days, the stench of
urine-coated feces, brown circular-shaped droppings that resembled miniature marbles, latched onto George's clothes so fiercely
that extra strength detergent couldn't completely remove the odor.
He began wearing only certain clothes when working in the barn
and wondered whether showers and dips in the swimming hole
adequately cleansed his body.

With rabbit cages stacked on more rabbit cages, making the walkways narrow and requiring a step ladder to reach the highest row of
cages, the barn felt even more claustrophobic. During the day, horse
flies and mosquitoes circled. At night, the crickets and bullfrogs
sounded like they were plotting an invasion. Paperwork and carting
away rabbit droppings could be put off for a while, but George
couldn't escape the barn until the rabbits had food and water.

Other Salt Point kids milked cows, sheared sheep, slopped pigs, and cleaned up. George reminded himself that those kids' chores were no different from his daily routine, especially the cleaning, which remained the lowest task of them all. Something always needed to be cleaned and kids were always candidates. George even grew tired of mating the rabbits. He found the humping repetitive. Rabbits didn't hump like humans, and he was a human who needed better role models.

George Sr. worked most evenings in the barn. Sensing his son's growing disillusionment with the chores, the elder Johnson began assuming part of his son's workload. On August 8, father and son finished watering the rabbits early in the evening.

"Let's go in and watch Nixon's speech," George Sr. said. "I can brush and hose down those cages over the weekend."

Inside the house, over a beef stew dinner, young George blurted out, "I haven't been to church since Easter and I don't miss it."

"Really, that long? I'll drive you there this Sunday."

"Don't bother. Hey, Dad? Are you ever gonna tell me why you don't go anymore?"

"When you're old enough."

"I'm fifteen. I'm old enough *now*."

George Sr. paused, studying his son's eyes, bright green like his own, yet with a see-through quality altogether different.

The TV flickered. George Sr. scampered over and turned up the volume when Nixon's face appeared. Father and son listened, each noticing the tension growing in the puffy-cheeked, self-right-eous speaker's voice. Visibly shaken, Nixon was struggling to uphold his dignity.

"Hooray, the bastard's resigning!" George Sr. exclaimed.

They watched until Walter Cronkite's face replaced Nixon's. "He didn't even mention Watergate as a reason for stepping down,"

George Jr. observed. "Everybody knows why he's quitting and he won't even admit it."

"Yeah, he was unbelievably audacious," the elder Johnson said, basking in the self-imposed glory of using a multi-syllabic word. He'd heard Mr. Woo use that word during a recent anti-union talk, and the word stuck in his head.

"Do you think Nixon'll go to jail, Dad?"

"Naw, the President of the United States? The underlings will all take the fall. He'll probably go off to California, sit on the beach drinking ten-year-old scotch. Just collect his fat pension and erase the rest of the tapes."

"So, in the end, Nixon ends up having no boss. He collects a big paycheck, but doesn't have to answer to anybody. Right?"

"Well, he's a disgrace now."

"If he's so bad," young George said, "Then why'd you vote for him?"

"There wasn't anybody else. Eighteen-year-olds can vote now, so you're gonna face the same dilemma in a few years. Who would you have voted for, smart ass?"

"Charlie Finley, that's who."

"The A's owner?"

"Yep. He raises hell. He pays his players to grow beards and mustaches. They wear high stirrups and yellow socks. He wants to use orange baseballs next spring. Boy, he'd really wake people up."

"Come on, he wasn't even running."

"I would've wrote him in. You can do that." Young George rose and turned off the television. "Hey, Dad?"

"Yeah."

"That story why you don't go to church. I'm ready for it."

"Listen, if I tell you, you have to promise not to repeat it to anybody. I don't want it getting around, okay?"

"Yeah, okay."

"Alright. Look, you're not gonna have any brothers or sisters. I'm not gonna have children with any woman besides your mother. I had this operation called a vasectomy. You know what that is?"

"No, but it doesn't sound like fun."

"It wasn't. It's an operation—a procedure—that makes it so you can't have babies anymore."

"How does it work? I mean, are you telling me that you can't doink anybody anymore?"

"Doink! Where'd you pick up that word?"

George shrugged. "Around. Kids use it."

"Anyway, I still can have sex with women, but I can't get them pregnant. I don't need to use any birth control."

"So you can still doink. That's good. Can I ask you another question?"

"Sure."

"When you doink ladies, do you face 'em?"

George Sr. gulped. "What?"

"Do you look at them. Rabbits don't look at each other. I wanna know whether people do."

"Well, there's different ways to have sex."

Young George sat up straight. "Oh?"

"Let me finish explaining the vasectomy."

"I wanna know whether you face ladies when you doink them?"

"Alright, listen. Usually, when men and women have sex, they face each other. But sometimes they don't."

"How come rabbits don't face each other when they're doinking?"

"I honestly don't know."

"You think that it's because rabbits all look the same?"

George Sr. stared at his son.

"Humans all look different. You think that, because rabbits all look the same, they already know what the other ones look like so they don't need to be face to face?"

"I don't know. I just don't know."

"I've got another question."

"Okay." George Sr. said.

"Was Mom the first lady you doinked?"

"Yes," George Sr. answered, suddenly steeped in memories of a night a decade and a half earlier. He saw Mary in a sleeveless violet dress and black pump shoes. He felt the wind blowing dewy air inside the Chevy. He heard the relentless cicadas buzzing nearby. Soon it all became a blur. George Sr. focused on his son sitting on the living room floor. "Can I get back to why I don't go to church anymore?" he asked.

Young George sighed. "Okay."

"Having a vasectomy is a big sin. So I'm not in the state of grace anymore. I haven't received absolution for it, so I can't receive communion."

"You can still go to church, can't you? I mean, is God blocking the door?"

"No, I can still go. But not receiving the body and blood of Christ, well, it's like not going at all. So, I made a pact with God that I would pray every night by myself until I could receive communion again. Then I'll go back to church."

Young George scratched his nose. "Will they ever let you back in?"

"I think so. Things change. I didn't do anything wrong. Back in '66, the same year your mother and sister died, the Church lifted the ban on eating meat on Fridays, except during Lent. That was a pretty big deal. So, we'll see what happens. It's really up to the Vatican. But, I want you to make up your own mind about church. I don't want you not to go just because I don't. I want you to decide for yourself what you wanna do."

"I don't get anything out of it. I'm bored there. I don't wanna go, except maybe at Christmas and Easter."

"You still believe in God, don't you?"

"I think so. I mean, you can't see Him or anything, but everybody seems to think He exists. What a waste of time if He didn't."

George Sr. grunted through a closed-lipped smile. "Yeah, it sure would be."

"Hey, Dad? Priests aren't allowed to marry. Ministers are. Why's that?"

"Catholicism requires priests to remain single and unmarried. And celibate. The Church says priests can't have sexual intercourse."

"Well, Reverend Mason over at the Netherwood Baptist Church has kids. So he must have sex. How come priests can't?"

"Because Catholics have a different belief system."

Young George rolled over onto his side. "I've heard stories that priests and nuns doink on the pews when the doors are locked. Is that true?"

"No! Where'd you hear that?"

"In Sunday school. Some kids used to say it."

"I doubt that's ever happened. Priests and nuns take vows to remain celibate. That's taken seriously. What you heard was just speculation. Don't believe it."

"But everybody sins. How can priests and nuns not sin?"

"Oh, they sin. They just don't commit grave sins because they agreed with God not to."

"I can't believe it's never happened between a priest and a nun."

"Believe it."

Young George stared at the ceiling, wondering how a nun would look in *Playboy*. He pictured the sagging breasts of a frumpy woman wearing a habit, holding a ruler in her hand. "What happens to the church money after the ushers collect it all?"

Relieved, George Sr. answered, "It goes to support the Church."

"How come there's two collections at every mass?"

"Because one goes to the Church and the other one goes to support worthwhile charities."

"When you were taking up the collections, did you ever take any money for yourself?"

"Hell no! That would be stealing. I'd never do that. People give their hard-earned money to the Church. I can't believe you'd ask me such a question!"

"I was just curious. There's a basket full of cash sitting around. They'd never miss a few bucks. You think any of the other ushers do it?"

"Absolutely not! It'd be like stealing from God himself. Let me ask you this," George Sr. said. "When you collect money on rabbit sales, is that what you do, take a few bucks for yourself and give me the rest?"

"No way! You're my father. I'd never do that!"

"Well, geez! That's how I feel."

"Okay. I'm sorry. I should've just asked if others did."

"Well, they don't!"

Young George stood up. "Okay. Thanks for telling me all this stuff."

George Sr. smiled. "You bet. Good talk."

"I'm going to bed. Good night."

❖

KEVIN WITHERSPOON WAS THE star halfback on Deer Creek High's junior varsity football team that fall. He and George became friends. George Sr. usually dropped his son at the Witherspoons' home in the Village after Saturday dinner so the boys could spend the night together.

In Kevin's room, while waiting for Mr. and Mrs. Witherspoon to fall asleep, Kevin said, "Man, we gotta score this year."

"By spring I'll have my license. Then I'm gonna get me some wheels," George asserted.

"Shit, man. You think wheels'll help?"

"Oh yeah. Chicks dig guys with wheels."

Kevin pounded his fist into the mattress. "I gotta get me some action. Lotsa guys on the team have already gotten some."

"Yeah, I know," George said, sighing. "Man-o-man, I don't care if I die when I'm eighteen. I just wanna make sure I got laid. That's why I want the car so bad."

"Whaddaya gonna get?"

"Don't know yet. Something with a big backseat."

"You got the bread?" Kevin asked.

"Yep, I got over five hundred bucks in my savings account from the rabbits. That'll get me a decent used car. I talked to Triple-R Jr. a while back. Said'll give me a job at his station up on the Taconic when I turn sixteen."

"You think he'll gimme one too?"

"Yeah, he likes athletes," George said. "But why doesn't your father just give you a job at Woo Labs? He's a big-time executive there."

"Because I wanna get my own job," Kevin said. "Hopefully Triple-R Jr. will gimme one."

Richard Robert (Robbie) Richardson Jr. owned the Salt Point Texaco station. Locals called him Triple-R Jr. He had a contract with New York State that allowed him to manage a second Texaco station on the Taconic Parkway, two miles north of the Taconic's intersection with Salt Point Turnpike. That gas station had no repair facilities because stations on the Taconic Parkway weren't allowed to perform repair work. Instead, the State awarded exclusive contracts for Taconic Parkway repairs to neighborhood gas stations. For a fifteen-mile stretch of the Taconic Parkway, Triple-R Jr.'s Salt Point Texaco was the only repair facility.

"Whaddaya gonna do 'bout the rabbits?" Kevin asked.

"I'm gonna have to get out. I haven't figured out how yet. My father's gonna be pissed. But I hate being in that barn. It smells. I just feel so…so crowded in there."

"Good thing you quit the Boy Scouts. You'd never score wearing that uniform."

"Man, I know it. Can you imagine me asking a chick out wearing those shorts? And how about those green socks coming up to my knees? Geez, she'd laugh right in my face."

Kevin chuckled. "You told Mrs. B yet?"

"Naw. I can't face her for a while. She probably knows I quit and is steaming mad about it. I'm surprised she hasn't shown up at my house to chew me out."

"I think my parents are asleep. You wanna head out?"

Outside in the warm air, George asked, "You wanna see if any other kids are still awake?"

"No, let's just get the beer."

The beer was housed in two refrigerators inside the Salt Point Firehouse. Salt Point firemen drank only Rheingold in cans. A fireman told Kevin about the beer's existence. A combination lock, with five black buttons protruding from a metal base, rested on the firehouse's front door.

George boasted that he'd be able to break the code and open the firehouse door. Applying a ninth grade algebraic formula for calculating the probability of an outcome, he knew that the door would open with one of sixty permutations. After ten minutes, he opened the door and led Kevin inside.

Kevin found the beer while George climbed into the driver's seat of the fire engine, examining the needles and dials. "Here's a six for you. Let's get the hell outta here," Kevin barked, returning from one of the back rooms.

The boys walked across Cottage Street onto the footpath that led up an embankment. They were near the back entrance to the

Salt Point Cemetery. The largest tombstone belonged to William Tydings, an animal trapper who preserved dead deer in salt in the early 1800s. Salt Point was named for his activities. At its base was a ten-inch ledge for people to kneel when remembering Tydings. Kevin and George sat down on the ledge and opened the Rheingold.

The boys didn't say much while drinking, except when Kevin talked about being elevated to the varsity football team before the season ended. He was hoping to play on Friday nights under the new lights. "It'd be cool to play in front of more people," Kevin said. "Especially the rowdy ones. Nobody really drinks during the day games." Between gulps of beer, George leaned back on his elbows and looked skyward.

The boys stumbled back to Kevin's house. With Kevin fast asleep, George sat up in his bed. He rose and walked down the stairs, taking a flashlight from the Witherspoons' kitchen. George jogged back to the cemetery and walked in the dark to the fourth row from the back, stopping in front of a six-inch high granite tombstone. He moved his right thumb upward. The flashlight awakened, shining its beam on the top of the small tombstone.

George thought of the intersection where the 1966 crash happened. He pictured the newspaper article in his shoebox. Tears rolled down his cheeks onto the tombstone's engraved letters. George flicked the light switch off and stood there for some time, alone in the darkness. Then he made the sign of the cross and looked up into the sky, grimacing as he tried to see where heaven might be past the faint stars. If you pray for your relatives in heaven, can they hear you? Can they make out your thoughts?

❖

THE SHORTEST MONTH OF the year, February, became a long month of reflection for the elder Johnson. His son's birthday, February 3, always reminded him that his son came into the world on the same day in 1959 that rock and roll musicians Buddy Holly, the Big Bopper, and Richie Valens were killed in an airplane crash in Iowa. His son's life began on the Day the Music Died. A kid's life started and a parent's dream faded. The dream-killing kid was born because a priest, Father Dombrowski, refused to allow an abortion. Then, eight days later in February, George Sr. faced the anniversary of the Day Half the Family Died. Yet he soldiered on, trying to raise the kid that, long ago, he didn't really want.

To celebrate his son's sixteenth birthday in 1975, George Sr. bought an ice cream cake at the Carvel Ice Cream store. When he rose that Saturday morning, his son was already eating cereal and turning pages of *The Hudson Valley Watch*. Nixon's top aides, even the Attorney General, had been convicted and would be going to jail.

"Hey! Happy sixteenth birthday!" George Sr. exclaimed, embracing his son and kissing the top of his head.

"Dad!" he shouted, trying to wriggle free. "Good thing no one's around. I'm too old for this."

"Can't I show my son a little affection on his important birthday?"

"Don't you get enough affection at Rondo's Go-Go?"

"I only go there 'cause my boss makes me."

"Yeah, I bet."

"How come you didn't make me bacon and eggs for breakfast?" George Sr. asked, walking into the kitchen.

"It's *my* birthday!"

George Sr. smiled. "You know, I got you that omelet pan over a year ago. You haven't even used it."

"You got it for me? Right! What was her name, that nurse? Miss Roth, she left it here. Why'd you stop seeing her, anyway?"

"It was all too much. Too crowded. But you could still use the pan and make me an omelet."

"I'd use it if you'd bring home some eggs once in a while."

George Sr. poured himself a bowl of cereal. "Pretty soon you'll have your license. Then you can go shopping and get whatever you want."

"Yeah, and I'll make sure we got more beer around here."

"Within reason, you can get what you want."

"Hey, Dad? Check out this article. Come here."

George Sr. read:

Local Youth Drowns in Hudson River

Lester Devonshire, a senior at Deer Creek High School, drowned last night when the car that he was driving broke through the ice covering the Hudson River. Lester, the youngest son of Mr. and Mrs. William P. Devonshire, 29 Havlon Road, Deer Creek, was attempting to drive his car across the frozen river. He left from the former New York Central Railroad Yard in Hudson County. The ice gave way thirty yards from the dock adjoining the Beau Rivage Restaurant in Highland. There were no passengers in the car.

Mr. Devonshire was pronounced dead on arrival at St. Francis Hospital. The Hudson County Sheriff's Department refused to comment on the incident, pending the outcome of its investigation. However, a well-placed source said that a number of students are being interviewed regarding allegations that drug use was a possible cause of the accident.

"DID YOU KNOW THAT boy?" George Sr. asked.

"Yeah, he's the one who shoved my head down the toilet," young George said. "That dummy, trying to drive a one-and-a-half-ton car on the ice. He got what he deserved."

"Don't be too harsh." George Sr. closed the newspaper. "A man loses his boy," he muttered, shaking his head.

"Hey, Dad? I got an idea for a birthday present you can give me."

"I already got you one. And a cake, too."

"How about another one?"

"What is it?"

"You're not gonna like it."

"I have experience with things I don't like."

"I've been thinking about the rabbit business. I need to get out. I don't like being in that barn everyday. I wanna get a real job."

George Sr. bowed his head. He set the teaspoon down inside the cereal bowl and took a few deep breaths. One of the reasons he'd broken off his relationship with Sarabeth Roth was her distaste for the rabbit business. And now his son no longer wanted anything to do with it.

Young George watched his father's sorrow. "I'm sorry, Dad. I gotta get out. Sorry."

George Sr. walked into the living room.

"Dad…where're you going?"

George Sr. said nothing. He started to sit down in the reclining chair, but thought better of it. Instead he opened the hall closet and fished around for a winter parka. Young George entered the living room as his father zipped the faded blue coat shut.

"Dad…"

"Look, you want out!" George Sr. shouted, raising his hands in the air. "You want out!" he repeated, slamming the closet door. "You can have out!" He unlatched the chain and opened the dead bolt on the front door.

"Dad, I— "

George Sr. turned to face his son. "Hey! I said you could get out! Okay? What more do you want from me?" Cold air rushed onto his face as he descended the front steps.

George Sr. let out a fierce scream that battled the January winds swirling around him like the thoughts racing through his head. "What the hell am I supposed to do?" he shouted, looking at the sky. "Whaddaya doing to me? My boy's quitting! My wife and the baby are gone!" George paused, barely catching his breath before shouting, "You ever feel any guilt up there?"

Except for when George had played high school baseball, he was somewhere along the expansive bottom of the pyramid, neck and neck with everyone else. Raising rabbits was his first original idea. His alone. He'd taken that idea and acted on it, turning it into a thriving business. He'd started with nothing. Two years later, he had nearly $11,000 in the bank, his only savings. The rabbits made him feel like he'd risen above his ordinariness, like he'd found a place all his own.

Plus he was saving money for his kid's college tuition. For his ungrateful kid's future. He didn't heed Father Dombrowski's advice on the vasectomy. Why did he acquiesce when the head priest said no abortion?

He stared at the stacks of rabbit cages saturated with white animals in various sizes and thought about his second idea that would now go by the wayside. He'd already decided that earthworms and rabbits would be the perfect combination. With his son's help, the worms could've lived in the rabbit manure. Over one million nightcrawlers could've multiplied in one-foot high by three-foot-wide-by-twenty-foot-long plywood bins that he planned to build in the basement. He'd already mailed out feelers to bait shops.

George reflected on the many hours he'd spent working with his teenage son, picturing him carrying a buck with two hands to a doe's cage. Those vapid rabbit chores once delighted his son. Now he'd probably have to sell all two thousand rabbits to the butcher and close down the business.

❖

WHEN THE ROADS CLEARED in late February, George Jr. took his road test. The elder Johnson had taught his son how to operate the pickup. The examiner remarked that he'd never seen a kid take a road test in such a large vehicle. While waiting for the official results to arrive in the mail, George scanned *The Watch*'s classifieds, looking for a good buy on a used car. As soon as he got his wheels, he could begin working at the Taconic Texaco.

When his father strolled in the kitchen for breakfast, George Jr. asked, "Can I take the Chevy around the corner? Just to Ring Road. A car's for sale that I wanna look at."

"You don't have your license yet."

"I know. But it's only a couple of miles from here."

"I'll drive you if you want," George Sr. said, taking the cereal out of the kitchen cabinet. "But you gotta wait 'til all the paperwork's done before driving on your own."

"Will you let me handle the guy then?"

"If that's what you want, I won't butt in. But I think you should let me look over any car you're planning to buy."

"Alright, you can come."

"What kinda car is it?"

"A gold Duster. 1968. Owner's asking seven hundred and fifty bucks. The ad says it's in great running condition."

George Sr. sat down to eat his cereal. "You think they'd say it was in lousy running condition? It's called puffing. Everybody does it. Is it a V-8 or V-6?"

"A V-6."

"That'll be a little better on gas mileage. After the oil embargo, the days of thirty cents a gallon are gone forever."

After breakfast, the Johnsons drove to Ring Road. A bearded man, dressed in a heavy gray parka with a synthetic fur-lined hood, met the Johnsons outside by the Duster, sparing them a glimpse inside the disheveled shell in which he lived with his pregnant wife and two infants. He emphasized the car's virtues: new air shocks, no body rust, good tires, and a recent tune-up. He skimmed right over the eighty-six thousand plus miles it had been driven.

"Okay to take her out for a drive?" George Sr. asked.

"Yeah, if you're serious," the man replied. He handed George Sr. the keys. "Just don't burn up all the gas."

George Jr. took the keys out of his father's hand. "I'm the one deciding whether to buy it. I'll drive," he said. George Sr. shrugged.

The Johnsons liked the way the Duster handled. Stopping on Netherwood Road, young George got out and opened the hood. His father examined the engine. "Not a bad buy for seven hundred and fifty. Mileage is kinda high, but the car's seven years old. The price is still under Blue Book. Can you afford what he's asking?"

"Yeah. I like this car. It's me. You know, fast and bad-looking. Plus it's gold. But I ain't payin' seven hundred and fifty bucks."

"Let's see what he'll do."

"Dad, let me handle it, okay?"

"Alright, alright. I won't say a word."

The bearded man, accompanied by his wife, waited for the Johnsons to return with the car. The man took back the keys. "Doesn't run too bad," George Jr. offered, smiling at the wife. "But she's got high mileage. I can only offer ya five hundred for her."

"Five hundred bucks! Whaddaya wastin' my time for, kid!" the man shouted in a raspy voice. "I'd come down to seven hundred. But that's it!"

"Five bills, that's my offer," George Jr. reiterated. "Take it or leave it."

"Forget it then. If you'd take her today, I'd let her go for six-fifty, but no less. Absolutely no less."

With a flair of practiced showmanship, George Jr. reached into his coat pocket. One at a time, he laid out each of the five crisp one hundred dollar bills face up on the gold Duster's hood. "Five hundred bucks, that's all I got. If you give me the title and registration, you can take the brand new Ben Franklins inside."

The bearded man said nothing for a few seconds, alternating his exasperated gaze between the five bills and his wife. "Honey, we sure could use the money," she said. The man went inside. After a few silent minutes in which three sets of eyes evaded each other, the man emerged from the trailer with two pieces of paper. The Johnsons watched him sign over the title, hand over the documents, and scoop up the five bills. He turned and walked back to the trailer, leaving the keys on the hood.

Two days later, George received his New York driver's license in the mail. He began to transform himself into an eighteen-year-old. He went back to the DMV and claimed that he'd lost his original driver's license. He paid five dollars to obtain a duplicate, which he'd show to a police officer if he was ever pulled over. George altered his original license by taking a single-edged razor blade and scraping off the nine in his year of birth and writing in a seven with a fine-point black pen. Then he became eighteen and could buy alcohol and gain admission to bars.

❖

YOUNG GEORGE BEGAN WORK in late March. He didn't have to show up for his first day until four on Saturday afternoon, yet he left home in his gold Duster at two-thirty. Driving up Fox Run Road, he felt and heard the gravel crunch underneath his car's tires until he reached the pavement on Netherwood Road. Five minutes later, he turned right off Salt Point Turnpike into Ursula Brombecker's driveway. She was unloading groceries from the trunk of her car. George remained in his Duster for a few seconds, knowing that Ursula couldn't see through its tinted windows and windshield. Finally, he opened the car door and shouted, "Whadja think, I was a robber?"

"You crazy son-of-a-bitch! You scared the crap outta me! Get your ass over here and carry these bags inside."

George strolled over to her. He set the bags on the car's hood and hugged her. She kissed him on the cheek. "It's good to see you, George," Ursula whispered, stepping back. "Come on, help me get these bags in and I'll fix you a sandwich."

"What I really want is some cream of mushroom soup."

"Of course," she replied, smiling. "I got plenty." George told her about the Duster, playing baseball, the new job, school, and quitting the rabbit business. "You're forgetting one thing," Ursula reminded him.

"I know. I hope you're not mad. I thought you might be. That's why I stayed away for so long."

"You coulda been an Eagle Scout. You were ahead of most kids who made it to life."

"I couldn't wear that uniform to high school anymore. No girls would talk to me."

"So that's what this is about. Girls, huh?"

George shrugged. "Yeah, I guess."

"I think being an Eagle Scout would impress some girls," Ursula offered.

"Not the kind I wanna impress. Really, Mrs. B, you're out of touch on this one. Trust me."

Ursula sat down across from George at the kitchen table. "So, what's this new job gonna do for you? You seem in an awful hurry to work."

George squirmed in his seat. "I just wanna make some money. I mean, with money I can pretty much do what I want."

"But weren't you making decent money with the rabbits?"

George took a swig of soup. "The money wasn't bad," he acknowledged. "But the whole scene was getting to be too much. You know, kinda cramped. I smelled like rabbit shit."

"Gasoline and oil smell better?"

"But this is a real job. It's not every day. It's not morning and night. And it's my job. I don't share it with my father. Or anybody else." George looked at his Timex. "I gotta run. I'm due at work in fifteen minutes. I'll stop by again."

Triple-R Jr.'s Taconic Texaco was between the northbound and southbound lanes of the Taconic Parkway. Ingress was limited to motorists exiting to the left off the winding road. Three sets of gasoline pumps greeted those in need. A plastic bottle filled with diluted cleaner sat on top of each set of pumps, which attendants used to wash every customer's windshield.

A small brick building next to the pumps contained an old, large vanilla cash register with a sliding black drawer. The building also housed bathrooms and soda and candy machines. Triple-R Jr. appeared at four that Saturday to explain to George how everything worked. George worked the 4:00 p.m. to 10:00 p.m. shift on weekends, which didn't conflict with school or baseball practice.

Triple-R Jr. was a slightly built, middle-aged man with a mole on his left cheek. He paid George two dollars and ten cents an hour, the minimum wage. George noticed a few dark hairs growing out of that mole. He tried to count the stray hairs, which made it hard to concentrate on the instructions. Despite the distraction, nothing prevented George from noting the loaded .45 pistol, wooden billy club, and razor-sharp machete that were kept on the top shelf of the counter, right under the cash register.

"You're gonna get weirdos in here, especially on Saturday nights," Triple-R Jr. warned. "If somebody tries to rob you, just take the gun out and shoot the bastard. Make sure you keep the safety off or you won't have time to shoot. If the safety's on, you'll just have to cut him up with the machete." Triple-R Jr. removed one of the floor tiles, exposing the safe. A slot allowed attendants to slip large dollar bills inside. "Don't ever keep more than fifty bucks in the drawer. That way, if you get held up and are too chicken to shoot, then he doesn't get that much."

"Yeah, right. And then he shoots me."

"You'll be alone, so just keep your wits about you. I'll be back at ten to show you how to close up."

George soon fell into a comfortable routine. One month into the job a woman, wearing a pink knit tube top and blue jeans, caught his eyes while he washed her windshield. Without any warning, she lifted the tube top from her breasts. George gawked and brushed his long hair away from his eyes. Then he smiled. He felt guilty taking the fifty-cent tip from her husband, who'd been in the men's room at the time.

George pulled his trousers up and stuck the two quarters into his pocket. The quarters rattled against each other until they settled at the bottom of his pocket, like the woman's exposed breasts had rattled against each other. A memorable moment for a teenager. Momentary attention for a young woman. But why she'd do that? Boredom, he figured.

George Sr. visited later that night. He sat on the sidewalk near the gasoline pumps. He opened a can of Shop-Rite cola and watched his sixteen-year-old son work. Selling gasoline instead of rabbits. Cleaning up after customers instead of rabbits. Wearing a collared Texaco shirt with his name on it instead of a tee shirt. He took a swig from the can and set it on the sidewalk. "Kid forced me out of the rabbit business," he muttered.

A Cadillac approached from the Taconic and stopped in front of the pumps. George Sr. stood up and chucked his soda can into the metal trash container. He waved good-bye to his son and walked toward his pickup. "Unemployment's over nine percent, and he's responsible for a whole business," he said to himself.

The second Saturday in May was quiet at 9:45 p.m. Not many customers usually came in after nine, and George Jr. used the time to brush up on triangular properties before the upcoming New York State Geometry Regents exam. Even though no car had pulled up, he heard the rusted bell jingle as the office door opened. A woman walked in. She wore a navy blue windbreaker, faded denim shorts, and sandals. When she walked toward the vending machines, George's eyes returned to his geometry notes. A minute later the woman appeared at the counter. He looked up. "Is there anything I can do for you, ma'am?"

The woman lifted her right hand to remove a few errant strands of unwashed brown hair from her face. As she perched the hair behind her right ear, George saw her right eye drooping lower than her left. She leaned over the counter, with her windbreaker open, exposing a bulging neon green halter. George took a step backward to expand his field of vision to include her face.

"I sure hope so," she answered. Her smile exposed small grayish teeth. "Say, you sure are cute. What's your name?"

"George. Ummm, what's yours?"

"Sandy. My name's Sandy. Say, Georgie, I have a little itty bitty problem here." She ran her fingers across the embroidered name on George's left front shirt pocket. "How come if your name's George, it says Robbie here?"

"Because they only gave me one shirt with George on it and that one's dirty. I'm kinda new."

"Oh," she whispered, "I see."

"Ma'am, uhh, ma'am. What's the problem that you have?" George asked, smelling her drugstore perfume.

"I'm just about out of gas. It's another ninety miles to New York City. And I'm all out of money."

"That sure sounds like a problem. I'm sorry, but I can't give you any gas if you can't pay for it. The boss'll fire me."

"Well," she said, "I was thinking maybe we could make a little trade."

"What kind of trade?"

She took off her windbreaker. "You can have me for a tank of gas!"

With his back against the wall and the woman advancing, George responded, "I don't know. I could get in trouble."

She untied the strings at the top of her halter and ran her tongue across the top row of her teeth. "I don't think you'll get in any trouble," she said, lowering the neon green halter to expose her breasts.

Sandy took the keys from George and locked the office door from the inside. He flicked the two switches that turned the pump lights off.

"Wh…where?" he asked.

"On the floor. Just you relax, Georgie. I'll show you how."

Which she did, quite well, though she wore an expression of studied indifference throughout. George would later laugh at how he lost his virginity, recounting that he had lasted longer than any of the male rabbits, but not by much. George pumped six dollars worth of regular gas into her Volkswagen Beetle. She waved good-bye. He took six dollars from his wallet and put the bills in the cash register. George closed the station and locked the door. He drove home, humming, "You can trust your car to the man who wears the star."

For the next week, he held center stage during lunch-time conversations, telling the other boys about the woman at the Taconic Texaco. "She just wanted me. She couldn't control herself," he'd say, omitting the part about how it cost him six dollars. "Wow, tell it again!" they'd shout. And he would oblige.

When school and baseball season ended, Triple-R Jr. increased George's weekly hours from twelve to thirty, giving him the 4:00-10:00 p.m. shift Saturdays through Wednesdays. So father and son ate dinner together only twice a week that summer. To George Sr. the house seemed empty with his son away so much. Some evenings George Sr. would open his son's final report card, which he kept in the top drawer of his bedside night table. "That kid sure is smart," he'd say, staring at the picture of Mary.

With his summer days free, young George palled around with Kevin Witherspoon. Kevin's father was in charge of human resources at Woo Labs. George Jr. overheard Mr. Witherspoon saying, "We're just going to have to hire more scum to work third shift on those grinding machines."

Over beers at the Clinton Recreation Park, George asked Kevin, "Doesn't your father understand that the workers actually make the glass products that bring in the money to pay his salary?"

Kevin shrugged.

Mrs. Witherspoon hated the thought of her son riding with a long-haired boy in a gold Duster with mag wheels, air shocks, and tinted windows. One afternoon she went to the mailbox and noticed that George's Duster, parked behind her Mercedes in the driveway, had a bumper sticker that read, "Don't Laugh, Your Daughter May Be Inside." The Witherspoons had twin daughters younger than George.

Mrs. Witherspoon rushed in the house to make sure that George was nowhere near her daughters. She took them shopping for the rest of the day. "What can we do?" an exasperated Mr. Witherspoon asked later that night. "Ban Kevin from seeing George? How could we enforce that? Besides, George is a straight-A student. And he doesn't have red eyes or dilated pupils like the scum at the plant."

❖

KIDS IN DEER CREEK did most of their partying on the eastern shore of the Hudson River at an abandoned boat landing. They reached the boat landing by driving down a dirt access road behind Happy's AMC Jeep dealership. Since the road began on private property, the police didn't know about it. That all changed when Lester Devonshire died. The sheriff department's investigation led to the discovery of the access road.

After Lester's death, kids still partied at the boat landing, but they had to pay attention to every set of headlights winding their way down through the woods. The rule was that all arriving cars had to flash their high beams three times, signaling to everyone near the river that the approaching car was okay. Whenever patrol cars arrived, kids threw their bottles and cans and joints into the woods. Since the spot by the river was public property, kids couldn't be arrested for just being there.

George drove his gold Duster all over town that summer. With the windows opened, his long hair flapping in the wind and music blaring from his new eight-track, power-boosted, four-speaker Blaupunkt stereo system, neighbors couldn't miss his approach. He came to know all of the corners on Netherwood Road by heart. He'd drive past Netherwood Baptist Church and the pastor's adjoining home (where he thought of Reverend Mason screwing his wife), Netherwood Acres (a horse breeding farm where he once watched a foal being born), and Netherwood Elementary School (which would later be plastered with signs declaring it to be drug free).

George felt a sense of freedom leaving Salt Point. He'd never been anywhere else, not even to New York City, though his father had tickets to an upcoming Labor Day double-header at Shea Stadium. The gold Duster was a ticket that allowed him to go anywhere outside the Village of Salt Point. Deer Creek was in the opposite direction, and that route took him over roads he'd rarely traveled before getting his driver's license.

In late August, Jennifer Conlin, a regular at the abandoned Hudson Valley boat landing, mentioned to George that her cousin would be visiting in a few days.

"So," he responded.

"Maybe you and me and Kevin can go driving," Jennifer suggested. "We could, you know, show her around."

"Okay. If you bring her down to the river, I'm sure we'll be around."

"I was thinking of setting up something now," she persisted.

"Alright. For when? If you wanna do it before ten thirty, it's gotta be a Thursday or Friday."

"How about next Friday? Will you pick us up?"

"Wait a minute. What's this cousin of yours look like?"

"She's very pretty. And she's seventeen, like me."

A week later, George and Kevin arrived at the Conlin home. The boys got out of the gold Duster but the girls quickly emerged from behind the front door. Jennifer had seen George's bumper sticker and knew her parents wouldn't appreciate it.

"George and Kevin," Jennifer said after the girls made their way down the walkway, "this is my cousin, Desiree." Each boy said hello and noticed that both girls were wearing skirts. Kevin and Desiree climbed in the back seat. Jennifer perched herself in the front passenger seat.

"Where do you wanna go?" George asked.

"I've never been out to Salt Point," Jennifer said. "Why don't you drive us out there?"

"Okay. I know a place where we can go. There's a park on Clinton Hollow Road. It's closed at night, but the gates aren't locked." George tapped the steering wheel. "We'll have to get beer in Deer Creek. There's no place out there."

They stopped at the 7-Eleven on Route 9. George picked out one six-pack of Heineken and one six-pack of Genessee Cream Ale. "Hey, Kevin," George called out. "Bring two more sixes of Genny Cream to the counter."

"You're sure we need four sixes?" Kevin inquired, hoisting the beer cans on the counter. "We didn't get any money from the girls."

"Don't worry about that, man," George replied, winking. "They'll pay us back later."

"What if there's extra? It'll go to waste."

"No, it won't. My father lets me keep beer in our fridge. It's better to have too much than too little."

"How come girls never pay for anything?"

"Look, stop whining. You still have the condom I gave ya?"

Kevin nodded.

"Good, tonight's gonna be your big night. Give me a few extra bucks for gas, okay? It's a long way out there."

George backed the Duster out of the 7-Eleven's parking lot. "Keep the beers down when a car approaches," he admonished. "Cops still might be able to see in through the front windshield with their headlights on."

George reached into his ashtray and retrieved a bottle opener. "You'll need this," he said, handing it over his shoulder to Kevin. "Open the Heinies first."

On the half-hour ride to the Town of Clinton Recreation Park, the girls yammered about some new perfume that was killing the air inside his car and would probably later seep its way onto his lips.

"Smells nice," he finally said when Jennifer stuck one of her dainty wrists under his nose. Multicolored costume bracelets dangled over her translucent skin, chiming in the wind.

When the group arrived at the park's entrance, George shut off the headlights. He knew the way to the beach by heart and didn't want to draw attention from other passing cars. The girls jumped out of the Duster as soon as it stopped. George signaled Kevin to meet him behind the car and handed him a blanket from the trunk. "Take this and a six. There's plenty of room past where the creek bends over there." He pointed the way.

"Right now? Shouldn't I wait a bit?" Kevin asked.

"Just walk up to her nicely, take her by the hand, and say that you wanna see what's around the bend." In the moonlight, George watched proudly as Desiree slid down the slope of the creek's bank with Kevin, safely out of sight.

George and Jennifer opened their blanket on the sand and drank parts of their beers. Without warning, Jennifer lifted her skirt for him. She snatched the condom from George's hand and put it on him. She thrusted a lot more than the Taconic Texaco seductress and instructed George to keep moving.

"How was it?" Jennifer asked, turning over to grab a beer.

"Fine. How was it for you?"

"You need more practice. It was too quick, almost as quick as when you lit that fire in Miss Mackey's class"

George sat up. "So you ratted me out."

"You're not mad, are you?"

George laughed. "Nah, it was probably good that I got caught and suspended. Slowed me down a little. Made me think more about the stuff I was doing."

Out of nowhere, Kevin came running toward their blanket, his beaming face flushed red. "George! George!" he whispered as low as he could. "I need another rubber. Where are they?"

"Kevin, my boy. Another one already?"

"Yeah, yeah. Where are they?"

"In the glove compartment," George answered, leaning back on the blanket with his hands clasped behind his head.

Kevin took a six-pack and ran back toward the creek. George watched until Jennifer rolled over on top of him. "Time to rally, Georgie."

"Okay, but don't order me around this time. It's distracting."

❖

AFTER THE BUTCHER PICKED up the last few hundred rabbits, The Johnson Rabbitry went out of business. George Sr. walked across Fox Run Road to examine his unused eight-acre swamp. Buddy followed behind. George remembered that he and Mary often wondered if any productive use could be made of those wetlands. When George Jr. began to walk, they avoided the place. That collection of stagnant water, broken trees, and thick vegetation held the possibility of serious injury or even death for their feisty little boy. Mary wanted to fence off the swamp, but the prohibitive cost precluded the Johnsons from doing anything other than keeping a watchful eye on their son.

George allowed himself a wistful smile. He turned around and crossed the street, walking with Buddy past his house to the backyard. He sat down on the cinderblocks bordering the well. On many nights he and Mary had rested on those same cinderblocks watching their kids play on the grass. Now George sat there alone, with no kids to watch and no wife to hold. He reached down and touched the inside of a cinderblock. He felt coarseness against the palm of his hand. The roughness reminded him of Mary's smooth hands and fingers. He took a deep breath, surprised that roughness could remind him of softness, of her.

A flurry of images rushed at George. Images of Mary and their kids as toddlers sloshing around in their blue plastic swimming pool. Images of him pushing their kids on the swing set with Mary, facing them, hands held out, letting their kids know that Mommy would catch them if they fell. As quickly as each image appeared it disappeared into the next one, until no more came.

He continued running his hands across the cinderblocks' abrasive pattern, feeling the bumps against his calluses. He examined the cinderblocks with his fingertips, searching for any imperfections, for any spots of softness.

❖

As a junior, young George was a benchwarmer on the varsity soccer team. He played in only three games, though never when the final outcome might have been affected by his performance. He thought many times about quitting, but the coach reminded him that he'd be a starter as a senior. "Why don't I quit now and just play next year?" George asked.

"Because, if you quit now, I'll make sure you sit again next year," the coach responded. But riding the bench made George feel like he was on the bottom of the pyramid.

Over dinner in late October, the elder Johnson announced that he wanted to watch a varsity soccer game. "I'm starting to understand the game. I'd like to see how the team is doing. I can *tell* you how the team is doing this year. You can *see* how it does next year when I'll be playing."

"You can tell me where I can go, and where I can't?"

"I'm *asking* you. Please don't come to any games this year. For me, okay?"

The elder Johnson clasped his hands behind his head. "Okay, if that's what you want. Whaddaya gonna do about baseball season? Do you have the same situation, a senior shortstop?"

"Yeah, there's a guy named Wendell Smith who rode the bench last year. I'm hoping that Coach Royce isn't gonna give him the position just 'cause he's a senior. It'll kill me to sit on the bench for baseball."

"When I was a junior, I was lucky because there weren't any seniors who played shortstop. So I sort of inherited the job."

"You were also great. I hear the stories from the other kids' fathers. They say you were a natural. Bobby's father says you fielded better than major league shortstops. Says you did everything, catching, throwing, all in one fluid motion."

"I don't know about all that." George Sr. hated reminders of past glory. Maybe someday they'd be pleasant recollections, and he could retrieve the scrapbook Mary used to keep in the attic. But now they were reminders of lost chances.

"How come coaches will start a senior over a junior?" young George asked, staring out the window.

"When you're a senior, it's your last hurrah. Coaches think a junior has to be much better before they sit a senior."

"I think if a junior's better, the junior should start. None of this last hurrah crap."

"You're gonna learn that the world doesn't work like you think it should. So, if you wanna chance to start at short this season, you better practice in the gym this winter."

"I will. I'm not gonna let any senior beat me out."

George Jr. practiced every day, but Wendell Smith became the starting shortstop. George didn't sit on the bench, though. Coach Royce moved him over to second base.

Since George had become a starter, he didn't try to stop his father from attending home baseball games. And the elder Johnson didn't miss one. For the first home game against Kingston, George Sr. left work early to be there at 4:00 p.m. Deer Creek High traditionally set up a public address system for the first home game. Every player was introduced, and George Sr. wanted to see his son run onto the field and tip his cap to the fans. George Sr. had also agreed to throw out the first pitch.

"Batting eighth, playing second base and wearing Number one, the son of the most honored athlete in our school's rich history, George Johnson Jr.!" the PA speaker called out. An exuberant young George waved from the field to his father, who was sitting in the bleachers.

After the player introductions, the elder Johnson strolled out to the field.

"Ladies and Gentlemen," the PA speaker began. "Let me direct your attention to the pitcher's mound. We've got a special treat for you all today. The time was the 1950s. The Dodgers were playing at Ebbets Field in Brooklyn. The Giants were playing at the Polo Grounds in New York. One hundred miles upstate, Deer Creek had its very own baseball star. He is still, yes that's right, still to this day the holder of six career Deer Creek baseball records—highest batting average, most hits, most runs batted in, most stolen bases, most assists, and best fielding percentage by an infielder. But that's not all! In 1958, while leading Deer Creek to the only state championship in the school's storied history, he was named the Most Valuable Player. Folks, please give a warm and gracious welcome to Ge-or-ge John-son, Seeeeenior!!"

What else was there for George Sr. to do but throw the damn ball to the catcher? A few hundred fans cheered, yet he probably knew only a few of them. The catcher offered George the baseball, but he refused to take it. He waved to the crowd, then walked off the field and shook his son's hand before taking his seat in the bleachers.

"Hey, Johnson, not a bad toss for a has-been!" a man yelled.

George turned and nodded to Daryl Edwards, Bobby's father. "I'm not a has-been," he replied. "I'm a never-was."

❖

OVER THE COURSE OF the season, George watched most games in the company of Daryl Edwards and Pauline Swenson, the mother of the senior third baseman, Brian Swenson. It was the top of the second inning when George arrived for the Wappingers Falls game. "Hey, G-man, you ain't missed nothing," Daryl yelled. "It's zero-zero."

George said, "I've got something to show the both of you."

"Yeah, what?" Pauline replied, her eyes fixed on the action in front of her.

George pulled a piece of white paper out of his shirt pocket. "Math—seven-nintey, Verbal—seven-thirty," he read. That totals fifteen-twenty, which is in the ninety-ninth percentile!"

"So, what's that mean?" Daryl asked.

"You dummy, don't you know?" Pauline interjected.

"I'll tell him, Pauline," George said. "Those are George's test scores for the PSATs."

"Oh, that tells me a lot. What the hell is a PSAT?"

"It stands for…" George paused to clear his throat. "They make it so hard to pronounce, Pre-limin-ary Scho-las-tic Ap-ti-tude Test. It's a test colleges require. George got in the highest two percent of the whole country!"

"Bobby ain't mentioned that test. Anyway, college is so damn expensive, I could never afford to send him." Daryl leaned forward and reached across George to tap Pauline on the shoulder. "Did your kid take that test?"

"No, he didn't. But he's goin' to Hudson County Community College next year or I'll throw him out of the house."

She turned to George. "That's great about your son. Can you afford to send him?"

"I'll take a second mortgage on the house if I have to. But colleges give financial aid these days. You can't believe how complicated the stuff is. It's like the colleges all get together and make up all these crazy rules and deadlines just so they don't have to give away much money."

The Deer Creek centerfielder made a shoestring catch for the third out.

"Check this out," George said, placing his arms on each of their shoulders. "The Ivy League schools don't even give out scholarships for sports. Nothing! This whole Ivy League thing is a conspiracy. Rich kids of alumni automatically get in. Plus, they charge unbelievably high tuitions. That way, even if the government makes them give out some financial aid, it still costs more to go there than a state school. So not many working class kids get to go. That opens up lotsa room for kids whose parents are gonna be making big donations. But where does that leave the smart, working class kids? Out in the cold, baby."

"Keep it down, Johnson, Bobby's up," Daryl said.

"Congratulations, George," Pauline said, clutching his elbow. "You should be proud of him. He's a good boy."

Bobby Edwards flew out to the leftfielder. Daryl tapped his right knee in disgust.

A loud voice laced with a slight German accent called out, "How's the little wise-ass doing so far!"

George recognized the voice. "Mrs. B, what're you doing here?" he shouted, peering down toward the field and waving to her.

Ursula Brombecker made her way up the steps and displaced Daryl from his seat. "What do you think I'm doing here?" she said to George. "I came to see the star baseball player. Then I'm coming over for dinner."

"Well, your timing's good. That's him coming up to bat now. The guy before him just walked."

Ursula stood up and shouted, "Come on, you can hit this knuckle head!" Spectators sitting closer to the field looked back over their shoulders. George Sr. winced. At home plate, the Wappingers Falls catcher asked, "Hey, batter, is that your old lady?"

"Naw, she's my girlfriend. I'm into older chicks. They do all the work for ya." The catcher laughed and missed the ball, allowing the runner on first to reach second.

Ursula cupped her hand over her mouth and asked George Sr, "Why does he wear the number one on his uniform?"

"Because that's the number his father wore."

Ursula smirked. "That's not why. He told me he wore the number one because it reminded him of an erection."

"He didn't say that! Did he?"

"No," Ursula confessed through a smile. "But just look at all these cute girls around here. They're here to check out your son. Why else would girls come to baseball games?"

"To watch them?"

"You've been breathing in too many fumes at work. Did Mary come out of love for the game itself?"

"Well, you have a point there."

"Let me fill you in on something else. Erections are what caused your son to quit the Boy Scouts."

"Will you keep your voice down! I know people here."

"It's true. Your son told me that himself. He quit scouts because of girls. He thought they'd laugh at the uniform."

After dinner that evening, Ursula placed her hand on young George's shoulder. "I hope I didn't embarrass you today by yelling while you were at bat."

"Naw. I'm glad you came. You wanna know what I said to the catcher about you?"

"I most certainly do," Ursula replied.

"After you yelled at me, the catcher asked if you were my mother."

"And what did you tell him?"

"I told him you were my girlfriend!"

Ursula laughed. Even George Sr. chuckled.

"Then he missed the ball," young George continued. "So the runner got to second. Then I singled him home. I got an RBI because you yelled at me. Even the umpire was laughing."

"Well, Mrs. B, you're helping my son's statistics."

While young George used the bathroom, the elder Johnson said, "It's good for him to have a female influence. He really respects you, you know."

Ursula beamed.

❖

TRIPLE-R JR. HIRED KEVIN Witherspoon to work the Friday evening shift at the Taconic Texaco during baseball season. Like George, Kevin learned to take the pump readings, recording the seven-digit serial numbers that corresponded to the volume of gallons pumped. Triple-R Jr. used the number of gallons consumed per shift to compute the shift's gross gasoline revenues. He then reconciled the shift's cash and credit card receipts with the gross revenue calculation.

One night, while reading the pumps closest to the office, Kevin felt the barrel of a gun pressed against the back of his head. The assailant marched him inside the office and told him to lock the door and turn off all the outside lights. When he ordered Kevin to open the cash register, Kevin grabbed the machete and swung it at the robber's face, grazing his neck. The assailant fired two shots, one that shattered Kevin's cheekbone and one that struck him in the chest. Kevin's lifeless body was found the next morning on the floor of the men's room.

Young George's nose was in a chemistry textbook the next day when his father walked upstairs.

"Son, I gotta tell you what happened last night."

George Jr. lifted his head.

"Kevin Witherspoon was robbed and killed at the station."

"What! Kevin's dead?"

George Sr. described the murder to his son.

Young George sat back and stared at his bedroom ceiling. "Wow. Kevin was a great guy." George saw a vague image of his own mother on his bedroom ceiling. Then a likeness of his baby sister. He dreaded reading Kevin's obit in the newspaper.

"I'm uncomfortable about you going to work tonight."

"I'll be okay. It's my last weekend. Next week I start at Richardson's in The Village."

"I'm sorry for Kevin's parents. It coulda just as easily happened to you. God, it makes me nervous thinking about you alone, with those crazies that come in. If it happened to you, I'd be all alone."

George Jr. walked over to the edge of the doorway. "Hey, it's okay. Nothing happened to me." He grasped his father's biceps and gently shook them. "Dad, I know. It's scary. I can't believe Kevin's gone. What if the guy had robbed the station on Saturday instead of Friday?"

"Then you'd probably be the one dead."

"But you said they found a machete on the floor. Kevin was probably trying to cut the guy's head off. Me, I'd just give him the money.

And I keep a lot more than fifty bucks in the drawer. Five, six, seven hundred bucks. I keep the whole night's take in there. I don't want some lunatic shooting me because he only got fifty bucks."

"I figure you can handle any situation."

"Right, you gotta think about things in advance—"

"But that's not the point. The point is you shouldn't be exposed to that stuff, those risks. You're only seventeen and you're worrying about being robbed and shot. In my day, we didn't even think about stuff like that."

They looked into each other's eyes for a few seconds.

"Hey," George Sr. said.

"Yeah?"

"Would it be okay if I spent the last couple of hours at the station with you? Tonight and tomorrow night? I don't want you closing up alone. That's the most dangerous time."

"If that'll make you feel better."

Holding him tight, not ever wanting to let him go, George Sr. whispered in his son's ear, "Yes, it will. It sure will."

George Jr. pulled back, again grasping his father's biceps. "Promise me one thing, though."

"What's that?"

"That you aren't gonna spread this around. I'm really old enough to look out for myself."

"Okay, sure. And let's bring some pizzas over to the Witherspoons' house tonight."

The Johnsons ate pepperoni pizza for two consecutive nights at the Taconic Texaco.

Richardson's Texaco in The Village stayed open until midnight. George Jr. worked the four to midnight shift five nights a week during the summer before his senior year of high school. Most of the customers were regulars, not the transients who filled up at the Taconic Texaco. Richardson's Texaco got the occasional shunpikers, but they always seemed friendly, different from the Taconic Parkway motorists speeding to reach their destinations.

Triple-R Jr. spent most of his days at Suzie's Tavern on Clinton Hollow Road. Suzie's was one of the few places left where patrons could still buy a glass of draft beer for twenty-five cents. Even though the two hundredth anniversary of the signing of the Declaration of Independence generated price increases throughout the Hudson Valley, Suzie kept hers the same. For another quarter, customers could play a game of pool, shoot darts, or roll ten frames on the bowling machine. Triple-R Jr. usually sat next to the beer tap. But his Texaco employees knew that their absentee boss could appear unannounced at any time.

When George switched to Richardson's Texaco, he found ways to make a few extra dollars. K-Mart sold Texaco motor oil for sixty-nine cents a quart. Triple-R Jr. sold a quart for a dollar and fifty cents. George always kept a case of oil in the trunk of his Duster. He'd keep a mental record of how many quarts he sold each shift and almost never rang up oil sales. If he sold ten quarts of oil during a shift, he'd replace Triple-R Jr.'s cans with ten from his trunk, pocketing over eight dollars on the deal.

George also made extra money by selling receipts to business customers, usually salesmen. They'd purchase a small amount of gasoline, pay cash, and ask for a receipt in a greater amount so they'd have the documentation for their expense reports. Sometimes people asked for a receipt without even buying anything. George charged these customers a cash fee of twenty-five percent of the receipt's amount.

❖

IN THE FALL OF George's senior year, his English teacher handed him an unsigned, typewritten note: "Instead of your fifth period study hall, report to Mr. Shostankovich's office." George entered the main office. "Go right in," the white-haired woman behind the counter said.

"Oh, George! Please come in," Mr. Shostankovich said, waving his hairy-knuckled hand. "Sit down."

He chose the chair farthest from the principal's desk. "What is it?"

"Relax. This is a pleasant get-together."

"Okay."

"I have to tell you, young man, that in the three years since you were last in this office, you've come a long way."

"Thanks, I guess. So…"

"So," the principal intoned, "I want to commend you on your advancement." He smiled and lifted a piece of computer-generated paper from his desk top. "After three and a quarter years, you're the number one student in your class. You will likely be the class of 1977's valedictorian."

"Really?"

"Yes. And the valedictorian gets to give the traditional commencement address."

"Would I get any money for it?"

The principal laughed. "Of course not. But you'd get the honor. And it's a very impressive honor, if you win it."

"May I have that piece of paper with all the grades on it?"

"I can't give out other students' confidential grades."

"Well, can you rip the paper in half? I don't need their names, only the grades."

"What do you want this for?"

"So I can calculate the size of my lead and figure out what I need in the next three quarters to stay in front."

"I see. Okay, sure."

The principal gave the portion with the grades on it to George. "Let me ask you this. You're planning on going to college next year, yes?"

"Yeah," George said, looking over the printout.

"Any idea where?"

"Don't know yet. I got fifteen-twenty on the PSATs, so I'll probably score at least that on the SATs. Maybe Harvard or some other Ivy League school. But that depends on how much financial aid I get. I didn't play soccer this fall so I could work forty hours a week at Richardson's Texaco. But I might have to settle for Albany or something like that."

"SUNY Albany is a fine school."

"Yeah, but it ain't Harvard."

"George, let me say one thing to you about giving the valedictory address."

George looked up from the printout. "I'm listening."

"I'd require you to cut your hair before graduation. We simply can't have a commencement speaker with shoulder-length hair. There'll be a couple of thousand people on hand, including most of the community's dignitaries."

George scowled. "My own father doesn't even make me cut my hair. You can't order somebody to do that."

Mr. Shostankovich leaned forward in his chair, hands clasped. "I'm the principal. I can."

George glanced at the maple tree outside the principal's window. "What if a fat guy won it? Would you make him lose weight?"

"That's different. You can control the length of your hair."

"Well, I don't want to cut it."

"If you become valedictorian, you *will* cut it."

George rose from his seat. "Yeah, and if you make me cut it, then you'd better watch out." George smiled. "Because you never know what I might say to all those people."

"George, I really called you in here as a peace offering—"

"Peace offering? You called me in here to make me cut my hair. Why's that? So you can boss me around?"

"Young man—"

"You're just trying to be nice 'cause you might have to deal with me at commencement."

"I thought you'd matured in the last three years."

"If being mature means being you, then I haven't!" George shouted, storming out of the office.

George was scheduled to work that day, but called in sick. Instead he drove with his new girlfriend, Shannon Thompson, to Fox Run Road after school. George and Shannon had been dating since a mid-September football game. She was a spry blonde, thin in appearance, and she had perfectly straight white teeth.

George pulled into his driveway. Instead of going inside with Shannon, he opened the rear car door and allowed Buddy into the back seat. The three of them drove to the Clinton Rec Park. George opened two cans of beer and told Shannon about his talk with the principal.

"You're really special," Shannon said, taking his hand and repositioning his wind-blown hair. "You know, people think you're wild, really unpredictable."

"They do?"

"Yes. Part of it's your long hair. But people have told me that you're nice to them one day and the next day you won't even say hello in the hallways."

"Really? I guess I just have stuff on my mind a lot."

Shannon set her beer down on the Duster's hood. "What kind of stuff?"

"Oh, whatever stuff gets on my mind. It's hard to explain."

She touched his jaw. "What kind of stuff? We never talk."

"Yeah, well, you don't seem to mind not talking when we're over at your house or mine."

"Don't get mean. I know you talk with your father. Tell me what kind of stuff is on your mind."

George tossed a tennis ball into the creek. "Fetch, Buddy!" He turned toward Shannon. "I didn't like what went down today. I get this note. It's not even signed. The principal just orders me to his office. It's just part of his power trip. He knew I was gonna think it was something bad. And he liked knowing I was gonna think that. He actually loved it."

"Adults do stuff like that. My father, he's the head of the county's health department. And he loves to call people into his big office and tell 'em what to do. People love power."

"Yeah, I'd like to be in a position to make that principal squirm."

She sighed. "You'd like to do what everybody else does. Get some power and stomp on somebody because somebody else stomped on you."

Buddy brought the tennis ball back. George took it from his mouth and threw it in the creek again.

"You're wrong. I just wanna stomp on the guy who stomped on me. That's revenge. The bastard deserves it. On top of everything else, he wants me to cut my hair. I've had this hair since I was in the sixth grade. He's trying to control the way I look."

"I agree on the hair part. People are into appearances, instead of what's inside."

George took a swig of beer. "I suppose."

"Look on the bright side. You could give the big speech at graduation. That would be exciting."

"I guess."

"What do you mean? That would be awesome."

"I don't know. If I have to cut my hair, I'm gonna be pissed. The whole thing could get ugly. I think, maybe I shouldn't do it. Say I'm not cutting my hair, get somebody else. But my father'd love to see me up there. You know, I ran the numbers on everyone's grades at lunch. I have a big lead. As long as I keep my grades in the low nineties, I'm pretty much a cinch to be valedictorian."

George leaned back on the hood. "Hey, Buddy!" he screamed. "Come." He rolled on the grass with his dog for a few seconds, then threw the tennis ball along the creek's bank. "Fetch." Buddy scampered after it.

"Is that as far as you can throw?" Shannon asked.

"I don't wanna ruin my arm before my last season of baseball. This is the big year. We got ten seniors coming back. And yours truly is gonna play shortstop."

"Are you gonna to try to play baseball in college?"

"I'm not good enough. Maybe if I go to an Ivy League school, I'll get to play. They don't have very good sports programs. My problem is, I can't hit. Limited power. And I can't make the throw from the hole to first base. My father, he can still throw harder than I can."

"What are you gonna major in?"

"I don't know," George said, pounding his right fist into the palm of his left hand. "I think you gotta have money if you wanna really be somebody. *The Wall Street Journal,* they're only writing about people who have money." George shrugged. "So, I'll probably major in business. That way, I can be some power-hungry boss like your old man, giving out orders to everybody. Then I'll get married and have a daughter like you who resents me and rebels by going out with long-haired hicks."

Shannon laughed. "You really are crazy, you know that?"

"Hey, as long as we're doing this talking thing, can I tell you something else?"

Shannon flung George's hair back. "Yes, my long-haired hick, you may."

George took Shannon's hand. They sat down with Buddy on the bank of the creek. "Look at this Vietnam thing," George said. "We finally got the soldiers out last year. The college kids, mostly the rich ones, got these education deferments. They didn't have to go at all. So lotsa poor kids who couldn't go to college died in some little-shit country because President Johnson sent them there. Funny thing about LBJ, though, he was poor, once. He musta forgotten what it's like."

George shook his head. "People who have money get treated better than those who don't. I see it at the gas station. The people who have money get their cars done faster. It even affects me. I'm quicker to get out there and pump someone's gas if it's a Cadillac, as opposed to some old jalopy."

Shannon hugged George. After a few seconds, she tried to pull away, but George wouldn't let her go. Shannon nestled her head next to his. He smelled the beer on her breath. Another few seconds passed before George slid his head down, resting it on Shannon's breasts. He kissed the nape of her neck. Shannon opened her eyes and saw Buddy sleeping on the grass. George nuzzled his head back into Shannon's embrace. A tickling sensation caused Shannon to wiggle free. Slowly, George raised his head and stared into her eyes.

"What is it?" she asked.

George took a deep breath. "Can I tell you a secret?"

"Of course."

"Alright. You know how I was making you hold me. How I was cuddling up against you."

"Yeah. I liked it."

"Can you remember your mother ever holding you like that? You know, in that protective way."

"It's been a long time since my mother held me."

George shook his head sideways. "I don't mean recently. I mean when you were a kid. When you were hurt, maybe."

"Oh, yeah. If other kids were making fun of me. Or if my father yelled at me. Then Mom would hold me real tight."

"You remember what it felt like?"

Shannon thought for a moment. "Yeah."

"Tell me."

"Okay. It felt like…like I was safe. Like if other people hurt me then I had a place to go where no one could hurt me anymore. I had someone who could make the hurt stop."

George buried his head into Shannon's breast. She wrapped her arms around him.

"It's okay, George," she whispered. "What's the matter?"

George looked up. Tears rolled down his face. "I can't remember my mom ever doing that. You know, just holding me close. She musta done it before she died. But I can't remember. I was too young, I guess."

"Oh, I bet your mom held you close a lot. A real lot. You're the type of guy a mother would want to hold close."

"You think so?"

"Yeah." Shannon kissed his cheek. "For sure."

❖

WES BROWER WAS THE mechanic at Richardson's Texaco in the Village. He'd graduated from Deer Creek High in 1971, after finishing the automotive mechanic program. He was six and a half feet tall and wore his long blonde hair in a ponytail.

"What the hell's another long-haired guy doin' at my station?" Wes asked when he first met George.

"Man, I just love dirt 'n' oil."

Wes extended his grease-stained hand and George shook it. Both laughed at the black grime covering George's palm. At night, George had to sweep the day's gunk down the station's main drain. All the tools had to be wiped clean. The floors had to be hosed down and cleaned with a large squeegee. Wes seemed to manufacture dirt, leaving his tools scattered all over the workbench and floor.

Despite the filth, Wes the Mess had the uncanny ability to attract girls like a dead woodchuck attracts flies. Guys stopped by the station for updates on their way to Suzie's. After work, Wes sat in the bays, covered with grease, flinging his blonde ponytail back and forth, telling of his conquests.

Wes rode the disco wave until it crested. By the mid-1970s, Wes had mastered all the moves that Arthur Murray taught. He played disco music nonstop at work. Customers standing by the pumps could hear the beat echoing from the bays.

Wes introduced George to the Lucky 7 Club, where Wes danced with any girl he wanted. Girls danced well, George saw, but most guys were clumsy on the floor. Before disco, a guy could shake his body from side to side on a crowded dance floor. But when spins, dips, flips, and slides came into vogue, a guy had to have some training in the moves. In his lime green leisure suit, French cologne, and black platform shoes, Wes was Deer Creek's disco king.

George pulled into Richardson's Texaco a few minutes before four on a Thursday afternoon. "Hey, Wes. I brought you a couple of sixes of Genny Cream."

"What for?"

"Just for letting me hang with you. Here, take it."

Wes took the beer. "You gonna drink with me?"

"Yeah, as soon as the customer traffic dies down." George paused. "Could you show me some of those disco moves?

Wes shrugged. "Sure."

"You're just amazing with chicks. You always score. I wanna learn to dance so I can get some of your table scraps."

"Scoring's the whole point of goin' out. You'll see. As you get older, it gets easier to score."

"Really?"

"You bet. Because the available pool of babes grows."

"Huh," George said.

Wes patted George on the shoulder. "You're seventeen. It's hard to score with girls your age. That's because the eighteen-year-old guys get the chicks who're putting out. But when you're twenty, your pool becomes chicks between sixteen and the mid-twenties. I'm twenty-four. I can do sixteen-year-olds, girls my age, even ones in their thirties. There's more prospects out there."

"Wow! What's the oldest one you've ever done?"

"A forty-two-year-old. A few weeks back."

"Forty-two! With all those wrinkles? Where'd you do her?"

"In the back room," Wes said, pointing. "On my bed behind the gate."

"You got a bed back there!"

"Yeah, man. How else could I take advantage of what comes in here?"

"Can I see it?"

Wes led George into the back room, behind the bays. They walked past the sink, through rows of air filters, fan belts, and tires. When Wes stopped, George saw ten cardboard boxes on the floor, laid out in two rows of five. Each box held a case of Texaco motor oil. A pillow and crumpled-up blanket rested on a nearby metal shelf next to the spark plugs. "That's where I hosed her," Wes said.

"Awesome! Right there?"

"Yep. Remember the lady who brought in the green Volvo? The one you helped me get the old exhaust system off of?"

"Yeah."

"Well, that was her, the forty-two-year-old. She liked the music I had on. After I washed my hands and showed her some spins, she was all mine."

"But wasn't that lady kind of big?"

"Because I like you so much, I'm gonna let you in on my secret. Fat chicks are where the action is."

George gulped. "Huh?"

"I've watched you in the Lucky 7. You always go for the attractive babes. Bad strategy. They're all stuck-up. There are plenty of guys willing to go home with them. They know it, so they jerk your chain."

"But Shannon's cute and—"

"Shannon's different, man. She's your girlfriend. I'm not sayin' get a fat girlfriend. What I'm sayin' is, for just one night, you gotta lower your standards. Everybody wants to screw good-looking chicks. With them, you gotta get in line. Fat chicks don't get many chances to put out. So, when they do, they're gonna come through."

"Man, you serious?"

"You play baseball, right? So, look at it this way, I'm telling you how to raise your batting average."

That night, for hours, Wes and George practiced dancing with each other in the bays, taking breaks to guzzle Genny Cream Ales and wait on customers.

❖

GEORGE WORKED ON COLLEGE applications and financial aid forms with his father. It was a tedious process that became an obsession with the elder Johnson during the winter. George Sr. immersed himself in catalogues and promotional literature, creating his own tables for comparing schools and programs.

Young George liked making money. He saw how the world revolved around it. So he decided to study business. With the number one class ranking and a 1570 SAT score, he had his choice of colleges. The Johnsons narrowed the list down to three: Harvard and Yale for their national reputation and SUNY Albany as the best New York state school. Albany was a distant third in the Johnsons' rankings, but they needed a safety school if Harvard or Yale offered meager financial aid.

After the application deadlines, spring baseball practices began. George cut back his hours at Richardson's Texaco. He continued to spend many afternoons with Shannon.

The Deer Creek Wolves started slowly and never lived up to their pre-season potential. They were eliminated from the title chase with four games left in the season. Shannon brought her camera to the last home game and snapped pictures of father and son together. On the bench, young George turned to his father, "Dad, thanks for everything. I love you." He then ran onto the field.

George Sr. froze. His mind replayed his son's words in slow motion. He looked at the ground, rewinding the sound track and listening again. He wished Mary could've heard them.

"Mr. Johnson, are you okay?" Shannon asked. "The game's about to start," she continued, motioning him to join her in the bleachers.

After an inning, George Sr. shuffled his feet in the stands. "Shannon, if I tell you something, will you promise not to say anything to George?"

"I guess so."

"Okay, listen. Woo Labs has a college scholarship program. Some years the company gives a full academic scholarship to a child of an employee. They don't give it away each year, only when they think they've got a worthwhile candidate. George won it! I just found out today."

"That's great! So he doesn't know yet?"

"Nope. I got called into Mr. Woo's office right before lunch. I thought I was in trouble because I've never been in there before. But he just stuck out his hand and said, 'Congratulations, your boy won our scholarship.'"

"That's so exciting!" Shannon hugged her boyfriend's father. "George never told me that he'd applied."

"That's because I applied for him. He doesn't even know about it."

"How'd you do that?"

"I got the application and filled it out. I just typed in one of the Yale essays he wrote. When he was signing other stuff, I slipped in the Woo application. He just signed it."

"He's sure gonna be surprised." Shannon leaned back in the bleachers. "Wow, a free ride for four years."

"There's one catch, though."

"What's that?"

"The winner of the scholarship has to go to a New York State school. To use it, George's gonna have to go to Albany."

"How come?"

"Because they're cheaper. A four-year scholarship to an Ivy League school costs a lot, even for a company like Woo Labs."

"He's pretty psyched to be accepted at Harvard, though. Is he still waitlisted at Yale?"

"Yeah, but he doesn't much care. He just wanted one of the two. They cost the same. I think that Yale would be better than Harvard because it's closer." George Sr. paused for a few seconds. "You've talked to him, Shannon. What do you think he'll wanna do?"

"I don't know. He did mention that Albany had a good business program. He really wants to make money. But he says you're more likely to end up rich if you go to an Ivy."

"It's true. The Harvard name will follow a guy around for the rest of his life."

"I wouldn't mind him being at Albany State, since I'll be at College of St. Rose," she admitted.

George and Shannon turned their attention to the game. Newburgh didn't score in the top half of the seventh inning. Deer Creek was losing six to three, so it was Deer Creek's last chance. George was due to bat sixth. If his teammates didn't rally, he'd already batted for the last time as a high school baseball player. Slouching on the bench, George grimaced, watching the dirt scatter as he pounded his bat into the ground.

But his teammates rallied. By the time George stepped up to the plate, two runs were in, the tying run stood on third base, the winning run on second base, and there were two outs. Taking his warm-up swings with a practiced determination, George knew the situation he faced. His at-bat would determine who won the game. With a count of one ball and two strikes, the Newburgh pitcher threw a curve ball, low and away. Saddled with two strikes, George had to protect the plate. He lunged at the pitch and tapped a weak groundball toward the hole between first and second. The first baseman reached out and snagged the ball in his glove. He raced to first base and made the unassisted putout, stepping on the bag well ahead of George's head-first slide.

The season-ending game was over. Newburgh had won six to five. With dirt in his mouth, George remained on the ground. He spat saliva-soaked dirt on first base. No one bothered him. The Deer Creek team manager picked up second and third base, placing them in the team utility bag, but left first base undisturbed. Soon the field was empty. George Sr. and Shannon began walking toward first base, but Coach Royce waved them off.

Coach Royce strolled over to young George and stood above him for a few seconds. "You know," the coach said in a throaty voice. "I've never seen a player want to win a game as bad as you wanted to win this one." George remained speechless. "We almost pulled it out," the coach said.

"We would've won if I'd a gotten a hit."

"You gave it your best shot." Bending over and patting George on the back, Coach Royce continued, "That's all anybody can ask. It's been a pleasure coaching you for the last two years. You always came on the field and held nothing back."

George pushed himself to his knees and turned over, sitting on first base.

"You've gotten the most out of your ability, kid. You're a tough competitor."

Over dinner that night, George Sr. told his son about the Woo Labs scholarship. "It's a great deal. But the choice is yours. I've got twelve grand in the bank. That'll at least cover the first semester at Harvard."

Even with Harvard's aid package, the Johnsons still would need to come up with ten thousand dollars for George's. freshman year alone, and more than forty thousand dollars for four years of an Ivy League education. By comparison, the Albany State education would cost nothing. The scholarship even provided a hundred dollars spending money each month.

"I don't know what to do, Dad. I really don't."

"Look, it's a hard call. A Harvard degree will never leave you. It's like making Eagle Scout. But the money difference between the two schools is pretty large. Whatever you decide, I'll help out all I can."

Young George smiled at his father. "I know you'll help out. But the rabbit money's yours. Besides, if I went to Albany, I wouldn't have to work. It'd give me more time to study. I'll probably get better grades."

"And Shannon will be nearby."

"She'll be at a different school. Anyway, I'm eighteen years old. You think I'm just gonna hang with one girl?"

"She's very sweet, you know." George Sr. said, looking at his plate. "Why don't you pass the salt?"

George did. "Lots of important people went to Harvard. presidents, congressmen, doctors, lawyers. I bet there're great connections to be made."

"Bet there are."

Young George sighed and rubbed his eyes. "But the scholarship's too awesome a deal to pass up. I gotta go to Albany. It'll be a good education. And you'll be able to keep all your rabbit money."

❖

AT THE WOO LABS award dinner in young George's honor, the elder Johnson beamed like an accomplished parent, one who'd steered his son around life's obstacles. A week later, final grades were compiled. George Jr. became the valedictorian of the class of 1977. Mr. Shostankovitch even backed down from his demand that George get a haircut to speak at commencement.

George Sr. invited everybody he knew at work to the outdoor event. Ursula Brombecker invited the entire Deer Creek Town Council. George Sr. sat on the porch of his tiny, white Cape Cod house. He noticed the peeling white paint. He studied the stars in the sky, pondering his good fortune. Petting Buddy, he said, "I guess everybody'll be at commencement 'cept you."

On graduation day, George Jr. insisted on driving himself to school. Ursula would give his father a ride. Shannon drove with her parents. George arrived an hour-and-a-half early and parked his car in the neighborhood across the street from the school. He closed his eyes for a few minutes, then took a last swig of warm beer.

Ursula Brombecker tape-recorded his commencement address.

Fellow graduates of the class of 1977, your families and members of the faculty. I am honored to stand before you as valedictorian....As I thought about what the experience of high school graduation means, and what I would like to say to everybody, my mind kept drawing blanks. I really don't know what graduation means. I also don't know what lies ahead for me, let alone for any of you. And if I had anything worthwhile to say, you'd probably soon forget it anyway.

DIGNITARIES ON THE OUTDOOR stage, including the county executive and the president of Hudson Valley Community College, began glancing at each other. With his voice cracking, George continued:

The person who I'd really like to be talking to is not here today. She can't be. She's my mother and she died in a car accident with my sister eleven years ago....So, I wrote her a letter last week, and I'd like to read it to you.

GEORGE RETRIEVED TWO FOLDED pieces of paper from his back pocket and flattened them out on the podium.

Dear Mom:

I'm graduating high school next week and I'd give anything if you could be there. I'm the valedictorian and I know you'd be proud of me. It's been a long time since I got to talk to you. I remember the last thing that you ever said to me. I was seven years old when you told me to pay attention in class. Well, I've been paying attention in class for the last eleven years and look where it got me. Then, you handed me my favorite lunch pail—the one with Underdog bursting out of the phone booth—and sent me on my way to catch the bus. I don't have the lunch pail any more because I stomped it flat when Dad told me that you and my baby sister were dead.

A lot has happened in the last eleven years and I wonder if you can see it all from up there. I have to tell you that Dad has done a wonderful job of raising me. As proud of me as you might be, you'd be ten times as proud of him. All by himself, he's fed me, clothed me, taught me, and encouraged me. He's done all this while letting me develop my own identity, which, by the way, I'm still working on. I've made mistakes, but Dad never seems to give up on me. He's been the greatest father a guy could have.

You know, he still keeps an eight-by-ten picture of you and Susan in his bedroom, and I go in there to look at it most days after school. I miss you, Mom. I miss you more than anything. And I miss my sister. It hurts, but I go on, because I know that's what you'd expect of me.

Now I'm getting ready to go to college. Harvard accepted me, but I've been awarded a full scholarship to Albany State. That's just too good of a deal to pass up. Dad tells me you both dreamed I'd go to college. Well, Mom, your dream is coming true.

I guess I'm expected to be an adult now, but I don't always feel like one. Sometimes I feel like I know everything and nothing at the same time. Sometimes I think I'm going out into the world naked, in need of protection. And sometimes I think I'm omnipotent. Sometimes I feel like I can achieve anything if I work for it and sometimes I wonder how a hick like me is going to be successful at anything. Right now, I'm very anxious about the future.

Mom, graduation is a cause for celebration. I wish with all my heart that you and Susan were here to celebrate with me, but I know that it just can't be. You are here in my thoughts. As always.

All my love,

George

Desire

GEORGE SR. STORED THE valedictory letter between two hardcover books on his dresser. Ursula Brombecker took a snapshot of father and son hugging after the speech. She enlarged it to an eight-by-ten and gave it to George Sr. The framed photo assumed a position on the night table next to the picture of Mary and Susan.

Three weeks before Albany's fall semester classes began, George drove his father to the Lucky 7 Club for a goodbye drink. George Sr. bought a beer for himself and a scotch for his son. They walked upstairs to the second level to escape the dance floor crowds. Neither of them recognized the music blaring from the club's speakers, but both still moved their heads to the beat.

"When did you start drinking the hard stuff?" George Sr. asked.

"Oh, recently." George Jr. made eye contact with Wes the Mess on the dance floor and waved to him. Wes flashed a smile.

"When's the first time you were ever in a bar?"

George Jr. pointed to the dance floor. "Wes the Mess took me. I'm not exactly sure when."

The elder Johnson tapped his son's glass with the beer bottle. "The hell you aren't. You probably snuck in before you were eighteen, right? I did the same thing."

"Well, yeah…"

"I was fifteen. Used somebody else's license."

"I was sixteen. You beat me, just like at baseball."

"How'd you work it?"

"Got a duplicate license and altered it." George Jr. took a deep breath and exhaled through his nose.

"It's amazing how some things stay the same. We had the same scam going. In the fifties, mind you."

George Jr. guzzled the rest of his scotch and ordered another. George Sr. signaled for another beer with his empty bottle. When the waitress returned, George Sr. again tapped his beer bottle against his son's glass. "To you," he said.

"Can we leave after finishing these, Dad?"

"Why, you not feeling well?"

"I'm okay. It's just, well, a little strange being at a meat market with you."

The elder Johnson laughed. "Meat market," he said. "Where'd you hear that one? It makes me think of how we sent all those rabbits off to get slaughtered."

George Jr. didn't answer.

"I never used to come to places like this when I was married to your mother. I just went to work and came home. Now, I come to 'em often. Sometimes I have a real good time. Other times, I feel real lonely. Like I'm with all these other lonely people. They're talking to each other, but I wonder if they're really saying anything. Know what I mean?"

"Yeah, I know people like that." George Jr. paused before continuing. "You think you'll ever get married again?"

"Who knows? I've been alone for over ten years now. Your mother was real special. Once you've had a top-flight woman, it's hard to move down. I might never marry again, but I'm only thirty-seven." George Sr. shrugged. "Who knows?" he repeated. "Seems people don't want to be married as much any more. Back in the nineteen fifties, marriage was the big thing. Everybody wanted kids, a house, a car, a job. That was the big ol' American dream. Then came the nineteen sixties and all this free love stuff. Marriage sorta went by the wayside." George Sr. hesitated. "Why? Would you like it if I did?"

"Don't do it on my account. I just want you happy."

"That's nice to hear." He put his arm around his son. "A man needs a woman for certain things. But nowadays you don't have to marry 'em to get those things." George Sr. studied his son for clues to the extent of his sexual activities. Hazy images of fornicating young boys and girls entered his mind but receded. He looked up and down his son's body until the strobe light spun faster. "Look at all them girls hoverin' around the dance floor." He swayed. "You see 'em down there?"

"Yeah."

"Whaddaya think they're looking for?"

"I don't know."

"Guess."

"Dad! Really, I don't know."

"All those women, they're looking for one thing. One thing only! For *companionship*. That's what they're here for."

"Uhh, my drink's finished. Time to go home."

❖

FOR YOUNG GEORGE, IT seemed to take forever before he'd get to leave Salt Point for Albany. He daydreamed about waking up in a strange bed in a new place. He tried to picture what Albany State would be like, but really had no idea, never having visited a college campus and never having set foot in New York State's capital city. He'd miss his father and Buddy, as well as Shannon, but he still couldn't wait for the trip north.

George grew up with virtually no restrictions, a car, and money in his pocket. He didn't view college as a place where he'd acquire new-found freedom. But he wanted to find freedom on a grand scale. And more money, too. College meant emancipation from the town where he was born and raised. He'd never even been to another state. Jennifer Conlin's cousin Desiree was the only person he'd ever met who'd lived outside of New York. Albany State had students from all over the northeast, even some from foreign countries. Still, George couldn't fight off the tears when he said good-bye to Buddy.

On most of the drive north, neither father nor son spoke. With the rain beating down hard and the wiper blades cranking at full speed, young George confined his view to glimpses of fields, barely discernible through the car's rain-blurred windows. At sixty miles an hour, the images, flashing one after another, seemed surreal. The rolling hills, with so many trees, seemed so filled with life. Trees and humans have an important similarity—they both have no say in where they're born and grow up. Some are born in rich national forests. Others are born in the way of rich shopping mall developers.

The Johnsons drove past Catskill, where Rip Van Winkle had slept, and past Hudson, which missed becoming the state capital by one vote. George Jr. studied the buildings that occupied land once inhabited by trees. Some years back, he wanted to go to the American Museum of Fire Fighting. He didn't go and wondered if he could see it from the highway. The thought receded with the buildings. North of Hudson, George wondered about the greatness of the explorer who had so many places named after him—the Hudson River, the Hudson Bay, the Hudson Valley, and the Town of Hudson.

The Johnsons' truck made its way past Coxsackie, past the sign to Climax, and past the Thruway interchange. They could've made better time on the Thruway, but George Sr. hated the eighteen-wheel tractor-trailers.

George Sr. stayed on Route 9W all the way to Albany. "It's been quiet the last hour or so," he said.

"Yeah, I kinda feel happy and sad."

"Me, too. This is a new chapter for you. And for me, too. We've never really talked about what you wanna be."

"Whaddaya mean?"

"What it is you wanna do with the rest of your life."

"C'mon, Dad. That's a hard question. When you were eighteen, did you know what you wanted to be?"

"Yeah. When I was fifteen, I wanted to be a professional baseball player. That was my only dream. But I had no fall-back plan. It's great to chase after dreams, but you gotta be looking over your shoulder for that something that's always out there. That something that's trying to steer you off course."

"Yeah, that's how I feel about Salt Point. I feel crowded by it. Like I just gotta get out."

"You do. I'm glad you're gettin' out. You need to."

"Dad, you know, you can get out, too."

"Naw, not really. I've thought about it. But I'm stuck. I've got no skills, no education, no connections. You'll see that this world works on connections. Not always ability, but connections. I see it at work all the time. Guys get promoted because of connections. It's really a game, and you gotta play it. But it sure helps to have credentials. Just look at the Harvard thing. They took you without ever meeting you. All they knew was that you're number one in your class, and that you got over fifteen hundred on the SATs. Plus you can write a good essay or that you're smart enough to have someone write it for you. To them, all you were was just a piece of paper."

"I know. That's why I'll be getting good grades at Albany. So I can get a good job or get into a top-flight grad school."

"I'm glad you're thinkin' that way. Because, to a future employer or a grad school, all you're gonna be is just another piece of paper."

"But, Dad, there're things you could do. You don't have me to worry about any more. I'll study hard, like I always do. Plus, I got a free ride."

"True. My financial responsibility's pretty much over. That scholarship is a real bonanza." He touched his son's knee. "Thanks for working so hard to earn it. I'm really, really proud of you."

"Yeah, well, you tricked me into signing up for it."

George Sr. laughed. "That was a good one. Chalk one up for the old man." His smile receded into a grimace. "You ever been in an arcade room and played one of those race car video games?"

"Yeah. Why?"

"Because they're kinda what life is like. You're driving down that highway. The road curves and you steer the car to keep from crashing. Then there's slower cars in your way and you have to pass 'em. There's also accidents, oil slicks, other obstacles. If you accelerate, the obstacles come at you faster. So you gotta be even quicker to avoid 'em. If they hit you, they knock you off the road. But the faster you drive, the more exciting it is. You get a higher score. That is, if you stay on the road. Now, you could drive real slow and not get knocked off, but then the game ends before you score lotsa points."

George Sr. grasped his son's arm. "You got a real good chance of ending up with lotsa points. Me, I'm the car that's been knocked off the road too many times. My quarter's already spent. The game's over."

"Just put another quarter in."

"Yeah, well, I might be able to. But I doubt it."

"I hate hearing this. Makes me feel guilty."

"Hey, I'm not tryin' to do that. I'm just trying to teach you not to make the same mistakes I made. You're supposed to learn from your own experiences, but life's too damn short to recover from big mistakes. So learn from mine."

Young George leaned over toward his father and tapped his shoulder with a closed fist. The elder Johnson's shoulder absorbed the warmth, and it traveled throughout his body.

"My race car may be knocked off the road. But I'm on this big hill, and I can see this baby race car zooming down the highway. Really cruising along. And it lifts my heart. I'm one of the pit crew guys. I call out 'Hey, look out for that oil slick' or 'Come in for some more fuel.'"

"Well, your baby race car is picking up speed," young George said.

"Good, son. Just keep it on the road....Seriously, whaddaya think you wanna be?"

Young George scratched his head. What's a kid supposed to say to that? "Somebody important," he answered. "Somebody who makes lotsa money."

"That's a good start. But what kinda job you think goes with bein' important?"

"I don't know what's out there yet. Don't rush me." Young George cracked his window, breathing in the cool air. "I wanna be somebody who tells people what to do. So nobody makes my life miserable. I don't want anybody owning me."

"I've noticed that about you."

The Johnsons stayed on Route 9W until it became Delaware Avenue. Near the heart of the city, the rain stopped and the visibility improved. Young George turned his head quickly, looking over each shoulder in an effort to take it all in. The buildings were taller than he'd ever seen before, except for those in New York City. The closest he'd gotten to the Manhattan skyline was the view from the Whitestone Bridge when his father drove him to Shea Stadium.

They arrived at Albany State's Eastman Tower, the dormitory that would house George Jr. during his freshman year. George Sr. found a parking space. Father and son unloaded George's suitcases and milk crates. It took two trips up the elevator to move all of

George's possessions into Room 902. While young George stored the luggage, George Sr. walked through the living room area into one of the bedrooms. Virtually all of the walls consisted of cement cinderblocks painted white. Kneeling on the bare mattress covering an unmade twin bed, he glanced out a window that overlooked the center of Albany's campus. Two students were playing frisbee next to a fountain. Other students lounged beneath trees, talking in small groups. Still others sat alone reading books.

"Hey, Dad," George called out. "Wanna get something to eat? I can unpack this junk later."

George Sr. returned to the main room. "Yeah, sure," he responded, preoccupied. "What's the deal here? Three bedrooms?"

"Yeah, two guys in each room, plus one bathroom." Father and son walked through the three bedrooms. "We're the first one's here," young George observed. "That means I get first choice, huh?"

"I'd take the bedroom to the right," George Sr. advised. "It's got the best view of campus."

"Good idea. And it's close to the can. Give me a hand moving my stuff? If I put some of it on the bed by the window, the other guys'll know it's already taken."

"Sure." While the Johnsons moved the suitcases, George Sr. asked, "What's your roommate's name again?"

"Marty Goldberg. From Long Island. I can't remember the other four guys' names. It's in the materials."

"A Jew?" George Sr. asked.

"Yep. Half the kids here are Jewish."

"Wow. Never knew that."

George Jr. smiled. "I've never even met one before."

"Well, I hope this Marty is a good guy."

George Jr. nodded, then stared out a window at the parking lot. An insidious, flaky rust had spread throughout his father's blue truck bed. The lot was filled with Cadillacs, Mercedes, Saabs, and Volvos, all seemingly hand-waxed in comparison to his father's pickup.

An attendant in the dormitory's lobby directed the Johnsons to the Campus Center, where they could get lunch. The ten minute walk took them past the Earth Science, Fine Arts, Performing Arts, and Physics buildings. Inside the Campus Center, the Johnsons entered the Ratskeller, where the light barely reflected off the dark wood. They each took a red plastic tray from the stack on the counter. George Jr. ordered a burger and fries; his father substituted onion rings for fries. George Sr. paid.

"I guess this is the last meal you'll sponge off me for a while," George Sr. remarked. No response. "When will ya be coming home?"

"I don't know," George Jr. mumbled. "There's always Thanksgiving." George Jr. looked away from his father, thinking about how parents say you should get out into the world on your own, yet they still want to look out for you.

George Sr. stared at his onion rings. College would make his son feel more independent, but he didn't want to give up parental control. He thought of the Woo Labs executives who had kids in college. Many of them viewed the money they spent on their kids' education as an investment that must provide a decent return. Transcripts were like quarterly earnings reports, the only important measure of performance. Pretty soon, the kids became part of their parents' portfolios. If they performed well, they got mentioned in hallway conversations.

"I certainly hope you'll be home before Thanksgiving," George Sr. finally said.

"I probably will, but I'll see how the school work goes."

They finished their meal in silence.

With the storm that accompanied the Johnsons on the drive from Salt Point to Albany gone, they walked through the damp air back to the dorm. Tilting his head skyward, young George could see the dark cloud cover moving north in the direction of Canada, a country that he hoped to visit sometime in the next four years.

As they neared the low-level buildings that surrounded Eastman Tower like a fortress, George Jr. said, "I'll walk you over to the truck."

"Isn't there anythin' you need me to do? Like help you unpack? I'm not doing anythin' the rest of the day. It's only an hour-and-a-half drive back home."

"Look, it's okay. I'll be able to handle everything by myself. Let's just walk over to the truck and say good-bye."

George Sr. followed the footsteps of the young man he'd raised alone for the last eleven years. George Jr. pivoted on the ball of his right foot. He faced his father and touched his left arm. "Thanks for helping me get all my stuff up here."

"I'm your father. What else am I supposed to do?"

"I just want you to know I appreciate it. I love you."

George Sr. hugged his son. "I love you, too. And I'm damn proud of you."

George Sr's slouching shoulders reinforced his sorrow. He started the engine and rolled down the window. "Call soon and let me know how you're doing."

George Jr. nodded and watched the truck back out of its parking space. "Hey, Dad!" The truck stopped. "I meant everything I said in my speech."

The elder Johnson waved good-bye.

An exuberant Albany State freshman, with his loping stride gaining momentum, made his way back to his room. There was much to do: unpack, meet his roommates, register for classes, and figure out the best way to conquer a fresh environment.

❖

THE GOLD DUSTER WAS parked at the end of the windowless barn, next to the garden. Gone from the house was the sound of heavy-metal music rumbling from the upstairs bedroom. Gone were the dirty dishes in the sink, crumbs on the counter, clothes on the shag carpet, shoe-prints on the linoleum floor, skid marks on the driveway, beer in the refrigerator. But Buddy was still there and Thanksgiving was only two-and-a-half months away.

At seven firty-five the following Monday morning, George Sr. figured that he was eight to ten minutes away from parking his truck in Woo Labs' employee-only lot. The two-minute differential depended on whether he made the light on the corner of Randolph Road and Route 55. He'd learned all the nuances: the timing sequence of traffic lights, how fast he could take each corner, where the police hid out, where to brace for potholes.

George knew he'd be able to punch his card in the timeclock before eight. As he breathed, the numbness that infected him during the weekend returned. Even the bleached blonde he'd met at Lucky 7 couldn't shake his loneliness. Her name was Sunshine, Sunrise, Dawn, or something like that. He couldn't remember. A feathered earring was her most memorable feature.

The prospect of eight hours in a clean room heightened George's hollowness. Mondays held a familiar gloom, especially after a long weekend. But on that Monday George seemed more morose than usual. The country music on the radio didn't help. Turning left past the "Woo Labs—A Company of People Working to Better Serve People" sign, George decided to stop by a couple of auto dealerships after work. Maybe a new car would help. The truck was run-down, and the four-year scholarship was an unexpected windfall. With inflation outpacing the passbook savings rate, the rabbit money on deposit at the Hudson Savings Bank was depreciating in purchasing power.

❖

MARTY GOLDBERG ARRIVED WHILE the Johnsons were at the Ratskeller. A stocky boy of medium height with black, curly hair, he placed his belongings on the remaining bed. When George returned, the boys shook hands and unpacked in the midst of sporadic conversation. The four other incoming freshmen arrived later that afternoon.

Marty asked George if he wanted to look around campus. The two boys grabbed their wallets, walked to the cement-covered center of the main quad, and sat down near the fountain.

"So," George began. "Where're you from?"

"Oiyysta Baayy."

"Huh?"

"Oiy-Sta-Bay," Marty repeated. "It's on the nawth shaaw of Long Island."

George shook his head. "I'm having a hard time with your accent."

"You'll get use to it around heah. Wheh are you from?"

"Salt Point. It's ten miles east of Deer Creek."

"Wheh's Deer Creek? I mean, what state is it in?"

"New York, same as you. It's south of here."

"Oh," Marty smiled, "like in Westchestuh County?"

"No, Westchester County is south. Deer Creek's an hour north of there. It took me an hour-and-a-half to get here this morning. How long did it take you?"

"About faw-and-a-half owhas." The boys stared at the fountain. "Do you have any brothuhs or sistuhs?" Marty asked.

George looked down at the ground. "I used to have a sister, but she died in a car accident."

"I'm sorry."

"It's okay. You have any?" George asked.

"An olda sistuh. She lives in Stuyvesant Towuh, on the Dutch Quad."

"She goes here?" George confirmed.

"Yeah, right ovuh in that building," Marty replied, pointing. He stood up. "I'm hungry. You wanna eat?"

"Sure," George said, even though he wasn't hungry. "Where to?"

"I know a place you'll like. Follow me." The boys walked across the quad, careful not to interrupt the Ultimate Frisbee game in progress.

"Why's your sister live on campus if she's a junior?" George asked.

"Because her friends do. Lots of JAPs live on Dutch Quad."

"What're JAPs?"

Marty bucked back and forth, laughing. "Jewish American Princesses," he said. "They wear fancy clothes, heels, lots of makeup, bright lipstick, nail polish. They also have dis 'I'm da centuh of da univuhse' attitude."

"Man, I gotta see this."

"You can't miss it."

The boys entered Sutter's Mining & Mill Co., a dimly lit pub filled with cigarette smoke. Muffled sirens, whistles, and shots echoed from the game room. Spilled beer stuck to the bottom of their sneakers. Seated in a booth, each boy ordered a draft beer, burger, and cheddar fries.

"My parents are already asking when I'm comin' home," Marty complained. "I'm goin' back to da Island in two weeks. And dey wanna know when I'm coming home aftuh that."

"You're going home in two weeks? What for?"

"My cousin's bar mitzvah."

"What's a bar mitzvah?"

"It's a Jewish ceremony. When Jewish boys turn thirteen, they go through this ceremony that means they become men."

"I say you're not a man until you get laid."

Marty smirked. "It's a religious thing. What're you? Johnson sounds like a Protestant name."

"I'm Catholic. Which means that the girls in my religion have been raised to be prudes." George took a swig of beer. "I think I'm gonna like this JAP scene. Will JAPs go out with Catholic guys?"

"Most of them ah unduh pressuh from their parents to marry a Jewish guy. But they'll date a non-Jew."

"Excellent! Man, I'm eighteen and living on my own. Hey, let's get another beer. I can't believe you gotta go home in two weeks. Five hours each way. That's a lot of driving."

"Oh, I'm flying."

"Wow, just for the weekend?"

"Sure. I'll fly to La Gwadia Friday and come back to Albany on Sunday."

"Doesn't that cost a lot of money?"

Marty shrugged. "My parents pay."

"Wow. I've always wanted to be up in the sky, above everybody else. Must be powerful."

❖

GEORGE KNEW HIS FATHER was right when he said that four years of college would be condensed into a one-page transcript. He wanted to create a glittering piece of paper and use it as a springboard to wealth. He also wanted to pack a host of other experiences into his schedule. Aware of the tension between succeeding academically and socially, he took his father's advice and studied hard. Soon he discovered that keeping current with schoolwork made studying easier.

While pursuing JAPs, George occasionally wondered whether Shannon dated other guys. He saw less of her as the semester wore on. A relationship, even a sexually active one, constricted George. His desire for freedom couldn't be contained or channeled, not now.

Shannon visited George at the Johnsons' house during the winter break. "I came over because I've been thinking about us. We only saw each other twice last semester. We seem to want different things like…"

George tried to listen, but couldn't. He focused on her chest, which appeared to have added bulk. Images of her laying naked on Wes the Mess's oil can bed at Richardson's Texaco the previous summer, with a bottle of wine next to the spark plugs, appeared in his head. In the stillness, he muttered, "Uh huh."

Shannon stayed quiet until George realized she deserved a response. "Look," he began, fumbling for the words, "I haven't treated you very well the last few months—"

"Tramping around while I waited by the phone in my dorm? You've treated me like crap!"

George maneuvered the reclining chair forward. "Alright, I have. But I didn't mean to. It's just hard being away at school."

"We don't live far from each other in Albany."

"Hey, I'm sorry. I hurt you. You're the last person I wanted to hurt. But, when you go to college, things change."

"Maybe we should just go on with our lives separately."

"Look, I feel bad," George said, staring at the ceiling, relieved. "We're too young for a serious relationship. It's kinda confusing—I love you—but I just gotta do my own thing."

"What's your fear about seeing only me?"

George shrugged. "I'm not sure. But, most college kids, they don't marry the person they were dating in high school."

"How do you know what'll happen if you don't try?"

"Well, if I love you even more, and we break up, then it'll hurt even more. It'll hurt a lot instead of a little."

Shannon dropped her head in her hands.

"Hey," George said, reaching out to touch her elbow. "There's something I learned from my mother's death."

Shannon looked up. "What's that?"

"That if you love somebody too much, they end up leaving you too soon."

Shannon lifted herself from the couch, signaling George to rise from the recliner. Both hesitated, wondering what to do with their hands. "Hey," Shannon said, wiping away a tear from her left eye. "One night when I was sad, I wrote a poem about you. I want you to have it." She reached inside the pocket of her jeans and handed George a folded piece of paper.

"Wow," he said, taking it. "I hope yours is easier to understand than Robert Frost's."

"Well…"

"Yeah, you're going. I know."

"If you ever wanna talk about anything," Shannon offered, "You can always call me."

"Thanks. You turned me into a talker. Thanks for that."

George watched Shannon walk down the dirt path to her car. He sat down on the blue reclining chair, opened the piece of paper and read:

> How I miss the tender touch of your hand,
> And yearn for the sweet kiss of your lips
> Just to say good-bye
> Or maybe hello?
>
> How will I spend those empty nights
> With no hand to take away the loneliness?
> Now I watch the moon disappear tonight
> While time softly slips into tomorrow.
>
> Can my sun become a star?

❖

GEORGE MADE HIS DAILY pilgrimage to the mailbox. He'd been waiting for his transcript from Albany State. An oversized white envelope appeared a week before winter break ended. He ripped it open and read the computer printout twice to make sure: Astronomy–A; Calculus–A; Economics–A; English–A; Psychology–A. That made a perfect 4.0!

George let out a ferocious scream. Buddy yelped into the sky. George sprinted up the embankment to the front of the house, where he stopped. He turned to view the swamp across Fox Run Road through the leafless trees, glanced at the transcript again, pivoted in the crusted snow, and resumed his jaunt. Buddy followed. Crunching his way through the snow-covered backyard, George grabbed an icicle from a maple tree and flung it as far as he could. A mystified Buddy started after it, then stopped and barked when George hollered, "Yes! Yes! Yes!"

George sprinted again, reaching the nearest point where the cow pastures ended and the woods began, where he collapsed onto his back in the snow. With his free hand, George pulled the Brittany close. "You know, Buddy," he said, "sometimes you can just feel so good that the world can't touch you."

George showed his father the transcript as soon as he came home from work. "This is terrific!" the elder Johnson pronounced. "Your race car's aimed straight down that road."

"Heading right for the finish line. Gonna trade my As for dollars."

"It's been great having you home, seeing you every day. It's too quiet here without you."

Young George gripped his transcript with both hands. "My ticket to success."

The elder Johnson pulled his son toward him, then kissed the top of his head.

Five days later, the Sunday before classes resumed for the spring term, George Sr. drove his son back to Albany. The elder Johnson began thinking out loud. "This Chevy sure is getting up there in years," he said, tapping the dashboard. George Jr's head was bobbing, and the tapping forced his eyelids open. "I'm fixing to trade her in on a new car."

"If you get a new car, get one that rides smoothly. That'll help my hangovers," George Jr. advised.

"You did an awful lot of partying over the winter break."

"I had to make up for all the time I spent in the library during the fall term." George Jr. wiped his face with his hands. "The funny thing about partying is that I do more of it when I don't have a girl-friend. When I was with Shannon, I didn't drink much. Is that how it is with you?"

"A little. I stay home more when a woman's in my life. If we go out, it's more to movies and stuff like that."

"Exactly. And when a guy doesn't have a chick, he goes drinking at bars in search of one," young George said. "But geez, just to talk to most chicks at bars these days, you need to have a few drinks. How come there're so few girls a guy can actually talk to?"

"You ever wonder whether girls feel the same way about you?"

"You kidding me? The Jewish American Princesses in Albany, they love me. Except for Rachel, this hot super-rich girl."

"Rachel?"

"Yeah, her father flies to Albany in his private plane. Sometimes just to take her to dinner. I'd really like to go out with Rachel."

George Sr. rolled his eyes.

"She's probably planning on marrying a wimpy guy she grew up with on the Island. A guy who'll be a good provider. In the mean-time, I hope she wants to have fun."

George Sr. grinned. "Whaddaya gonna do about the summer job offer?"

"Probably gonna take it. This Woo Labs scholarship is sweet. I can't believe they're gonna give me three-and-a-half bucks an hour. That's eighty-five cents above minimum wage. Plus, I get to work over spring break. And I can probably still work Sundays at Richardson's Texaco."

"It's gonna be hard at Woo. Scrubbing mats for the machines is what you're gonna be doing."

"Yeah, it'd sure be nice to go to Europe instead. Just to screw around for the summer. That's what a lotta Albany kids are gonna do. Must be nice to be bankrolled." George slapped his father's right thigh. "Ahh, it can't be that bad scrubbing mats. Besides, we'll get to commute together. I might even take you out for beers after work once in a while."

"My son, buying me beers. I can't wait."

❖

GEORGE SR. BOUGHT A new 1978, gray Ford Pinto late that winter. None of his previous vehicles had been so luxuriously appointed. He was eager to use the air conditioner when the weather turned warm. He still kept the old Chevy pickup to haul stuff around, like his son's belongings. It wouldn't have brought much in the way of a trade-in anyway.

During spring break, young George worked at Woo Labs. The first shift workers viewed the honor student as they would view the boss's son. Even though George earned the first scholarship in three years, he still got stuck with the lowest and hardest tasks. And the workers distrusted him. By the end of the week, his legs and shoulders ached.

The summer following his first year at Albany, George studied the laborers he worked with. He watched how they ate, drank, and socialized. And he watched his father, the consummate loner, deal with them. He saw a throw-your-hands-in-the-air, shrugging your shoulders, way of behaving. Yet there wasn't anything wrong with conditions at the plant. Pay and benefits were decent, and there hadn't ever been any layoffs.

Something was surely absent from the faces underneath those cleanroom bunny suits. But how do you imagine an alternate future? How do you create one? Throw in a wife and kids and it gets really complicated really fast.

"I'd like to talk, Dad," George said on the porch one night.

"Yeah, sure. What about?"

"About working at the plant."

George Sr. sighed. "Alright."

"Well…"

"You wanna know how I do it? How I go there each day?"

"Yeah, I do."

"I got used to it, that's all. I go there to earn a living."

"But don't you gotta like what you're doing? I mean, don't you wanna feel satisfied?"

"I've never really thought you're supposed to like your job. My father never liked his. You're supposed to *do* your job, but you're supposed to *like* your family, your house, your weekends away from your job."

George looked into his father's weary eyes. "How about satisfaction?"

"How about it? I'm satisfied with how you turned out."

"I'm not talking about me. You were good about looking out for me. You taught me about the need to get ahead. But you don't look out for yourself like you look out for me." George Jr. paused. "How come you only get satisfaction through me?"

Averting his eyes, George Sr. confessed, "Maybe I've just given up on my dreams. Or maybe I figure you're the one who'll realize them. Or maybe I never had any 'cept for baseball."

Young George touched his father's shoulder. "You're too young to be raising the white flag."

"Yeah, well, I still gotta eat and pay the mortgage."

"You gotta like what you're doing," George Jr. insisted. "Look at me, I like what I'm doing."

"And who wouldn't? You got a full scholarship to college and lotsa girlfriends. It's a perfect set-up."

"Hey, I study seven days a week. I've worked hard for this set-up."

"I know," his father acknowledged. "Look, I'll be okay."

"But I don't want you to be like all those other guys on the lines. It's like some of 'em have their heads in a vice, and someone's turning the handle tighter. They look defeated. And they don't even care."

The elder Johnson looked his son in the eyes. "I'll think about it while you're back at school."

"Okay. Please?"

"I will. I'm different from most guys on the lines. I think about my life. They sorta exist. But I've got a real problem. Whaddaya you do when you're too dumb to amount to much, but smart enough to realize it?"

❖

GEORGE SR. APPROACHED THE remainder of 1978 with a sense that those were pivotal months in his life. His only surviving child was away from home. He was a single parent in the twilight of parenthood. As his son approached twenty, there was less to witness, less to see firsthand.

George had his most intense thoughts in his car; that Pinto drew insights out of his subconscious. At a red light on his way home from work, George read "Jesus Saves" on a car's rusted rear bumper. He got out and walked to the driver's open window. "What're you getting saved from?" he asked the woman.

She kept her eyes facing forward and didn't respond.

"Lady, how come you Jesus Freaks never drive a Mercedes? It's always these dilapidated cars. Does Jesus save you from failing inspection?" The light changed and George walked back to the Pinto, his heart racing. He tried to repel the fear that overcame him whenever he thought of God in a bad way. George turned into a Hess gas station. His gaze settled on a billboard. "Available GL2-2121," it read.

The following week, George approached line three's foreman, Henry Pepper. "Excuse me, Henry. Can I talk to you for a minute?" he asked.

"Sure. What's on your mind?"

"Are there any other jobs around here?"

Henry slapped George on the shoulder. "After all the years we been together, one of my best acid men wants to leave me?"

"It's not that—"

"Hey, listen," Henry interjected. "Why don't you and I go grab a couple of brewskies at Rondo's after work. Okay?"

"Uh, okay. Meet you in the parking lot after the shift?"

"You bet."

George jumped into his Pinto and followed Henry to Rondo's, where the sign exclaimed "Naked Girls!!!" They settled into two chairs next to a synthetic wooden table near the empty stage and ordered beers.

The Woo Labs baseball cap Henry wore branded them as laborers at the plant. "So, George," Henry said. "What's this talk of wantin' a different job?"

"I've been working the lines for almost twenty years. It's time I did something different."

"Like what?"

"That's what I wanna ask you. Are there any open jobs at Woo besides the lines?"

"You mean, like *my* job?" Henry bellowed. "I like you, George, but I ain't about to give you *my* job."

"Foreman's the next level up for me. I'd kinda like to be somebody's boss, get some more responsibility."

"You ever been anybody's boss before?"

"No, but I'd like to try."

Henry leaned forward. "Listen, I can't get higher up in the chain myself. You know what they're doin' upstairs now?"

"No."

"Two things," Henry said. His voice dropped to a whisper. "First, they're only hirin' people who got college degrees. Some of the newer ones, they even got master's degrees."

"Graduate degrees! In what?"

"Mostly business. But some of 'em got master's degrees in history or english or some other bullshit."

"Really?"

"Oh, yeah. That new gal workin' as an inspector on line two has a Master's degree in piano playing."

"A music degree and she's working on the lines? Wonder why."

"Because she can't get no other job, that's why. Woo pays the best in town. Hell, playin' the piano, you can't even do that at weddings."

Henry sat back in his chair and watched a dancer in a white cape appear on stage. "The girls here spend most of their time dancin' with their clothes on. Naked girls? What a bunch of crap."

"Why don't we go someplace else?"

"Show us some tit!" Henry screamed. With a practiced look of indifference, the dancer ignored him.

"The other thing that they're doin', George," Henry continued, speaking louder to overcome the music, "is hirin' broads for management jobs. Those ice queens, they're makin' it hard on fellas tryin' to move up in the world."

"Yeah, well, I guess they're entitled to jobs, too."

"Whaddaya crazy! How are ya gonna get ahead with that attitude? Lemme ask you this. What kinda broads you go for?"

"I don't know," George answered, put off by the question. "What about you?"

"Me, I like broads like my wife. She don't give me a hard time. And she feeds me regularly. When I get bored with her, I go for broads like the one on stage."

"Even though you're married?"

"Yeah. What's the big deal? Broads like these dancers, they're good for maintenance sex—"

"What?"

"Maintenance sex. To make sure all the parts are workin'. Like brushin' your teeth."

"You *pay* for sex?"

"Hey, get off your high horse. And don't be spreadin' this around, okay?"

George nodded. The men watched the end of the dancer's routine. George and Henry clapped.

"Johnson, what kinda broads you like?"

"Real ones."

"Whaddaya mean by that?"

"You know baseball?" George asked.

"Doesn't everybody?"

"Women are a lot like baseball fields. You got women who're like Wrigley Field. No lights or exploding neon scoreboards. They play outside on real grass. And it's a *field*, not a *stadium*. Then you got women who're like artificial turf, like the Houston Astrodome.

They're inside, playing on this fake surface. A lot of base hits on artificial turf would be ground-outs on real grass. How many times on
turf you seen a line drive single bounce over an outfielder's head for
a triple? You get true hops with real women. And the delicate things,
like bunting, they're hard to do on turf. Women like artificial turf are
just phony. I like 'em like Wrigley Field."

Shaking his head, Henry mumbled, "Man, okay."

Another dancer, wearing an oversized red and black hunting
jacket and a coon-skin cap, appeared on stage. She carried an imita-
tion shotgun on her left shoulder and spun around on four-inch
black heels. Centrifugal force lifted the bottom of the jacket to
expose her rear end.

"Gentlemen," the club's announcer said, drowning out the music.
"How'd you like to bag this trophy on a cold, early morning in the
woods? Please give a warm welcome to Large Marge the Sarge!"

"It'd be easier to drag a ten-point buck into a clearing, don't you
think?" Henry offered.

George looked at his watch.

"Have you tried talkin' to that ice queen vice president in
personnel? She's up on all the job openings."

"No. Good idea."

"If you do, watch out. She's about as pleasant as standin' in a
butcher's freezer. She's part of this new wave of broads with master's
degrees. You know the thing that really pisses me off about them?"
Henry asked.

"What?"

"They don't give guys like us the time of day. They think we're
scum. Just common laborers who ain't worth a shit. We'll never get
to screw one of 'em."

George grunted. "My kid's probably already done that."

"Yeah, Mr. Scholarship Winner. He'll probably end up marryin'
one of them. Bitch'll bleed him dry."

"Hey, Henry. Don't say that."

Henry stormed up to the dance stage, reached over the top rope and jammed a dollar bill into Marge's bra. She grimaced. Henry returned and yanked his chair away from the table. "You know what I'd like to do?" he barked. "Take one of those vice president bitches out behind the plant and do her Greek!"

"Time to go," George said, rising from his chair. "I'm splitting." He walked outside, past the bouncer. Henry stayed at Rondo's.

Despite the post-Thanksgiving onset of snow, George decided to sell the old Chevy four-by-four. Young George had moved to an apartment with two other students. And the boys signed a one-year lease, allowing them to leave their possessions in Albany over the summer.

Thelma Turgeson, an accounting clerk at Woo Labs, asked George to consider donating the pickup truck to the Netherwood Baptist Church. She explained that he could get the truck appraised by a member of her congregation for three thousand dollars, which would be the amount of his tax deduction. Since George was asking only four hundred dollars for the truck, he'd make more money from the value of the tax benefit than from selling it outright. "Besides," Thelma emphasized, "Reverend Mason has been convening a daily prayer group hoping to get a truck to haul around church equipment."

The following Saturday, George drove the truck to Netherwood Baptist Church to meet Thelma and Reverend Mason. They handed George a certified appraisal for three thousand dollars. Since the appraisal far exceeded the truck's Blue Book value, Reverend Mason also filled out IRS Form 8283, attesting to the fact that Netherwood Baptist Church was a charitable institution qualified to receive donated property.

Thelma even gave George a lift home. Winding his way along Netherwood Road in the passenger seat, George knew that the Church's involvement in the transaction didn't alter its essence. He sighed. There was little difference between what he'd just done and Spiro Agnew's kickback schemes. Everybody has schemes. When the guy next to him on line three realized that he couldn't make the payments on his silver anniversary Corvette, he drove it to Yankee Stadium and left the keys in the ignition. To cover the shortfall between the insurance proceeds and the loan balance, the guy told the insurance company there was five hundred dollars' worth of eight-track tapes in the trunk.

George eventually set up an appointment with Woo Labs' vice president for Employee Relations. She told him about a line opening in the Engraving Department. Since Engraving hadn't had any management openings in years, George declined that transfer. With almost twenty years' experience and a clean record, Woo Labs placed George on the short list for inspector and foreman job openings. He thanked the vice president. Two weeks later, George received an answer to another question that he'd posed during their meeting: his son's scholarship would be voided if he left Woo Labs and went to work elsewhere.

❖

THE LAMP POST, ON the corner of Washington Avenue and Quail Street, was one of the best places in Albany to meet Jewish American Princesses. Inside the doorway, the JAPs congregated on an elevated platform to see and be seen. The bathrooms were in the back. The best way to meet JAPs, George figured, was to place a chair next to the ladies room and heckle or smile at the girls coming and going to the bathroom.

Success at the JAP Post required an upgraded wardrobe; a polo shirt and tight Jordache jeans replaced George's sweatshirt and Levi's. He despised altering his appearance, but did what was necessary. He didn't have to change his clothes for the short road trips to finishing schools like St. Rose or Russell Sage, but those obsequious shiksas irritated him, and he stopped going.

On a Thursday night in March, George stood outside the JAP Post waiting for his housemates, who were meeting him after their evening history class. Ben Sawyer and Marty Goldberg were fifteen minutes late. George figured that Marty had cornered the professor after class to ask the questions he'd rehearsed the night before. Marty asked questions in all his courses, sucking up to the professors, trying to convince them that their courses were special so they'd remember him when computing final grades. By remaining in a liberal arts curriculum, despite having the grades to major in business, Marty had limited his options. A history degree with an emphasis on European revolutions would leave Marty with only two choices—working in his father's clothing business or going to law school.

"How'ya gonna get laid talking about that history crap?" George would chide Marty. "Chicks wanna be plugged by guys who talk about money and power."

George and Marty met Ben the previous year in Eastman Tower. Near the end of the spring term, the three boys decided to move off campus together. Five-five-six Park Avenue had a much more glorious address than it deserved. The unstable wooden columns supporting the sagging front porch seemed to portend the house's impending collapse. Three weathered metal and wooden chairs on the porch showed the effects of upstate New York winters. But each boy had his own room, and there was no campus security to deal with.

George glanced at his Timex. It read 10:35. He pictured Marty spewing words in the direction of a gray-haired professor in a tan corduroy sport coat.

Marty and Ben finally showed up in Marty's black BMW.

"Good," George announced. "Now, can we figure out how I'm gonna go out with Rachel?"

"Did you talk to her?" Marty asked.

"Yeah, I went to her room today. She's really into guys with money. She asked what kind of car I drove. What my father did for a living."

"Johnson," Ben said, waving his beer bottle. "You're trying to date out of your league. There are chicks who don't care that you drive a Duster. Or that your ol' man works the lines."

"Yeah," George said, "I guess. But I wanna date Rachel. She's classy."

"Hey!" Marty said, pointing toward the stage. "Check her out!"

The three boys eyed a bleached blonde wearing a tight-fitting, red lambswool sweater and matching red cowboy boots. She was the sort of full-bosomed girl who made George think that her breasts had siphoned off some of the cells that would have otherwise ended up in her brain.

George shook his head and ordered another beer. "I can't understand why money is everything to girls," he said. "But it is. There's no denying it."

"Whaddaya gonna do about it?" Marty asked.

"I don't know. I just don't know."

In George's spring term, business classes began replacing liberal arts courses on his schedule. He marked the shift by getting a student subscription to *The Wall Street Journal* and following the OPEC-driven rise in the Consumer Price Index. By year's end, it was the largest jump in thirty-three years. "Good thing I got the scholarship," he told his father during spring break. "Tuition's really going up next year."

The disco wave peaked in 1979—"Hot Stuff," "Ring My Bell," and "Good Times" all were number one songs by the summer. Wes the Mess ruled the Deer Creek disco scene. But he suffered a setback when a woman slapped him at Lucky 7, right in the middle of a dance.

The woman's outburst caused the band to stop playing. A bouncer intervened before Wes could hit her. Afterward, George caught Wes's smirk. George shook his head in disgust, shaking off several years' worth of admiration. He saw little of Wes after that.

Again that summer, Woo Labs gave George a job and even promoted him to assistant supply clerk. It was cushy work compared to the previous summer, and it allowed him to use his rudimentary accounting skills.

❖

ON A CRISP SUNDAY morning in October, George Sr. rose early. He threw his green winter parka over his PJs, slipped into untied boots, and walked with Buddy to the paperbox, where he picked up Sunday's *Hudson Valley Watch*.

Inside the house, the front-page headline caught his attention.

Carter Meets Pope in Washington

Washington, DC, Oct. 6, 1979—President Jimmy Carter welcomed Pope John Paul II at the White House today. The meeting was historic: President Carter became the first American chief executive to officially receive a Catholic pontiff. A member of the Pope's delegation was quoted as saying…

Another headline screamed at him.

Former Deer Creek High School
Valedictorian Arrested in Albany Drug Raid

Albany, NY, Oct 6, 1979—George Johnson Jr., a life-long Salt Point resident, was arrested on the evening of October 4 at his student residence, 556 Park Avenue in Albany. He was charged with three counts of criminal possession of a controlled substance with intent to sell.

According to an unidentified Albany City police officer, each count is a Class B felony punishable by a substantial term of incarceration. The same police officer told the *Hudson Valley Watch* that Mr. Johnson spent Thursday night in the local lockup and was arraigned Friday morning in the Albany City courthouse.

At the arraignment, Mr. Johnson's court-appointed lawyer, Saul B. Carlson of the Albany Public Defender's office, waived a reading of the charges. Mr. Carlson requested a preliminary hearing, which by law must be held within three days of the arraignment. Bail was set at $2,000 cash or a $20,000 secured real property bond. Although Mr. Carlson could not be reached for comment, his office confirmed that Mr. Johnson has not posted bail. He will remain incarcerated at least throughout the weekend.

Mr. Johnson is a graduate of Deer Creek High School, where he was the valedictorian of the Class of 1977. He gained fame when, delivering the valedictory address, he read a letter that he had written to his deceased mother. Mr. Johnson is attending SUNY Albany on a full scholarship awarded by Woo Industrial Laboratories, Inc. He is presently in his junior year. A spokesman for Woo Labs declined to comment.

George Johnson Sr. of Fox Run Road in Salt Point, the student's father, could not be reached for comment.

❖

"HOLY SHIT!" GEORGE SR. exclaimed, unable to decide what to do. He dialed his son's number.

"Hello," Marty Goldberg answered on what seemed like the fiftieth ring.

"Marty, this is Mr. Johnson! What the hell is going on? Where's George?"

"Uh, he's not heah right now, Mr. Johnson."

"Where is he?"

"I don't know."

"Like hell you don't! Stop covering for him. I just read in the newspaper he's been arrested." George fought back tears.

"I'm sohry, Mr. Johnson. I didn't want to lie to you. But I promised George that I would."

"Why didn't anybody tell me?"

"George didn't want you to know."

"Well, now that I know, I'm coming up. What's going on?"

"I don't know much. He's charged with selling cocaine to an unduhcovuh cop."

"Cocaine! Is it true?"

"I don't know. His lawyuh told him not to say anything. He's not tawking to anybody, even me."

"Was he dealing drugs?"

"I honestly don't know. I've nevuh seen him do it. If he was, he kept it from me. Honest."

"What a mess! Where is he?"

"He's still in jail, but I raised the two thousand dollahs bail from some friends. We should get him out tomorrow. We can't do anything today because it's Sunday. The preliminary hearing is at ten tomorrow morning."

"Where at?"

"In the city cawthouse."

"Where's that?"

"Downtown. I don't know the address, but it's across from the Capitol building. The judge's name is Sandburg."

"Alright, I'm driving up now. I should be there in a couple of hours. Will you be home?"

"Yeah, but you can't do anything today. There aren't even any visiting owhrs."

"Even for fathers?"

"Only lawyuhs."

"I'm still coming."

As soon as George hung up, the phone rang. He picked up the receiver, but couldn't bring himself to say anything.

"Is anybody there?"

"Oh, hi Ursula. Sorry."

"Have you seen today's paper?"

George pounded his fist into the refrigerator door. "Yeah."

"What's going on?"

"I don't know for sure. I just talked to his roommate. I'm going up there now."

"You want company?"

"No. I think I better handle this myself."

"Well, keep me informed then."

❖

THE POLICE OFFICERS AT the lockup refused to allow George to see his son. "If he don't make bail tomorrow morning, you can see him at two," the duty officer said. George resigned himself to passing time by watching the day's football games at his son's house. He slept in young George's bed that night.

The next morning, George reached the city courthouse, a time-worn brown building. He entered Judge Sandburg's empty court-room at 9:35 a.m. Fifteen minutes later, Marty poked his head in. He motioned George to follow him into the corridor.

"See that guy ovuh theh in da suit," Marty said, pointing down the hall. "That's Mr. Carlson. He's George's lawyuh. Theh's a problem with George makin' bail."

"George ain't gonna get out today?"

"I don't know. Go tawk to him."

George walked over and introduced himself. Saul Carlson was an energetic young man three years removed from Albany Law School. Mr. Carlson told George that unsealed indictments concerning the drug sting would be opened before the preliminary hearing, and that those indictments might further implicate George and affect the amount of bail. He promised to speak with George again after the preliminary hearing.

At 10:20 a.m. the bailiff shouted, "People versus Johnson!" George watched the door open where detainees entered the court-room. That Johnson was another man charged with arson. One hour later, George heard "People versus Johnson!" again. The marshal led his son into the courtroom and removed the handcuffs from his wrists. Dressed in prison garb, George Jr. marched in without taking his eyes off the floor. He whispered to his lawyer.

George Sr. didn't grasp all of what took place in court that morning. Apparently, the indictments unsealed earlier in the day hadn't further implicated his son. Judge Sandburg held a preliminary hearing. A police officer testified that he bought a gram of cocaine from George on at least one occasion, that the transaction was tape-recorded, and that marked bills were exchanged and recovered from the accused. The officer confirmed that he'd taken George into custody after the buy.

To a stunned father watching and listening, it seemed obvious that his son was guilty. He was torn between wanting to support his son and wanting to punch him out.

"I find the probable cause requirement has been satisfied," the Judge bellowed. "Accordingly, the defendant is bound over for action by the grand jury. This case is transferred to the Supreme Court of New York, Albany County. Call the next case."

Just like that, it was over. George was re-cuffed and led back to the holding pen. George Sr. and Marty cornered Mr. Carlson outside the courtroom.

"The Assistant DA will present your son's case to the grand jury in a few days," the lawyer said. "The grand jury will indict him, though it's unclear on how many counts. After that, there'll be a deadline to file motions and a trial date will be calendared. We'll have to decide about the possibility of a plea after we see the evidence. Any other questions?"

"When's my son gonna get out?"

"Today. Sometime this afternoon. It takes a while to do the paperwork, but the two grand has been posted by your son's friends. He'll be out by five o'clock."

"Can I see him before that?"

"Yeah, just go to the lockup. I gotta run."

Following the "Visitors" sign, the prisoner's father found himself swept into the maelstrom of an America he'd never seen: scores of filthy and unruly people were lined up waiting to see other prisoners. As soon as George took his place in line, others filled in behind him. It was hard for him to unravel the dialects. The visitors all moved single-file through a metal detector, offering their purses and bags to the guards for inspection. Men and women were separated so their cavities could be searched by an officer of the same sex. Then they were herded through a barricaded door into a large room to meet the prisoners. All movements in the visiting room were monitored by officers on elevated platforms and those watching closed-circuit television.

Despite the protections, George marveled at the visitors' ability to smuggle drugs inside the lockup. Before subjecting themselves to strip searches, people placed cocaine in pre-folded, paper packets. They inserted the small packages in their mouths under their tongues, keeping the packets hidden when they opened their mouths during the search. Females transferred the packages when kissing; males coughed the packets into their right palms and transferred them while shaking hands. George lowered his head.

When the line's forward movement drew a shaken George closer to the entrance, and closer to his son, he took a deep breath. He knew what to do but couldn't control the direction or intensity of his careening emotions. After seeing his boy barely fifteen feet away— his features partially shrouded by the dusty plexiglas barrier separating the caged from the free—his anger gave way to despondence.

Visitors could reach over the plexiglas and shake hands or kiss. That contact evidently lasted for days in a prisoner's thoughts. George's child was clad in gray cover-alls that had a Sunday school sameness about them. George Sr. extended his hand. Young George bypassed the outstretched hand, yanked his father toward him, and groped with all his might, bear-hugging his father until the plexiglas vibrated. A guard with a vacuous expression ordered the Johnsons to sit down.

George Sr. studied his son. He pictured the boy being sucked down a large sewer pipe by the weight of dirty sludge, his screams for help inaudible, buried by the slime. Toilet after toilet flushed.

George Jr. wiped tears away with his prison shirt. He thought about their first trip from Salt Point to Albany. He thought about the rabbits in the mink cages. He said, "I've been hoping that you wouldn't find out about this. That you wouldn't see me like this. Every time the guard came and told me I had a visitor, my stomach knotted up. I was hoping it wasn't you. But I was glad to see you in court this morning. When the guard came to my cell a little while ago, I knew it was you." Tears streamed down his face. His body convulsed.

"You'll get out later today," George Sr. offered.

"You're my family. It's lonely in here. I feel all alone."

"It's okay, George. It's okay," the elder Johnson repeated, rising from his chair and reaching over the plexiglass barrier to grasp his son's shoulders. "It's okay."

"I need you, Dad. I can't get through this all by myself. I mean it. I can't."

"Okay, I'm here." He turned. "Let me see about getting you out, okay?"

Young George watched his father leave without turning back to wave good-bye. Some choices leave you all alone. Consequences result from those choices, consequences you didn't see. Or perhaps you really saw them but just ignored them because another thing you saw, easy money, crowded out what could go wrong. You try to get what you think you want, but instead you go from half free to not free. Everybody living you care about will now judge you. Except Buddy. Does the Church teach that your dead mother will ever find out? Your dead sister?

A little over two hours later, George left the lockup. He'd been on the roof for the mandatory half hour of fresh air during the previous four days, but the soft wind and outdoor light now seemed richer, almost soothing.

On the short drive to 556 Park Avenue, he covered his face with his hands and thought about the tenuous line between freedom and imprisonment. The War on Drugs drew people closer to a line that marked people once it was crossed. Forced enclosure. Restricted movements. Verbal abuse. Physical abuse. Scars. In those four prison days, George slept without dreams. The confinement virus lodged in and spread throughout his mind. Infection.

"Dad, I'm guilty."

"Why? Just tell me why?"

"I'll try. Give me time."

They drove the rest of the way home in silence. Inside the apartment, they walked into George's bedroom. The elder Johnson closed the door while his son sat on the bed with his legs crossed, holding a pillow in front of his chest.

"Dad, just so you know, I wasn't using any drugs. There's only one reason I dealt. Money. I did it for the money."

"But you've got a full scholarship. You're not hard-up for money. I feel like I don't know you at all."

George Jr. tucked the pillow under his chin and sighed.

"I musta messed up raising you. I tried to be tolerant, even lenient, but this is beyond anything I ever expected. There musta been more in those suspensions than I saw."

"I was just mad then—"

"What are you mad at now?"

"I really don't know how to explain it. There's just something different about being up here. I mean, everybody's got money. Ben's got plenty of it. Marty's swimming in the stuff. There's all kinds of fancy cars up here. Most kids come from families who're loaded. It's totally different from Salt Point. I just got caught up in it."

"But selling drugs!"

"Hey, it's not like I was going down to the local junior high school and pushing 'em on kids. I was selling to college students. They're recreational users."

"This really frightens me. Don't you know the difference between right and wrong? Selling drugs is illegal!"

George Jr. covered his face. He remembered that his father didn't pay taxes on cash sales of thousands of rabbits. He also recalled that

Spiro Agnew didn't go to jail for tax evasion. But it didn't seem right to mention any of that now. Instead, he said, "Just because something's illegal doesn't mean it's wrong. And just because something's legal doesn't mean it's right."

"That's bullshit and you know it! You didn't decide doing drugs is morally right and then supply 'em to people."

"Alright! I already admitted it. I shouldn't have done it but I did. The money was just too good to pass up."

"How good?"

"Well, I could buy an ounce of coke for fourteen hundred bucks, and sell it by the gram for a hundred. There's twenty-eight grams in an ounce. So, I doubled my money. If I cut it with aspirin or mannitol, I made even more. That's where the big money was, in cocaine. For pot, I could buy it for three hundred and eighty bucks a pound. I split it into ounces and sold 'em for fifty bucks a piece. That's a profit of over four hundred bucks a pound."

"Unbelievable! I can't believe my son was selling drugs."

"Drugs are everywhere. Take a walk through the dorms. On the weekends, everybody's getting high. Coke is everywhere. So is acid. But everybody goes back to classes on Monday. It's all part of the college experience."

"Yeah, but those kids aren't going to *jail!*"

Young George took a deep breath and thought of the army cot he slept on. "You're right. I took a risk. And I got caught. Now, I'll probably have a record, like Johnny Cash."

"You might go to jail."

"I doubt it. It's my first offense. And who knows, my lawyer might even come up with a way to get me off. But it's gonna be really hard to face people like Mrs. B. I can't believe I was in the Sunday paper."

"I don't understand. You had everything going for you."

"Yeah, well," George Jr. responded, looking down at the stained check pattern on his bedspread. "I got impatient. I was thinking about it in jail. Every city in America has a drug trade. Dealing drugs is the lower class form of capitalism. Dealing drugs lets you be a business man. It's kinda weird, this class stuff. The dollars were so great that I jumped in. Felt forced into it. Like I couldn't say no. Dealing drugs seemed like any business, like the rabbits, even. I guess the ones who aren't successful get arrested."

George Sr. slammed the bedroom door shut. "You're a damned criminal. And I've given my life for you."

"Oh, c'mon." George Jr. squeezed the pillow against his chest. "I did this. Not you."

"How much did you make in this illegal business of yours?"

"All in all, a little over fifteen thousand bucks."

"Jesus Christ! Is it in a bank somewhere?"

"Hell no. They can trace that kinda thing. It's buried in two plastic bags in Lincoln Park."

❖

THREE DAYS LATER, THE grand jury indicted George on two counts of possession with intent to sell. *People v. Johnson* was assigned to Albany County Supreme Court Judge Simon Lewis, a cagey octogenarian known as a tough sentencer. The judge conferenced the case.

George continued to attend classes. But his preoccupied, wandering mind couldn't be reined in. He tried to fake attentiveness but, more often than not, stared into space. He couldn't escape the feeling of being carried away by events, having others determine his fate. The elder Johnson's frequent telephone calls didn't help.

Mr. Carlson told George of the dim prospects for reducing the felony counts to misdemeanors. "And the chances of prevailing at trial are remote," he advised. George instructed his attorney to open plea bargain discussions. He wanted the ordeal resolved, so he agreed to plead guilty to one felony count in return for the State dropping the other count. The prosecutor also agreed not to recommend a jail term, but wouldn't agree to recommend probation or community service.

Mr. Carlson estimated that George stood better than a 50 percent chance of receiving probation without a jail term, but mentioned Judge Lewis's unpredictability. A couple of weeks later, George stood before the judge in open court to revise his original plea. "Guilty, Your Honor," George said, his voice cracking. "I plead guilty." George answered the litany of questions designed to satisfy the judge that the guilty plea was voluntary. Judge Lewis scheduled the sentencing hearing for a few days before Christmas, which left enough time for the preparation of a pre-sentence report.

Young George begged the probation officer to recommend community service, but received no information about the recommendation. During moments of deep fear and desperation, George considered fleeing. He could've repaid the bail money to Marty out of his drug profits. But sooner or later, he realized, the law would catch up to him. Better to just face the consequences now.

George Sr. drove to Albany the afternoon before the sentencing hearing. Before reaching his son's apartment, he made his way to the east entrance of the Cathedral of the Immaculate Conception, one of Albany's oldest Roman Catholic churches. George veered toward the last pew. Kneeling down, he stared into the quiet, wide expanse. A priest was puttering around near the altar, arranging his accoutrements for the day's ceremonies.

"In the name of the Father, the Son, and the Holy Ghost," George began in a hushed voice, making the sign of the cross. His prayer asked for forgiveness of sins and begged God to spare his son from prison.

❖

FIVE-FIVE-SIX PARK AVENUE WAS quiet that evening. Marty and Ben vacated the house so that father and son could be alone. The elder Johnson inflated an air mattress and placed it beside his son's bed. He reflected on the stillness in the heavy air and sobbed into the pillow.

"Dad, please don't cry. Please. I can't stand being reminded that I let you down."

George Sr. cleared his throat. "Whatever happens tomorrow, I just don't want this thing to defeat you. It's serious. But it's not the end of the world. You're young, you'll come back."

George Jr. sat up in his bed and leaned over toward his father's silhouette. "No matter what happens, I'm tainted. I mighta done something lots of people do everyday, but I got caught. This could be one of those mistakes you can't recover from. Everybody looks at you differently. Friends, professors, people in my classes who don't even know me, they'll treat me differently now. I can feel the weight of their eyes."

"That stuff will pass. Trust your old man. It will."

"You know, I was wrong. I broke the law. I won't do it again. That's what I'm gonna tell the judge tomorrow. But it burns me up that some of these people, the ones who've gotten stoned or done lines the night before, are condemning me. Where do they get off acting that way?"

"Human nature. You gotta let go of that. Just be strong."

"I gotta be at Mr. Carlson's office at nine o'clock, so we can go over what's gonna happen at the hearing. You wanna just meet me at the courthouse a little before ten?"

"Yeah, that's fine."

George Sr. entered St. Mary's Church an hour before his son's sentencing hearing. He recited both the Our Father and Hail Mary that morning. He also lit a candle and dropped a dollar into the donation slot. He asked God to save his son from his family's ghosts.

On the way outside, George stopped to bless himself with the same holy water that his son dipped his fingers into less than an hour earlier. Walking toward the courthouse, George stopped in the chilly air to take one last look at the church. He stared at the weather vane on top of its tower; it depicted Gabriel, the Archangel, blowing his trumpet of judgment.

Father and son met outside the entrance to Judge Lewis' courtroom. They embraced before Mr. Carlson led George to the defendant's table.

"All rise!" the clerk ordered. "The Supreme Court of New York, Albany County is now in session. The Honorable Simon Lewis presiding."

"We'll do the sentencing first," the judge muttered to his clerk. The bailiff called young George's case. The Assistant District Attorney appeared at the podium to announce that his office took no position on the appropriate sentence. With George at his side, Mr. Carlson stressed George's lack of previous criminal involvement, admission of guilt, superb academic record, and the absence of any family except for his father. Mr. Carlson urged probation.

The judge removed his black reading glasses from the tip of his nose and rubbed his left hand over his face, resting his thumb and index finger on top of his closed eyelids. "Mr. Johnson," the judge began. "You are a young man who makes an old man sad. You are very different from most of the drug dealers that I've had the occasion, in increasing numbers, to sentence. You're not addicted to drugs, so you weren't selling them to feed a habit. You apparently weren't even using them. And you certainly weren't selling them to feed a family. It seems you sold them only to make money."

Judge Lewis leaned back in his chair. "Greed can be condoned only within the bounds of the law. Mr. Johnson, I am mindful that I'm sentencing you on only one felony count. But it's a very serious offense to which you've pleaded guilty. Oh, you make me feel sad. Your situation reminds me of Percy's Paradox. You know what that is?"

The question caught George off guard. "No, Your Honor."

"Then you have a lot to learn. Percy's Paradox is the pitfall described by author Walker Percy in which people attain straight As in school but fail life's larger tests. You've fallen victim to Percy's Paradox."

"Your Honor," George began. "I broke the law and deserve to be punished. I've paid a price already. I believe that community service and supervised probation would be the best sentence for me—"

"I'm not surprised that you feel that way," the judge barked. "Most defendants have similar beliefs. I'm prepared to sentence you. Anything else that you want to add?"

"Yes, Your Honor. With all due respect to Mr. Percy, when you see most everybody's on the take, it's hard to resist the temptation to grab something for yourself. You figure everybody does it and you're not hurting anybody. I know that sounds like Richard Nixon's defense. But I watched the Ervin Committee hearings a number of years back, and my situation is different from Nixon's. He was the President of the United States. Me, I'm just a kid. And, Your Honor, I've learned my lesson." George stepped back from the microphone.

"Alright. So you've learned the lesson that a poisonous preoc-cupation with money or power can lead to a person's downfall. But I'm still left with a responsibility to the community to punish you. Accordingly, I hereby sentence you to two years in state prison. Because of the presence of some factors in mitigation, I will suspend eighteen months of that sentence." The smacking sound of the judge's walnut gavel stunned the Johnsons.

Mr. Carlson jumped to his feet and shouted, "Your Honor! Mr. Johnson lives downstate. His father's the only living member of his immediate family. May we have an order that the six-month sentence be served at Edgewood Prison? It's across the Hudson River from where the defendant's father lives."

"Yes, I'll allow that."

"Your Honor," Mr. Carlson interjected again. "One more item. Can the defendant spend the Christmas holidays with his father and report to Edgewood shortly thereafter?"

"The defendant may report in early January. That's all."

"Thank you, Your Honor."

George Jr. stood up. With his head down, he walked out of the courtroom into the cold air.

❖

IT WAS A SOMBER Christmas season at the Johnsons, exceeded in despondence only by the first few holiday seasons following the deaths of Mary and Susan. Neither father nor son felt much like decorating a tree. The decade-old, artificial evergreen remained in its cardboard box in the attic.

Never much of a reader outside of the classroom, young George turned toward books. Cable television hadn't yet found its way into Salt Point, so it couldn't help pass the time. Friends and well-wishers called or dropped by, but George often pretended to be asleep or didn't answer the telephone. Whenever George Sr. called from work, he'd have to hang up in the middle of a ring and immediately call back to signal that it was him. Ben and Marty visited, and their two-day stay at the Johnsons' house the weekend before New Year's Eve reminded George that the bonds of friendship kept things from completely unraveling.

Unwilling and unable to face old friends like Wes the Mess during the winter break, George hibernated in his room. He'd already faced enough sets of judgmental eyes in Albany. The solitude of his room became a steadying influence. So did escaping, through books, into other worlds. He immersed himself in Hawthorne's stories of sin and guilt and Milton's *Paradise Lost.* He did venture down to his father's room on occasion to stare at the picture of his mother and sister, who now more than ever seemed like distant relatives from another life.

It was 9:00 p.m. on New Year's Eve when father and son saw the reflection of headlights in the living room window. The Johnsons were watching the last college bowl game of the day. George Jr. glanced over his shoulder out the picture window. A large figure opened the car's door. When the visitor struggled to her feet, George Jr. rose from the couch and exclaimed, "Oh! It's Mrs. B! I'm going to bed. Tell her I'm not here."

"She can see your Duster in the driveway. She wants to see you."

"Then tell her I'm sleeping."

George Sr. greeted Ursula at the front door and helped her up the last few steps. "I figured that you'd be home, so I'm paying you a visit," she said. "Is your son home?"

"Yeah. He ran upstairs when he saw you coming."

"Trying to avoid me, huh? It's not the first time." She handed George her coat. "You got any bourbon?"

"Yeah, whaddaya want with it?"

"Nothing. Just straight." When George went into the kitchen to retrieve a glass, Ursula continued, raising her voice, "I came over here because I'm concerned about two men who are very dear to my heart."

Sitting on the edge of the stairway on the second floor, George Jr. heard her.

"Glad for your concern," George Sr. replied before handing Ursula her drink. "We're doing about as well as can be expected."

Setting her glass of bourbon on the coffee table, Ursula grasped the elder Johnson's biceps with both hands. She shook him a little. "Hey, I know it's hard on you. You're the parent. You gotta be strong, otherwise the kid'll fall apart. I know it hurts, but you'll get through it. You've been through worse, you know."

"Yeah, I know. But it makes me feel like I've failed. There were things I coulda done better."

"That's nonsense," Ursula replied, tightening her grip on his arms. "Being a parent is like those You Make the Call ads. There's tough calls to make. You only have a fifty-fifty chance of being right. Besides, you can't control everything he does."

"I don't know. It's just—"

Like a burst of light, young George scampered down the stairs into the arms of Ursula and his father. The three of them, all meshed together and hugging one another, looked like a team huddling before the opening kickoff. When they broke apart, George Jr. said, "Don't take this on yourself. I messed up. All by myself. I'm just thankful you didn't abandon me."

"Well, that's the last thing I'd ever do. But, maybe I shouldn't have started a business with you. Maybe I got you thinking too much about money at a young age—"

"That's garbage!" George Jr. insisted. "That business was about a lot more than money. And you know it."

"Damn right!" Ursula observed.

"Maybe I should've seen something like this coming," George Sr. said. "I should've disciplined you when you got those suspensions. I shouldn't have lied for you to the principal that time. And I should've paid taxes on the rabbit money. Your mother would've handled those things differently."

"Look, Dad," young George said. "You can second-guess almost anything. You did your absolute best raising me. But I've got to take responsibility for what I did."

"George," Ursula interjected, peering into the elder Johnson's eyes. "Your boy's right. You did your level best. Parents give what they're capable of giving."

❖

JANUARY 4, 1980, WAS a Friday—the last day on which Judge Lewis permitted George to report to Edgewood Prison. George insisted on driving there himself. Ursula and his father would visit over the weekend. One of them would drive the Duster home.

Edgewood was a forty-five-minute drive west of Newburgh, reachable by Interstate 84 and Route 3. On the drive to the compound, visitors saw the lush land on which the prison sat. The low lying plain was bordered by a cluster of pine and spruce trees. A chain link fence topped with barbed wire surrounded the buildings.

Edgewood was hidden from view of the approaching road. Its only marking on Route 3 was a small green sign with white letters that read "Edgewood Facility" and an arrow that pointed to the right. Most motorists didn't know that a prison existed just three quarters of a mile away from that sign.

Unlike Attica or Sing Sing, Edgewood was a minimum security prison. There had been only a handful of reported rapes and no prisoner rebellions like the one at Attica in 1971. To George, Attica symbolized brute force. He knew it was the bloodiest one-day encounter between Americans since the Civil War.

George's cellmate was a middle-aged, Hispanic man who spoke only broken English. George had no desire to talk to anybody. He deferred to the Edgewood prison officials and kept quiet at group meetings, offering no grievances. He refused to attend the religious services.

In early February, George taped a sign, handwritten in black magic marker, on the wall above his bunk. It read:

"Every morning in Africa, a gazelle wakes up. It knows it must run faster than the fastest lion or it will be killed.

Every morning in Africa, a lion wakes up. It knows it must outrun the slowest gazelle or it will starve to death."

During his months at Edgewood, George read reference books, political memoirs, business and economic texts, even a few more novels. His father delivered whatever wasn't kept in Edgewood's library. Wherever George went he took a book with him. He had books with him at his job in the machine shop and at the supervised outdoor sessions. He even took books into the bathroom. All his meals were eaten with the company of a book; he shut out the other inmates. After five weeks, the assistant warden gave him a job shelving books in the library.

Besides the regular visiting hours, Edgewood allowed visitors on the third Thursday evening of each month. Ursula visited in March, sitting on a metal chair across a card table from George.

"You seem quieter," she said, extending her hand to touch his forearm.

"There's not much to say. I'm just killing time."

"It won't be long before you'll be out."

"Yeah," George shrugged. "Then I'll be an ex-con."

Ursula removed her hand. "That's what you deserve to be. You screwed up."

George sighed.

"Use the time to reflect on what happened."

"There's lotsa time to think in here. But that can be bad. 'Cause my mind just races on and on until I'm on a racetrack. During the day, I can look at something to stop the racing. But at night I can't see anything. The racing's really fast."

"What's on your racetrack?"

"Mostly I'm slouched in the backseat of somebody else's car. Nobody's driving. But the car's going fast, careening around corner. Missing stuff. Hitting stuff."

Ursula frowned, her eyes tracing the faded checkered pattern on the card table.

George shrugged. Funny thing, he thought. You try to escape your God-given cage, then you find a smaller one, a real one.

❖

THE EDGEWOOD LIBRARY CONTAINED a poetry section that George came across while shelving books. That led him to T.S. Eliot's *Selected Poems*, as well Alan Ginsberg's poems. He even studied Shannon's poem, wondering why his emotions at the time of their relationship weren't any deeper. Somebody who loved him thought he would be a star. Somebody people would look up to. They did look up for a few minutes when he gave the 1977 valedictory address. Now they look down, if their eyes are even open.

He spent many nights scratching out poems. Most of his verses followed the trail of angst previously traveled by many others. Some traced a you-hunt-or-be-hunted theme. George wrote one poem, though, that he taped to the cinderblock wall above his lion-gazelle sign. Whenever a guard asked him what this poem meant, he wouldn't say.

There is a clamor in the cells.
"The Warden has resigned!"
But the prisoner in cellblock one knows
better;
For he is the prisoner of freedom.

Confined to a cell with windows,
The shades are never drawn.
The fettered mind is the free mind.
The paradox lingers on.

There is a clamor in the cells.
"The Warden has resigned!"
But the prisoner in cellblock two still weeps;
For he is the prisoner of darkness.

Windows closed, shades drawn,
No sunlight seen at all.
A life that gropes in darkness
To know a prison wall.

There is a clamor in the cells.
"The Warden has resigned!"
But the prisoner in cellblock three hears
nothing;
For he is the prisoner of reflection.

Windows turned to mirrors,
Reflecting self-portraits only,
No need to draw the shades;
The life is eternally lonely.

There is a clamor in the cells.
"The Warden has resigned!"
But the prisoner of freedom knows better;
For the Warden never 'was'.

❖

GEORGE SERVED FOUR MONTHS of his sentence at Edgewood. He spent the remaining two months at a Poughkeepsie halfway house, which allowed weekend passes for good behavior. He spent two weekends at home before being discharged in early July.

George Sr, Ursula, and Buddy drove George home. Two days after being released, George bought a motorcycle, complete with a fairing, crash bar, and backrest for the passenger. Using a plastic milk crate held in place with bungee cords, George transported Buddy throughout the Hudson Valley on the back of the motorcycle. In the rear view mirror, George could see more white hair on Buddy's face, more yellow covering the enamel on his teeth.

George had two more months to spend by himself. He learned that Albany State planned to take no disciplinary action against him for the drug bust. The events leading to the guilty plea occurred off-campus, and the school reasoned that the State judicial system appropriately resolved the matter. As far as SUNY Albany was concerned, George was on a leave of absence for the spring term. He paid the deposit to register for the fall term.

But Woo Labs decided in August to revoke George's academic scholarship. Mr. Woo felt it would be wrong for his company to continue providing scholarship money to George. The elder Johnson protested to no avail.

In early September, George Sr. opened the rectory door in the back of St. Stanislaus. Father Dombrowski rose from his desk. His weary eyes lingered on George for a few seconds. "Dear God!" he exclaimed. "It must be ten years since you were last in here."

George extended his hand to the head priest. "It's been longer than that, Father."

"That wouldn't surprise me," Father Dombrowski replied, shaking George's hand. "Sit down, please." George obliged. "The years have served you well, my son. I can remember when you were my altar boy. Must have been around thirty years ago, right?"

"That's about right."

"Many fine boys have come and gone since you. When you get to be my age, their names and faces run together. But I can still remember your face. It was solid. You always had an eagerness about you. How are you holding up?"

"I got some wounds. But, all in all, I'm okay."

"I heard about your son. What's he doing now?"

"He's back at Albany. Woo Labs took away his scholarship. But he got some aid and loans. We're swinging it alright. I think he's gonna be okay, but it's hard to tell with him."

"It's a shame."

"It is. But I think he's learned his lesson. He'll graduate one semester late, which a lot of parents tell me is pretty good for college kids these days."

"This must be more than visiting an old friend," the Father said. "Have you been thinking about rejoining us?"

"I'm thinking about it," George answered. "But I haven't made up my mind."

"Tell me."

"Basically, I feel like I wanna come back and do some church ceremonies. I've been praying at home, but I'm thinking about worshiping more formally now. I'm just not sure that I wanna do it in a Catholic church, that's all."

"Why do you feel that way?"

"Mostly, because of all the rules. And the political positions. You know, like birth control, abortion..." George went on, but Father Dombrowski tuned him out.

"...you know, the Jews even let women become Rabbis now," George noted, before pausing.

"I'm aware of that," Father Dombrowski said.

"It's weird," George continued. "I'm only Catholic because my father was. I could've just as easily been raised in another religion. But I don't know if the Catholics have the whole religion deal straight."

"I see," Father Dombrowski said.

"That's the kind of stuff I'm thinking about, Father. I wanted to drop by and say hello and tell you what's been on my mind. I won't take up any more of your time."

Father Dombrowski stood. "It's healthy to question things. Glad you're thinking about these issues."

"Hey, Father? Glad you were here. Whaddaya doing working so late anyway?"

"I'm editing our *Engaged Encounter* manual."

"What's that?"

"It's something that post-dates your marriage, my friend. Couples who accept the sacrament of marriage now spend a weekend with priests and trained laymen learning about each other and about the role of the Church in their lives after the marriage ceremony is over with."

More propaganda, George thought. It's just like the Church. Taking celibate priests who can't marry and anointing them experts. "See you, Father," he called out, going through the doorway.

The following weekend, George drove to Albany. He joined his son, Marty, and Ben for drinks and a meal at Sutter's. "Here's to my son's roommates," George Sr. announced with an infectious smile, raising his beer mug. "They've shown him the true meaning of friendship."

By the evening's end, the Johnsons drank enough beers to take a taxi home, but not enough to fall asleep. From the air mattress in young George's room, George Sr. asked, "Ever think about going back to the Church?"

"I thought about it in prison. And I'm not going to. I'm disillusioned with religion. Especially Catholicism."

"Your smarts are God-given. So I wouldn't write-off the Church."

Young George rolled over and peered down from his bed at his father laying on the air mattress. "God-given, huh? You really think so?"

"There's no other explanation."

Young George smiled, then rolled back to the middle of his bed.

"You know," the elder Johnson volunteered, "I told Father Dombrowski all the bad things I thought the Church did. And he took it well."

"The old bugger must want you back in the congregation."

"Hey, son, you holding it together? Things okay up here?"

"Yeah, they are. School's going fine. I've gotten all As on my first set of exams. I'm more introverted now, a little more aloof than before. Some people see me and still think *jailbird*. But I've been having weird dreams."

"What kinda dreams?"

Young George studied the water-stained bedroom ceiling. "I have two kinds of dreams. In the first, I'm sitting in this clearing in the woods. The swamp in Salt Point is right behind me. New York City is on the other side of the woods. It's nighttime. And this huge, raging fire is burning all around me. It's windy. My hair is blowing all around my face. Then there's a big opening in the fire. So I start running through that opening toward the skyscrapers. I get partway through and the wind starts blowing in the opposite direction. Wham, the opening in the fire closes up, chasing me back to Salt Point. When I get back there, my pants and shirt are on fire. So I roll around in the swamp to put out the flames on my clothes. Then I wake up."

"Jesus! What's the second dream?"

"I'm at a surprise birthday party for me that my wife's thrown. I'm a lot older. We live in this fancy high-rise overlooking Central Park. It's got fireplaces and Victorian furniture with carved legs that curl up on the ends. My wife and I have just come back from dinner in our Porsche nine-eleven. All these people are waiting at our place to yell 'Surprise!' I'm wearing a three-piece, pin striped suit. She's got on a strapless, form-fitting dress. Oh, Dad!" George exclaimed, "You should see my wife! She's hot. So, anyway, I'm totally surprised by the party. Then I get this Carvel ice cream cake filled with candles. All these people sing 'Happy Birthday' to me. I blow out the candles. And they turn out to be those reigniting kind. So I blow a couple of times and they keep coming back. Then I blow real, real hard and they finally go out. Everybody claps. When I get up close to the cake to read the inscription, all the candles come back to life again and scorch my face. My eyelids and hair are on fire."

"Then you wake up?"

"Yep, with my heart in my mouth."

❖

AT AGE FORTY, GEORGE Sr. thought half his life was over. But he still harbored a primal fear of meaningful relationships. Part of the fear stemmed from the way his wife and daughter were taken from him. Zap, and the girls were gone. If George let another woman close to him, would that be disloyal? Would that be dishonoring his vows? Catholicism had all the answers when it came to dictating when and how parishioners could have sex, but provided little guidance on the question that George had wrestled with for more than a decade.

George's friends cautioned against high maintenance women, and they advocated sport-poking. Truck drivers at Woo Labs competed for conquests. If two guys had sex with the same woman, they bragged about being semen brothers.

Subjected to those influences, George couldn't block them out. Some of the games and remarks struck him as harmless. Some struck him as funny. Anyway, how could an assembly line worker change his environment? Especially one who'd received condescending glances from female executives.

But, late one Saturday at Lucky 7, a spry, redheaded woman with an angular jaw walked into the lounge and asked George to dance. She exuded warmth in her matter-of-factness, smiling in a way that made her appear glad to be dancing with him, but not in a smothering fashion. She wore a bowling glove on her right hand, and her absent-mindedness gave them both a laugh.

When the music stopped, she took off the bowling glove and extended her hand. "Annette Mackey," she said.

George raised his eyebrows as he reached for her hand. "You teach science at Netherwood Junior High?" he asked.

"Used to," she said.

"George Johnson," he said, pointing to his chest. "The father. Not the son who started fires in your classroom a decade ago."

"Oh my God!"

They stared at each other before breaking into near simultaneous smiles.

"Miss Mackey, another dance?"

They spent the rest of the night in each other's company. The lounge band played a few disco songs, and Annette led George through the moves. She made him feel competent. They were on the floor during every slow song, holding each other and kissing whenever the strobe light dimmed the dance floor. They continued their slow dance in the parking lot, using the easy-listening station on the Pinto's radio for music. Annette finally said good night.

The next day they shared a picnic lunch at Lake Taghkanic. As George held hands with Annette, he felt bolts of warmth traveling through his body. She maintained a contagious, euphoric expression the whole day. Never once did it disintegrate into the paradoxical little smile that George feared. And she didn't glom on to him after they made love on her cotton blanket, barely a hundred yards from the trail that ran near the Taconic Parkway.

❖

STROLLING THROUGH ALBANY'S MAIN quad on a cloudy September afternoon, George Jr. caught a glimpse of the voter registration stand. He suppressed the urge to veer in that direction and overturn the table. Instead, he took a deep breath and visualized himself lifting the table and throwing it into the fountain, with all the registration forms floating in the air.

New York State prohibited convicted felons from voting in elections. 1981 was the second year that George missed out on a Constitutional right not conferred on all citizens. 1980 should have been his first opportunity to vote in a presidential election, and it irked him when New York state denied his voter registration application. He'd heard about a process by which convicted felons could petition the governor to vote again, but it sounded so technical and time-consuming that he hadn't bothered with it. But George's felony conviction didn't prevent him from helping with a presidential campaign. John Anderson, the Illinois congressman, had won a place on New York's ballot as an independent candidate. His handlers welcomed George's help.

That fall semester was George's last at Albany. Marty had graduated the previous spring, been accepted to Columbia Law, and appeared headed away from the family clothing business. Ben was still around, and the two boys decided against filling the third room for the fall term. Since the prospect of working for a living didn't sit well with George, he decided to apply to graduate business schools, taking the GMATs that October.

Marty flew to Albany for a reunion. The three boys visited old haunts, including Across the Street Pub, a more upscale place than Sutter's. The pub was well lit inside and didn't attract the jeans and sweatshirt crowd that frequented Sutter's.

"So, Marty," Ben demanded as the three boys huddled near the bar, "Tell us about the law school babes."

"One thing I've learned at Columbia is not to call dem 'babes.' Dey want to be called 'women.'"

"No shit! How come?"

"Because they're oulda."

"That's something I've learned," George offered. "Call 'em women. I've run into these feminist types at Anderson rallies. They've decided it's now demeaning to be called girls." George shrugged. "Maybe they're growing up. But call 'em women. They'll be so grateful. Maybe they'll even think you're enlightened."

"Agreed, man," Ben said, raising his glass of beer. "Just GLP."

"Damn right!" George pronounced.

"I nevuh hehd of that," Marty said.

"Get Laid Politics," Ben said, slapping Marty on the shoulder.

Marty smiled. "Lemme tell you guys my new JAP joke. Name four words that a Jewish American Princess nevuh heahs?"

"We give up," Ben responded.

"Attention all Kmart shoppers!"

The boys howled.

"Guys, seriously," George said. "Wouldn't it be neat to have a girlfriend who understood you? I haven't had that since Shannon, in high school."

Ben rolled his eyes and turned to Marty.

"C'mon, Marty, give us a story."

"Law school's pretty dull. We just study for owhas."

"Glad I'm going to business school," George said.

George graduated summa cum laude from Albany State that December. He scored 780 on the GMATs, assuring him a spot in the fall of 1982's entering class at a top-flight business school.

To pass the time from January to August, George landed a job with a grand title: Special Assistant to the Hudson County Finance Commissioner. The county finance office was on Main Street in the heart of Poughkeepsie. He commuted there from his father's house in Salt Point. The job required George to wear a jacket and tie, sit at a gray metal desk, and perform revenue and expense projections for the commissioner. He also organized the ladies' racetrack bets, collecting their money and placing daily wagers at the Off Track Betting windows a block away.

The work was light, leaving George time to fill out his business school applications. He applied to seven programs. All required essays.

The Person I Admire the Most

The person I admire the most is my father, George Johnson Sr. I was conceived out of wedlock. The Catholic Church forced my father to marry the high school girl he'd gotten pregnant; six months later I was born. Seven years later my mother and younger sister were killed in a car accident. My grieving father then began an unyielding quest to become the best parent he possibly could.

Oftentimes, children do not fully appreciate their parents, if at all, until they reach a point in their lives that enables them to look back on their formative years from a distance. I have reached that point, and what

I see is that my father faced a daunting task, one whose enormity was exceeded only by the dispirited realization that he would have to raise his surviving child alone.

As I have grown, I've watched relationships between friends and their parents. What I've seen is that my father's unquestioning love and sense of commitment far exceeds the combined parental abilities of all mothers and fathers. There has never been an occasion when my father was too preoccupied, too tired, or too uninterested in something important to me.

The most poignant example of my father's superior parental abilities occurred two-and-a-half years ago. In the fall of my junior year of college, I was arrested for selling cocaine to an undercover police officer. I reacted with shame and humiliation; instead of calling my father and asking for help and for bail money, I pretended that I alone could rectify my predicament. But I learned that certain troubles are of such magnitude that only the love and faith of a parent can help resolve them.

Instead of learning about my arrest from me, my father read about it in the newspaper. He immediately drove to Albany. I had been in jail for nearly four days when I first saw his face in the visitor's room. I cried and embraced him; I didn't ever want to let go. My father's steadying influence, obvious hurt and disappointment, and constant encouragement all helped me conquer my fears. After that experience, I've come to see clearly the man who is my father.

I pleaded guilty and served a six-month jail sentence. I can still picture the headline in Albany State's student newspaper: "Down for the Count—Honor Student Headed for the Slammer." Almost everyone made me feel forever scarred; my father made me feel like I had made a serious mistake in judgment, but one that I could overcome. It's easy to fall into the trap of feeling sorry for yourself, but my father wouldn't allow me to do that. He has no rivals.

MOST MBA PROGRAMS WANTED George to work a full year, so they deferred his acceptance pending completion of that requirement. But the University of Pennsylvania's Wharton School of Business allowed him to matriculate in the fall of 1982.

"Well, Dad, I've finally made it to the Ivy League," George said, handing his father the copy of Albany State's student newspaper that Ben Sawyer had mailed. "From Jail to the Ivy League—Former Albany Ex-con to Enroll at Wharton" read the headline.

George Sr. put his arm around his son as they walked from the kitchen into the dining room for supper. "From my little hill I saw a baby race car that crashed from driving too fast. I thought the crash might be fatal, but you've repaired the car." He squeezed his son's shoulder. "Drive safely from now on."

Control

TWO MONTHS BEFORE GEORGE started graduate school, television brought a sacrosanct religious ceremony into the Johnson household—one whose magnitude had never been seen anywhere. The Johnsons had been to Madison Square Garden only to see Knicks games, but on July 1, 1982, Reverend Sun Myung Moon conducted the largest mass wedding in history. In a three-hour service, over four thousand Moonies took their marital vows. Most couples had met only a few days earlier. Father Moon hand-picked everybody's mate. During the ceremony, each person absorbed on his or her rear end three swings of the indemnity stick. Reverend Moon said this taught forgiveness.

Sitting in the living room of the Fox Run Road house, Annette Mackey and the Johnsons were mesmerized by the sights. "The thing I don't understand," George said. "Is why they have to wait three-and-a-half years to consummate the marriage. Those guys might as well be priests."

"Some of 'em will probably break that rule or end up kidnapped by deprogrammers," Annette offered.

"Whaddaya think makes kids do something like that?" George Sr. asked.

Annette started to answer, but young George spoke louder. "I think most people are gullible, non-thinkers," he said. "Those types have always been open to exploitation. When you start doing things in God's name, people just buy into whatever scheme's going. Just look at all these evangelical types running around. The Moonies are just one example."

Annette went into the kitchen for another round of beers. "I think faith-healers serve an important function," she countered. "They give people something to hope for. A sense of salvation."

"These evangelical types are a bunch of frauds," young George said. "Rather than pray for people, they prey on their weaknesses."

"How is that any different from traditional religion?" George Sr. asked.

"Traditional religions don't have their hands that deep in your pockets. And they don't make you marry someone you've just met because the top guy says you have to."

"How come you're not going out tonight?" the elder Johnson asked. "I hear Shannon's now a nurse at the hospital. You'd probably run into her at the Deer Creek Inn."

"Yeah, lotsa girls just adore you," Annette said. "How come you don't go out much?"

"I don't know. Some of my old friends, they're just not as fun anymore."

"How come?" Annette asked.

"Things are just different."

"Different how?" George Sr. inquired.

Young George shrugged. "I have less and less in common with old friends. People just grow in different directions, I guess."

"So, you can't still be friends with 'em?"

"I'm not saying that. But things that initially attracted me to them aren't there anymore. And things in me that attracted them, I've changed. When I come back to Salt Point, I'm excited to be here. I like goin' down to the station and saying hello to Triple-R Jr. and Wes the Mess. Those guys actually think it's cool that I went to jail. But

I have less in common with them. Our conversations are awkward, especially if we're not out drinking. Those guys are looking at me, wondering why they can't see the same ol' George. And I'm looking at them, wondering how can they stand doing the same thing year after year. Yet, I want to see them, because I'd feel empty if I didn't. But I can only stay for a little while."

"I just hope you don't forget about me when you're a corporate bigwig," his father said.

George walked over to his father, who was stretched out on the couch. "I could never forget all you've done for me. Never." He clapped his hands together. "I'm going upstairs to read for a while. Then I'm gonna hit the sack. Good night."

George Jr. pictured Annette's naked, freckled body sprawled out on his father's bed. Love can make life more bearable, he thought.

❖

THREE DAYS BEFORE BUSINESS school began, George Jr. stood on the corner of Thirty-fourth and Walnut Street in Philadelphia. He was dressed in an Albany State T-shirt, cut-off sweat pants, and high-top Converse All-Stars. He wondered how he was going to fit in among the elite. Thankfully, he'd secured a partial scholarship and low-interest loans. It was enough financial help that he decided against paying for Wharton with any of the fifteen thousand dollars in drug profits. Before leaving Albany, he'd dug up the plastic bags from Lincoln Park and brought them to Philadelphia.

Benjamin Franklin's legacy was everywhere. The university boasted that it was founded by Franklin in 1740. He was to Philadelphia what Henry Hudson was to the Hudson Valley, except on a grander scale.

George saw that Penn deserved its reputation as one of America's most beautiful campuses. It was filled with tree-lined walks, manicured lawns, brick walkways, and Victorian halls. George veered onto Locust Walk, trying to imagine it filled with students. He was surprised that Penn actually had more graduate students than undergrads, and he wondered whether that statistic's dating implications were negative or positive.

Steinberg/Dietrich Hall appeared sooner than George expected. He almost traipsed past the sign before catching a glimpse of the building to his left. He read that Wharton's undergraduate division used to be housed in Dietrich Hall, a dignified brick building in which many students felt at home lighting their first cigar. But some years back Wharton outgrew Dietrich Hall and the newer, modern Steinberg Hall was built around it. The architecture confused him when he first strolled through the hallways.

Penn prided itself on having the country's first business school. Walking through Steinberg Hall's corridor, George stopped to stare at the sign outside Dietrich Hall's entrance: "The Wharton School of Finance and Commerce—Founded by Joseph Wharton 1881." Signs abounded throughout the Wharton School; every lecture hall and classroom sported the name of an individual, foundation, or company. A NASDAQ Quotron machine in one of Steinberg Hall's passageways enabled students to monitor their investments real-time. A Money Access Machine was nearby.

Steinberg/Dietrich Hall developed the minds of undergraduates only. Graduate students were taught in Vance Hall, less than one block to the southwest. George made his way there. Like the undergraduate division, the graduate division's classrooms and lecture halls were all named for and funded by somebody or something. Even the admissions office had a sign that proclaimed: "This Office Provided by Salomon Brothers."

He was hungry. It was only three blocks to the apartment he'd rented for the year. Four-zero-five-five Spruce Street was a large, brick Victorian row house. It didn't have a turret or balcony like some of the other houses on the block, but it once served as a magnificent aristocratic home. Because of the building's proximity to a major university, it made sense for the owner to subdivide the house into small apartments. George rented the basement apartment. He stored the fifteen grand in his mother's old white suitcase, which he stashed in the back of his bedroom closet. It remained a hidden, yet visible, reminder of past wounds. And, perhaps, it offered him a future financial safety net.

After opening the refrigerator, George realized that he hadn't yet been food shopping. He took his keys and wallet from the kitchen table and walked outside into the sticky summer air. Thick wires were strewn above the road's surface. Railroad tracks were embedded in the pavement. He couldn't imagine that the wires and tracks were still in use, but on the way to lunch, he almost crossed the street in front of the electric trolley's path. Only the sound of the trolley's horn prevented him from being hit. With his heart in his throat, George sat on the curb, hyperventilating. He'd soon learn that the trolley only used the Spruce Street tracks when the mainline was out of service. But he never failed to check for the trolley's approach in the years ahead.

Ever since getting out of Edgewood, George wore his prematurely graying hair shorter, concluding that a more appealing group of women were attracted to men who conveyed a mainstream look. After all, the largest post-World War II economic expansion was under way, and men's magazines were advertising closely cropped hairstyles.

George's undergraduate accounting degree gave him an advantage over his competitors. He'd already learned parts of the eight core courses and was familiar with the material taught in certain electives. Although the actual business schoolwork wasn't demanding, it was time-consuming and shrouded in seriousness. During first year, many assignments were doled out as group projects. Wharton reasoned that students had to work with others in the corporate world and should learn how to reach a group consensus.

George's marketing project during the fall term was a group assignment designed to simulate Johnson & Johnson's response to the seven Chicago deaths in September that resulted from consumers ingesting Extra Strength Tylenol capsules laced with cyanide. Right after the project was assigned, an eighth death occurred in California. The students pretended they were J&J marketing executives and formulated a plan to stem the loss of market share.

George took charge of the project, overseeing a mock strategy to recall all capsules and a media blitz emphasizing Tylenol's advantages over aspirin as a painkiller, as well as a plan to shift capsule users to tablets. He launched a Lee Iacocca-style television ad campaign, in which the head of J&J personally promised that the tablets were safe and backed it up by swallowing a couple on national television. "Folks, use the tablets," George instructed during the class presentation. "They're entirely safe because they're white. Any tampering would be readily apparent since cyanide discolors tablets."

❖

WHILE READING ON THE blue reclining chair, George Sr. caught a glimpse of the dirt and lint under his toes. He tossed *Today's Sports* on the shag carpet. His relationship with Annette was getting closer to that inevitable directional fork where it would either turn serious or be derailed. More nights together. More presumed nights together. Sometimes entire weekends together. Sure it was meaningful and rewarding, even occasionally breathless. Unless interrupted, their relationship's momentum was trending toward full-time togetherness.

George sighed. *The Hudson Valley Watch* remained on his lap. He opened the paper and turned to the classifieds.

All You Could Ever Want

I'm a thin, shapely, 5' 7" SWF, 35, brunette, Catholic, and I'm intelligent, charming, witty, talented, spirited and romantic. For the right man, I'd create heaven on earth.

You must be handsome, well-educated, available, and capable of commitment. Drop me a note with a recent photograph. Let's not be alone.

GEORGE SCOFFED AT THE ad, noting that it didn't mention weight or employment. A few seconds later, his eyes returned to the classifieds.

NEW TO THE AREA

I'm adorable, affectionate, altruistic...

HE STOPPED READING. *ALTRUISTIC.* He studied the word before deciding against finding a dictionary.

He knew he'd have to make an appearance later that day at Henry Pepper's funeral. It had been a balmy Saturday night in early October when George last saw Henry at Lucky 7 in the men's room. George noticed Henry urinating through a partially erect penis. Henry stepped back to avoid splattering himself. "What's the cause of all the excitement?" George asked.

"I'm gonna get some definite action tonight! Keep it quiet around the plant, okay?" Those were the last words that Henry uttered to George.

Within an hour, Henry left Lucky 7 with a young woman on his arm who'd offered to drive him to her place. In the parking lot, her estranged boyfriend rushed over from behind the adjacent van and shot both Henry and her in the head at close range. Then he turned the gun on himself. The double murder/suicide was a front page story for days in *The Hudson Valley Watch*.

George looked beyond his bare feet and saw Buddy sleeping on the shag carpet. *Promoted to foreman after twenty-plus years*, George thought, *because my boss cheated on his wife with the wrong woman*. The dead can sure make room for advancement.

He considered calling Annette. He considered answering a personal ad. Instead, he walked to the hi-fi in search of the Barry Manilow album that he'd played often during the previous four years. George placed side two faceup on the turntable. He moved the needle to "Even Now," the first song.

As the piano intro began, George felt Mary's presence. He imagined her soothing, yet censorious eyes looking down from heaven. Soon Manilow's voice overtook both the piano and the crackling sound of the hi-fi needle on the dusty rotating album. George turned sideways and tried to bury himself in the reclining chair. Is she really up there, shadowing him? Can she please allow him to stretch their bond, not to break it, but to make a little space for someone else? When the song finished, he wiped away his tears with the sleeve of his flannel shirt.

George went to Henry Pepper's funeral in his reliable blue suit. A good portion of Henry's face and head had to be scraped from the inside of the woman's car, so the casket remained closed during the ceremony. Henry's widow seemed unfazed by Henry's death or the circumstances under which he died. Perhaps his behavior over the previous twenty-six years had left her numb.

Woo Labs' manual set out the protocol for funerals. The manager had to express sympathy for the widow's loss and say it would be difficult for the company to move forward in the deceased's absence. If an employee was particularly valued by Woo Labs, a corporate executive attended the funeral. At Henry's ceremony, owing to the media coverage, Mr. Witherspoon personally attended. Woo Labs also let anyone who knew Henry attend on company time, and the company's generosity swelled the size of the crowd. Mr. Witherspoon sat next to George. Each man had lost loved ones. The two men didn't speak.

George studied the square scuffed tiles on the floor, then looked at Henry's widow, clad in a long black dress that resembled a poncho. She was the epitome of chastity and obedience. He wondered whether she behaved like a nun and if that accounted for Henry's tireless pursuit of extramarital activities. He looked at the closed casket. The older George got, the more dead people he knew.

At home, alone with a glass of scotch, George knew he wanted more out of life than to raise a kid, work, and die. He just didn't know what, or where to begin to look. There were no role models. He rarely spoke to his own father, who was living in Florida. They got along, but there was something distant about the old man. George couldn't turn to him for guidance.

In the weeks following Henry's death, George's new duties as foreman didn't allow much time for self-reflection. The glass manufacturing and packaging procedures were routine, so scheduling and quality control proved to be George's major responsibilities. He didn't make any changes, hoping to build a solid rapport with the men.

A month after George was promoted, a group of guys working the lines offered to take their new boss to Rondo's. They wanted George to see Mimi Longu, the contortionist. She had been the talk of Woo Labs during the fall of 1982. A former gymnast at Deer Creek High School, she dropped out of Hudson Community College and began her dancing career. Her cropped brown hair and innocent smile sat like a bobblehead over her bony upper body and thick, muscular thighs. Each forearm bore a tattoo of a red rose.

With an offstage drum roll growing louder in volume, Mimi strolled on stage, paused, reached down and grabbed her right leg and lifted it up to her shoulder. Smiling, she placed it on her shoulder, behind her head. Next, she sat down on the stage and placed her left leg behind her head. With both feet sticking up behind her cranium like rabbit ears, Mimi propped herself up with her hands and began waddling across the stage on her rear end like a penguin. The sign outside Rondo's summed it up: "See Mimi Walk on Her Ass!"

On that November night in 1982, the appreciative crowd threw roses on stage and chanted "Mi-Mi! Mi-Mi!" until she reappeared on stage waving to the cheering horde. George joined in the applause, smiling at the men on whose work he now relied to meet his monthly production quota.

❖

GEORGE SR. OPENED THE door to his son's room. Young George, home for Christmas break, was asleep in his twin bed. Ruffled hair jutted out from his forehead. The stench of cigarettes lingered in the air. Judging by the odor, George Sr. figured that his son's last stop was the Deer Creek Inn, the only bar east of the Hudson River that stayed open until 4:00 a.m.

Although the faded blue curtains were closed, it was a little past noon, and the sun forced a lackluster patch of light into the room. George Sr. glanced at the small desk adjacent to the bed frame and pictured an eager elementary-aged boy with a crew-cut scrawling out his homework. He fought back tears when he recalled Mary whispering in his ear whenever they watched their children sleep. He stepped closer to the bed, careful not to spill the half-full glass of water on the floor or knock over the opened bottle of aspirin. He's got most of the Johnson features, alright. Same forehead with those three wrinkles. Same crow's feet and angular face. Hair going gray.

George studied the bridge of his son's nose, remembering early high school kisses with Mary when her nose got in the way. They became adept at approaching each other at more acute angles.

"Dad!" young George screamed in a hoarse voice, startling his father. "What the hell you doing?"

"I was just—"

"Whaddaya doin' standing over me while I'm sleeping? What's that smirk for?"

"I was just watching you sleep…"

"I don't even like it when girls do that."

"I came to wake you up. When you were sleeping, I got to looking at your nose. You got your mother's long one. That made me think of her…"

Young George sat up in bed. "It's okay. It's really weird how images of Mom appear. Happens to me, too. Usually in a supermarket. Got freaked out last month. Staring straight into my face in the Kmart lunchpail aisle was an Underdog lunchpail. Made me shiver."

"Wow, I bet. So, ya gonna get up?"

"Depends on what you're making for breakfast."

"Breakfast! How about lunch? And we gotta put up the Christmas tree today."

"Yeah, let's get the tree up. It'll make it feel more like Christmas. Wish there was snow on the ground."

"Sounds like you want to celebrate this year."

"Yeah, I do," George Jr. said. "I've already bought your present."

"I hope my present is you getting rid of that gold Duster. It just sits in the driveway, rusting out and running down the property values around here."

"I already told you," young George pleaded. "I wanna kept it around for old times' sake. If looking at it bothers you that much, I'll push it in the barn."

"Why don't you do that. The rabbits are all gone."

The Brittany spaniel pushed open the bedroom door. "C'mere, Buddy boy," George Jr. called out. Buddy bounded to the side of the bed. George began wrestling with the dog, mimicking his bark.

The elder Johnson watched for a few seconds. "Son," he cajoled. "Hop in the shower, huh? I'll fix us lunch."

"Alright." George sat up. "Buddy," he growled, "I ain't about to take one with you."

George, hair drenched and vaguely combed, walked downstairs to join his father in the kitchen.

"When your hair was long, you looked like a girl when it was wet."

"Yeah, Dad. The way you were looking at me this morning, it was like I *was* a girl."

"Well, if you were a girl, I wouldn't have just been looking… Hey, you going to midnight mass this year?"

"No, don't feel like it. But don't let me hold you back."

"We'll see. How come you won't go?"

"There's too much suffering. Mom's dead. Susan's dead. Plus all the famines, wars, natural disasters. Millions dead. Millions crippled. If God wants us to worship, then why's all this bad stuff never stop? Why're we expected to worship someone who shows his love for us like this?"

"Maybe bad stuff happens because people're not paying enough attention to God. Maybe you just need to have faith."

Father and son stared into each other's eyes. Soon they turned toward the stove. The grilled ham and cheese sandwiches were finished. They each carried a plate into the dining room.

"Didja meet any nice girls last night?" George Sr. asked.

"Not really. I was talking to this one at the Inn. But I didn't follow up with her."

"How come? What was she like?"

"She met my definition for one-night stand material."

"What's that?"

"She had a pulse."

George Sr. laughed, almost spitting out bits of his sandwich. "What was her personality like?"

"That was the problem. I couldn't tell if she had one."

"That's definitely a problem, alright. Did you spend time with anybody at Wharton?"

Young George shook his head. *Spend time* was his father's euphemism for *have sex*. Sometimes his father used *get together* instead of *spend time*, but they all meant the same thing. "I dated a woman for about a month. She was okay. It was fun for a while."

"Tell me about her?"

"There's one funny story."

"So, go on."

"Her name's Carly. She's a second-year at Wharton. I met her in the cafeteria. About a month goes by with us together, and I'm starting to get frustrated with her. One morning, she's at my place. We're in the bathroom getting ready for classes. I'm brushing my teeth. She's on the toilet. She's taking out her diaphragm. She gets up, sets her diaphragm on the counter. Then she flushes the toilet and reaches for the faucet to wash her hands. But her elbow hits the diaphragm and knocks it into the toilet. And the damn diaphragm gets flushed into the plumbing system."

"So, it's gone down the drain?"

"Yep. It really clogged the pipes. So I call the landlord, who tells me to call the plumber. You shoulda seen the look on the plumber's face when he finds this diaphragm in there. Said it was the funniest thing he'd ever seen."

"George," the elder Johnson whispered. "She did all that stuff right in front of you?"

"Yeah. What's the big deal?" After a pause, George Jr. asked, "So how's this promotion to supervisor working out? You liking it? Telling people what to do and all."

George Sr. swallowed the last bite of his sandwich. "It sure beats moving an assembly line every three minutes. I still have to wear the clean room get-up though. But I sorta oversee things now. At least I'm using my mind a little bit. What about you? What're you gonna do this summer?"

"Probably get a job in the city. Something related to finance. Or maybe a consulting firm. We'll see. I'll start interviewing when I get back to school."

"What will you actually do at one of those big outfits? You won't be making anything, right?"

"Right. I'm not gonna be in a production position. I'll probably end up analyzing something, or doing some limited type of strategic planning."

"So, you'll end up being some hot shot?"

"I doubt it. I'll just be a low-level schmuck. But I'll make good money. And I'll have to get fancy suits. It isn't gonna be that different from what you do at Woo Labs, except my uniform'll cost a lot more."

"Don't sell it short," the elder Johnson said.

Young George grunted. "A lot of my classmates have this over inflated view of how indispensable they're gonna be to some company. They're in for a rude awakening."

"How come?"

"Because nobody gets to start at the top right outta school, unless it's your own place. I mean, you and I were at the top of The Johnson Rabbitry. We ran the show. But, lotsa these guys think that they're gonna step right in and run some big company...ahh!"

George exclaimed, raising both hands over his head. "Maybe it's not their fault they think like that. Wharton encourages that sorta thing. Even on the freaking application, there's a question that starts out 'You have been named Chief Executive Officer of a large organization. Describe the most significant challenge you face.' So you ain't even started school yet, and they have you thinking you're gonna be a CEO somewhere when you graduate."

The elder Johnson didn't respond. His son rose from the table to turn on the TV.

❖

AS THE ECONOMY CONTINUED to expand that spring, Woo Labs received 30 percent more chrome-plated glass orders than the previous year. To accommodate the additional requests, the company widened the clean room. George Sr. had more workers to monitor and more operational decisions to make. The plant manufactured different sized glass pieces and outfitted them with different types of coatings. George's objective was to organize production runs of similar orders to minimize the downtime that accompanied changing over the lines. The size of quarterly bonuses hung on the outcome, creating a degree of pressure.

His son's life in Philadelphia was also hectic. Spring semester for first-year Wharton students was the time of year when they chose their summer jobs. Also, unlike second-year Wharton students, most first-years were still concerned about their grades. George filled out his spring schedule with electives, including a regulation course. He wrote and presented in class a position paper advocating a new tax deduction for the purchase price of engagement rings. Reasoning that Congress already used the tax code to promote marriage, George contended that, while some tax incentives for marriage were in place, society needed more. He argued that the tax laws should penalize divorce through a one-time tax surcharge, payable as a condition of obtaining a divorce decree.

When George finished, Professor Paul Rodgers, a former deputy treasury secretary, walked to the front of the classroom. "It's certainly not a synoptic argument," he began. "But it poses a valid, if unanswered, question about the proper role of the tax laws in creating incentives for certain types of social behavior. Whether Congress ought to be legislating at all in this area is something that Mr. Johnson could have addressed. A more thoughtful proposal, Mr. Johnson, would have been better received. Now, who's next?"

George hung his head. He replayed the professor's rebuke in his mind. Back in high school, George would have seriously considered plucking Mr. Rodgers' toupee from his greasy head. But now there was a future in view, a future less tolerant of adolescent misdeeds. After class, he bought a sandwich and diet soda from the lounge's vending machines, then opened *The Daily Pennsylvanian*, Penn's student newspaper.

"May I join you?" a confident voice asked. George looked up from the sports page. His eyes widened at the sight of Elby Bontawdle peering down at him through brown glasses. "Uhh...Elby Bon..." George tried to recall Elby's last name, but couldn't capture it, only remembering that she graduated from Sweet Briar.

"Are you planning on answering me?" Elby asked.

"Oh, sorry. Yeah, sit down. I was just digesting what Professor Rodgers said. The guy was harsh."

Elby sat down. "Would you like to know what I think?"

"Sure."

"I thought the manner in which you presented yourself was excellent. You were poised, and you spoke clearly. As for the merits of what you said, I agree with Professor Rodgers. There were gaps."

"Like what?"

"First of all, you failed to address whether your proposal would create *additional* marriages. That would be its obvious objective, but men will purchase engagement rings irrespective of the tax incentives for doing so. Now, your proposal might encourage purchases of *more expensive* rings, which would no doubt help the diamond industry. But you didn't make a compelling case that your proposal would result in more marriages, or even longer marriages."

George nodded. "Yeah, you're right. I should've done a better job."

"One other point. I think your proposal is sexist—"

"Really?"

"Let me explain," Elby said. "Setting aside the issue of whether engagement rings themselves are inherently sexist, your proposal only offers a tax deduction to men. Only men purchase engagement rings. Yet women purchase wedding bands for their prospective husbands. Why not allow that cost to be deducted? And, there are other marriage costs, like the wedding itself, which is usually paid for by the bride's family. Did you consider that? I don't think so. Your proposal is skewed in favor of men."

George stared at Elby's thick glasses. Brainpower was packed in behind them. "Point well-taken," he conceded.

"Thank you," she replied, smiling.

"No, thank you," George emphasized. "Thanks a lot."

❖

ONE SATURDAY MORNING, GEORGE Sr. stared at his first personnel memorandum. Until being promoted to foreman, he never typed anything on the clean room's IBM Selectric typewriter. Woo Labs had a typing pool, but it took upwards of three days for a foreman to get something turned around. Unwilling to wait for an available typist, George continued to peck away.

Sometimes, our employees can behave like the Colorado River, which runs wild and indiscriminately floods adjoining farmlands whenever it gets out of control. What we've got to do here at the plant is to impose certain restraints on productive people who might otherwise wreak havoc. Like the Hoover Dam, which ameliorates the destructive flooding and harnesses the Colorado River by turning it into cheap hydroelectric power, we can channel the raw energy of our employees into higher productivity rates.

GEORGE SMILED TO HIMSELF. A thesaurus had given him *ameliorate*. He hand-delivered the original memorandum to the personnel office, placing it in Mr. Witherspoon's box.

Woo Labs was considering a capital investment in robotics, and George sought to head off firings by appealing to the personnel executives. Although he knew Mr. Woo would make the final decision, he felt squeamish about sending a memo directly to him. Foremen just didn't communicate directly with the chairman.

George glanced at his watch. 11:20 a.m. He'd have to leave within five minutes to make the 11:55 a.m. train to New York City.

Young George waited for his father's train at Grand Central Station. He studied the vaulted ceiling, which, to him, possessed the ability to open up and let the time in. It was is if the future was up there in the constellations, friendly from this safe distance yet bound to change before it arrived.

When his father walked off the train, George hugged him and led the way to the downtown subway. They got out at the Christopher Street Station to drop off George Sr.'s bags at the Greenwich Village brownstone that George had rented for the summer. Then they got back on the downtown subway so George could give his father a tour of New York's financial district. The second-year MBA student secured a summer job with Jerson, Abernathy & McCall, a public policy consulting firm. JAM had eight hundred consultants plus an extensive support staff in four offices worldwide: New York, Los Angeles, Sydney, and London. Half of the work performed by JAM's domestic offices involved competitive bidding or single source US Government contracts.

JAM's New York offices were on the sixtieth and sixty-first floor of the Chase Manhattan Bank Building in Lower Manhattan. The elder Johnson was speechless as they entered the glass and aluminum structure, made their way past the security guard, and rode the elevator to the sixtieth floor. George Sr. stopped to take it all in—hardwood floors, Victorian furniture, brass fixtures, paintings, sculptures, oriental rugs. He moved closer to an oil painting of a girl sitting in a chair in an unadorned room, staring out a window at a barren cityscape. Next to that painting was another depicting a small, isolated figure in the corner of a deserted city. Young George joined his father in front of the paintings.

"Who's this artist?" the elder Johnson asked. "This Edward Hopper fella?"

"Beats the crap outta me," George Jr. whispered, turning toward the weekend receptionist to confirm that she wasn't watching them.

"I like his stuff," George Sr. observed. "We should go to a museum tomorrow. There's a bunch of 'em here."

"C'mon. Let me show you my office," young George pleaded.

The Johnsons continued down the hallway, making a couple of left turns. "Here it is," the proud son remarked, inviting his father inside the open door.

"Amazing! They gave you one with a *window*." George Sr. was drawn to the view. "Which way are we looking?"

"East, toward Brooklyn. See that first bridge," George Jr. said, pointing. "That's the Brooklyn Bridge. The one above it is the Manhattan Bridge."

"Jesus Christ! How do ya get any work done with this view?"

"It's tough. One of the problems is that it makes me wonder what I'm doing in a place like this during the day. It makes me feel cooped up."

"How many people have views like this?"

"Your view depends on your perspective. When I was in jail, all I saw was concrete walls and bars. I didn't really want to go outside. Now, in here, all I see is the sun and the traffic. People going places. Makes me feel like escaping."

"Don't you like the work?"

"Oh, it's intellectually challenging. I'm trying to figure out the most economical way to bring natural gas to market from Prudhoe Bay, Alaska to California."

"Who's the project for?"

"The Department of Energy."

George Sr. widened his eyes. "What're the options?"

"One is to liquify it and put it on tankers. Another is to send it by pipeline to Valdez." George Jr. sighed. "Ah, Dad. I don't want to talk about this boring stuff."

"How come?"

"C'mon, let's leave." He led the way back to the elevator.

Father and son tracked the elevator's descent until it reached the concourse. "How many people work in this place?" George Sr. wondered.

"Around fifteen thousand."

"Jesus Christ!"

After riding the subway back to the Christopher Street Station, young George asked, "What do you feel like eating tonight? My treat."

"Something that's not too foreign, okay?"

"How about Mexican?"

"American, okay? I want some place we can walk to. I don't wanna get on that subway again."

"Hey," George Jr. said. "Loosen up. You still seeing Annette?"

"Yep. Pretty much every weekend."

"I'm afraid you're stuck with *me* for the rest of this weekend," young George said, tightening the grip on his father's shoulder.

George Sr. tried to wriggle free. "You really shouldn't be doing that in this neighborhood. Won't people think we're, you know, a couple?"

"Probably. We're in the Village. If we walk arm in arm, nobody'll bother us."

"Jesus Christ, what a place. I'm hungry. Let's eat."

"Boy, what a whiner you've turned into. It's only six."

"I usually eat at five thirty. You know that."

"It's a Saturday night in New York. People don't eat for another couple of hours."

George Sr. stopped and gave his son a disapproving glance.

"Okay, let's eat now. I know a place on Bleeker Street."

"That's my boy."

❖

GEORGE JR. MADE $750 a week that summer, so he worked for JAM until the day before classes started at Wharton. He'd whisper to himself the summer's final gross earnings—$10,200! He'd earned half his father's annual salary in just one summer. George dwelled on his expected annual salary of $55,000 a year. All he needed to do was accept JAM's offer of full-time employment

On October 23, 1983, a suicide terrorist penetrated the US Marine Headquarters at Beirut International Airport, detonating a massive bomb that killed 241 marines and sailors. The US servicemen were part of the multi-national peacekeeping force in Lebanon. Among those killed was Sergeant Maurice Brower, Wes the Mess's older brother.

Virtually all of Salt Point's residents made an appearance at either the wake or the funeral. Triple-R Jr. closed Richardson's Texaco during the funeral. And the Marines sent a uniformed officer of Maurice's rank to deliver an American flag to the Brower family.

In the cold fall air, the funeral was held next to Maurice's grave in Salt Point Cemetery. Reverend Mason delivered the eulogy. The Johnsons escorted Ursula Brombecker to the ceremony. The three of them walked past Kevin Witherspoon's tombstone and stood in the crowd with their hands behind their backs.

Before the funeral began, George slipped away from his father and Ursula, moving backwards through the crowd that continued to form behind them. He hadn't visited his mother's and sister's gravesite since his high school valedictory address. But now, six years later, he thought he could overcome the forces that seemed to shield him from their grave. He stood over their tombstone. The piece of granite inscribed with letters and numbers made his stomach ache. The stone rising from the ground seemed to serve both as a link and barrier to the rest of his family. It reminded him of past and current pain and of dreams that didn't turn out like they should have. George knelt down and made the sign of the cross. A few moments later, he rose and walked back through the crowd. When George again stood beside his father, the elder Johnson took his son's hand and squeezed it.

Father and son listened to the head pastor at Netherwood Baptist Church begin the eulogy: "Maurice Brower died an honorable and heroic death. Like the good serviceman Maurice was, he placed his trust in his superiors. We, the servants of God, must honor Maurice's death by reaffirming our trust in God, our superior. But the problem with *trust*," the minister emphasized, "is that it requires faith and courage. Yes, that's right, trust requires faith and courage! Now, I've got to ask all of you a question." George Jr. glanced up to see if Reverend Mason was speaking directly to him.

"Can a coward have faith?" the Reverend bellowed. "Can a strong person have no faith?"

Young George grunted. "That's two questions, not one," he whispered to his father.

"Yes, friends and relatives of Maurice Brower," Reverend Mason continued, "faith and courage, two qualities possessed by our fallen hero, are required for trust."

Young George had trouble picturing Maurice as a hero. He remembered him as a bully. "Consider this, my fellow servants of God. Aren't you a coward if you're incapable of trust?"

George scanned the sky looking for an image of God, but couldn't find one. He wondered if an invisible path led from his mother's and sister's tombstone to heaven. The crowd was beginning to disperse. He saw Wes the Mess hugging his mother. George felt a tap on his shoulder. "Are you gonna stick around tonight?" George Sr. asked. "Or, are you heading back to Philly?"

"I'm heading back today," George muttered. "I've already missed some classes."

"That's what I figured. I have to go back to work now."

"I know. I can catch a ride back to the house to pick up my car. I'm gonna hang around here for a while."

"Okay," George Sr. said, sighing. "It's weird that I'm the one leaving you. You're usually saying good-bye to me."

"I know."

"Call me soon. And drive safe. Love you, son."

Young George embraced his father. "Love you, Dad."

A few people stayed to watch the two cemetery hands shovel dirt on top of Maurice's casket. Mrs. Brower clutched the triangular-shaped American flag with both hands. George stood for a few minutes, listening to the scraping sounds the shovels made as they penetrated the pile of dirt adjacent to the burial plot. There was a pleasing rhythm about the swish of the shovels dislodging the dirt before it thumped down on the casket. When the coffin was covered, George turned and walked toward Ursula.

"You got any food in that house of yours?" he asked, placing his right hand over her shoulders and kissing her cheek.

"You can't be thinking that this suave stuff is gonna work on me."

"Hey, I'm being sincere, Mrs. B. I'm only insincere with other women."

"C'mon, let's get outta here. You're hopeless." Ursula led George up the path from the cemetery to her house. "Whaddaya feel like eating?" she asked when they reached the back porch.

George opened the door for her. "You need some exercise. You're totally out of breath. I don't wanna be back here for another funeral."

"Ahh, don't worry about me. I'm just getting old."

"You got plenty of time to exercise. Even just walking would be okay. Me, I run twenty miles a week now."

"Whaddaya think I do all day? Sit around playing with myself?"

George tried to picture that, but couldn't. Besides, he was hungry. "What's going on these days?"

"Oh, I'm still involved with scouting, mostly the Cub Scouts. And I volunteer at the Poughkeepsie Literacy Center."

"Doing what?"

"Teaching people how to read. The federal government says that twenty-three million Americans are functionally illiterate. That's ten percent of our population."

"Geez."

"So, Mr. Bigshot, what's happening with you? You wanna eat some cream of mushroom soup?"

"Naw, that stuff is loaded with calories. How about chicken noodle?"

"Yeah, I got that. It ain't nothing but chicken-flavored hot water. I'll make you a sandwich, too. How's ham?"

"Fine. But use mustard, not mayo."

"You order your girlfriends around like this?"

"Yeah," George answered with a grin, "and they love it!"

"What a dreamer you are. So, where are ya gonna work after you become Mr. Bigtime MBA?"

George took his accustomed seat at the kitchen table. "In the city. Probably with the same consulting firm I worked for last summer."

Ursula moved back and forth between the refrigerator and stove, stirring the soup with an ancient wooden ladle. "You don't sound all that excited about it."

George leaned back in his chair. "You're right. I'm not."

"So, why are ya gonna take that job?"

"I don't know." George's body stiffened. "It's better than going to work for Goldman Sachs or some other investment banking house. There, all I'd do is crunch numbers. JAM's one of the leading consulting firms in the world. It's really hard to get a job with them. Besides, they're paying me fifty-five grand a year to start."

Ursula poured half the steaming liquid into a bowl and placed it in front of George. "Take it from an old lady who's been around. One of the biggest problems people have is money running their lives. Look at your old man. He's slaved away for twenty years with a clock dictating what he does and when he does it. Twenty years on the lines. And why? Because of money. What else could he do? Nothing."

"I know all this—"

"Let me finish!"

George slid his chair backwards, away from the table.

"If you knew all this already, you'd be acting differently. Your father's worked hard so you could have a better deal. He doesn't want money trapping you like it's trapped him. So, if you're gonna work at this hotshit consulting firm because of money, you're not gonna be that different from your old man. You'll just get a bigger house with a bigger mortgage, a Mercedes instead of a Pinto, eat in fancy restaurants instead of diners, and vacation in Europe instead of the Jersey Shore. You'll just end up trapped with nicer trappings."

George took a deep breath and placed his forehead flush on the table. A few seconds later he raised it. He felt hot.

Ursula set the ladle down and took a seat across from George. "Hey," she said, touching his elbow. "I just care, that's all."

"I know," George groaned. "You have a way of putting stuff in focus. Lotsa people just don't get a chance at real living. Look at those guys on the lines at Woo Labs. They're only in their thirties and forties. But they're already dying, little by little. Even my father. Every time I see him, he looks more worn down. It's hard to live for anything else but your job because you put so much into it."

Ursula smiled.

"There are some people who're born in a ditch, while others are born on level ground or a hill. They have a natural headstart. Sometimes, I feel like people keep throwing dirt on me. Like they don't want me gaining ground. If you don't get too much dirt heaped on you, you got a chance at that hill. A chance to improve. It's funny," he reflected. "With the drug dealing, I threw a bunch of dirt on myself. All because I wanted to strike it rich."

"You'll make your money, if that's what you want. But success isn't becoming a big-time capitalist. Success is doing what you want with your life."

George sighed. "I'm climbing a ladder, but it feels shaky. All I keep finding is another rung." George gulped a spoonful of soup. "Mrs. B, what's on top of the ladder?"

Ursula laughed. "Only you can decide. It's important not to let others decide for you. Define your own success."

"Okay," George agreed. "I just want to get up every day free enough to do what I want. Not what someone else wants. I guess for me, that's what success is."

"Good. Anything else on your mind?"

"I've gotten my ticket punched. And now I have to make all these decisions. Simpler people, they don't have much to worry about. Those guys on the lines, they're probably happy because they don't know what's out there."

"Don't delude yourself," Ursula warned. "Those people just haven't had the opportunity to become complex. It'd be a sin to let your complexity go to waste." Ursula walked behind George, placed her hands on his shoulders, and squeezed them. "Live the life you wanna live. Yours. Not somebody else's. Make it a promise, not a trap."

❖

During their second year at Wharton, George and Elby Bontawdle often ate lunch together. When it was warm, they took their sandwiches outside. "You know," Elby said, "it annoys me that this country hasn't ratified the Equal Rights Amendment."

"Congress let the time run out," George said, standing up from the table. "They're a few states short."

"The Constitution just doesn't afford the same safeguards to women as it does to men. That really bothers me."

"The opponents say the protections are already there, just in other laws. Well, if they're already there, why not put them in the Constitution?"

"Exactly. Perhaps then even the Catholic church would let women be ordained as priests."

"Elby," George said, slipping his arm over her shoulders, "I'd vote for you for President. That is, if I were allowed to vote."

George accompanied Elby to a few of Wharton's Executive Dinner Series functions, where chief executive officers and chairmen of corporate recruiters traveled to Philadelphia to dine with pre-selected groups of students. He marveled at the ease with which she could discuss foreign currency fluctuations. After one dinner, Elby told George that his polyester clothes, even in the summer, were not commonplace in New York's financial district. "Give the suits and ties to the Salvation Army, if they'll even accept them," she quipped. "You'll even get a small tax deduction."

Elby took him to Brooks Brothers, where he parted with over twelve hundred dollars, buying two suits, four cotton shirts and silk ties and a pair of leather dress shoes. It was the most money he'd ever spent in one day. If he went to work on Wall Street, the shopping spree would approximate one week's gross pay. A fairly minor investment in becoming a Corporate Bigwig. The suits wrapped him in self-importance. A uniform, yes. But a uniform bespeaking dignity. A uniform worn by someone with an elevated rank.

In the spring, George had to decide whether to accept JAM's offer to become a consultant in its New York office. He interviewed at other firms and investment banking houses, getting offers from Booz Allen and Salomon Brothers, but decided that investment banking was too narrow a field. JAM offered a broader exposure to public and private clients. The decision to join JAM settled and dissolved inside George like sediment descending to the bottom of a liquid container.

George called in his acceptance to the managing principal of JAM's New York office, Ronald Ziegler. "Glad you're coming aboard," was all that Ziegler said.

Then George called his father. "I took the job at JAM," he announced.

"It's sure a lot of money," the elder Johnson said. "How do you feel about it?"

"I really don't know."

"I'm glad you'll be close by. But Mrs. B is gonna be disappointed."

"You tell her, okay?"

"Alright."

"Let's take a trip this summer. Just you and me."

After hanging up with his father, George called Elby. "I took the job at JAM," he said.

"It'll be good for you," Elby offered. "You'll be exposed to a broader world."

"I've already been exposed to it. Now I'll have to live in it."

That night, George dreamed he was the only passenger riding a freight train. He was dressed in Edgewood prison garb when the train took a sharp turn and derailed in a secluded mountain region. The railcar flipped over and began rolling down a steep embankment. Boxes of heavy cargo emptied on top of him before the entire train exploded.

The dream rewound itself. Again, George found himself in the same boxcar of the train. This time, sensing the locomotive beginning to curve around a bend, George opened a window just in time to see a rock formation jutting out from the mountain, but not in time to prevent the approaching monolith from decapitating him. When George saw his head bouncing along the railroad tracks, dust attached to his distended green eyeballs, he woke up shivering, the sheets damp from sweat.

❖

OFFICIALLY LISTED IN WHARTON's 1984 commencement program was "George Johnson Jr.: Jerson, Abernathy & McCall." He savored the sound of his name echoing through the damp air at May's graduation exercises. His father and Annette watched with pride. Ursula declined her invitation. Donald Trump, himself a Wharton graduate, spoke at commencement. Trump's self-promoting, proverb-filled pep talk held little interest for

George. Instead he daydreamed about removing the dusty milk crate from the old rabbit shelves in his father's barn, strapping it to the motorcycle, and driving Buddy throughout the Hudson Valley.

Thirteen years of baby boomers were lined up ahead of George in the work place. Five more years of boomers would stalk him throughout his career. Yet he knew that Wharton was capable of hurling him up the ladder and farther away from that ditch.

After graduation, George went home to see Buddy. The Brittany had been in declining health for months. He'd given up on walks across the Johnsons' property. The coat on his face had become even whiter. George took Buddy on one last motorcycle ride. Buddy barked with excitement when George began dusting off the milk crate, and the dog's movements became even more animated in anticipation of being hoisted onto the bike's seat. Yet Buddy's burst of energy soon wilted. The dog was barely able to keep his eyes open. Buddy just nestled his head under George's armpit as the two of them drove back home.

As Buddy's health eroded, the Johnsons wouldn't let him out of their sight. "He's lived here his whole life," George Sr. said. "He's got the right to die here." The Johnsons found Buddy one July morning laying lifeless in the barn. They buried him in the backyard, on the spot where he always laid down while watching George play catch with the elastic pitchback. That Brittany's life had spanned George's entry into manhood. Something steady. Something comforting. Something that wasn't taken away too soon.

❖

BEFORE OFFICIALLY MOVING OUT, George treated his father to a week long vacation in Florida. Marty Goldberg's parents owned a condominium on Miami Beach. They lent it to George in recognition of his graduation from Wharton.

It took the Johnsons two-and-a-half hours to drive from Salt Point to Newark Airport. They parked the Pinto in the long-term lot. From Newark, they caught a non-stop flight to Miami.

On the plane, George Sr. removed a pack of gum from his shirt pocket. He chewed, then retrieved the wad from his mouth, split it in two, and placed one chunk in his left ear and the other in his right.

Young George pretended to read a magazine. "What're you doing?"

"I'm fixing up my ears so they don't hurt. It's the cabin pressure. I've heard that once you get up in the air, your ears hurt."

"Dad—"

"Oh yeah, sorry. I shoulda offered you a stick." George Sr. extended the package of gum.

"Hey," young George snapped. "Take this crap out of your ears before somebody sees you. You chew the gum. The swallowing action keeps your ears clear. You don't plug your ears with it."

"Oh," George Sr. said, removing his gum. "Hope I didn't embarrass you, Mr. Bigshot."

"I don't think anybody saw you. Jesus, where'd you ever get a crazy idea like that?"

The elder Johnson didn't answer. Soon he settled into a nervous sleep.

The Johnsons picked up their rental car and drove to the Goldberg's ocean-front condominium complex. A private security guard handed them a temporary pass. For one week, the Johnsons did nothing but sunbathe, swim, eat, and drink.

On their last night, George treated his father to dinner. They walked down the beach to the Fountainbleu Hotel and sat down at a marble table overlooking the pool.

"You'll be staying at places like this from now on," George Sr. observed.

"Lotsa cocaine cowboys stay here," George said, winking at his father. "Hey, are things with Annette getting serious?"

"Yep. She might move in."

"You up for that?"

"Makes me a little nervous. But I'm all alone now. You're gone. Buddy's gone."

Young George stared at the bow-tied pattern on the floor. He suddenly felt melancholy. "She's pretty cool, I guess."

"She is. You'll have to hear her play the piano sometime. Whenever I hear her playing those keys, it feels like my heart opens up."

Young George smiled. "That's good."

"I ran into Shannon last week in the Shop Rite. She had her nurse's outfit on. Looked really cute. She asked about you."

"What'd you say?"

"That you'd gotten a big Wall Street job."

"And..."

"She wanted to know how prison had affected you."

"And you said..."

"I said you'd recovered."

"Hmmm..."

"She said to say hello."

❖

YOUNG GEORGE SPENT THE remainder of the summer commuting between Salt Point and New York City, trying to find a suitable apartment. JAM provided leads, but George had to see the buildings for himself. Only the naive and uninformed paid two thousand dollars a month for a two-bedroom Manhattan apartment without inspecting it. George eventually found a rent-controlled apartment on the Upper East Side. The rent was only three hundred dollars a month, but buying the lease obligated him to make a five thousand dollar cash payment to the building's landlord. George could stay in the apartment for as long as he wished, and the rent would increase only in minute increments each year.

That July, Democratic presidential candidate Walter Mondale chose Geraldine Ferraro, a Queens Congresswoman, as his running mate. The next morning, *The New York Post* summed it up: "Gerry Gets It." Elby was on a business trip to New York on the evening of Ferraro's debate with George Bush, the Republican vice-presidential candidate. George carried a copy of *The Post* when he entered The Waldorf-Astoria Hotel. Dressed in jeans and a T-shirt, he nodded in the direction of the doorman.

The Waldorf's lobby contained elegant chandeliers, brass fixtures, dark wood, oriental rugs, and well-dressed patrons. The lobby reminded him of JAM's downtown office. George called Elby from a house phone. She told him her room number and invited him up.

George lunged forward to greet her with a hug, but she stepped back, extending her hand. George shook it, picturing Elby slouching under the weight of a gem-encrusted tiara, wearing a sign that said, "Do Not Touch My Royal Person."

"Come in," Elby offered. "It's great to see you again."

George set his knapsack on the bed and looked outside the window to St. Patrick's Cathedral. "What brings you to town?" he asked.

"One of my firm's clients is purchasing a retail conglomerate here. It's all hush-hush, so I can't say much about it."

George stepped over to the bed and opened his knapsack. "I thought you'd enjoy this," he said, handing Elby *The New York Post*.

"The sexual innuendo in this headline is disgusting," she said. "And patronizing."

"C'mon. They're just trying to sell papers. What do you think all the blue-collar workers in America are saying when they talk about Mondale picking a woman for the ticket? Most of 'em are Democrats, you know."

"It'll open up people's minds, if only a little bit. It's a barrier that had to fall."

"I agree. But I can just picture a bunch of factory workers having beers and saying 'Hey, yo, there's a broad runnin' for vice president. What's gonna happen when she's on the rag?'"

"Spare me the derisive descriptions."

"I've heard a lot worse."

"No doubt."

"On the cab ride here I was thinking about the time you and I first met. You said my tax presentation was sexist, remember?"

"Yes. But you're getting better."

Elby and George ordered room service and watched the Ferraro-Bush debate. "It's pretty obvious that Ferraro was trounced," George said when it ended.

"I have to agree. She didn't help Mondale with her performance tonight."

"Yeah, and this problem with her husband the slum lord isn't helping either."

"I'm curious," Elby said. "Who are you going to vote for?"

"Nobody. Remember, I can't vote. I'm just like a Watergate burglar."

"Oh, sorry. I forgot."

"Yeah, one mistake, and they take away your right to pick who represents you."

"Have you started work yet?"

"Not yet. Just trying to avoid it for as long as possible. So I can enjoy my last summer of freedom."

"Freedom from what?" Elby asked.

"Freedom from somebody else telling me what to do."

Elby pushed her chair back and stood up. "I can't see this fear being connected to your mother. Or sister. Is it related to your father?"

George shrugged. "Before I was born, my father was a great high school baseball player. His dream was to play in the majors. He had college scholarships. Then he got my mother pregnant. He traded his dream for a line job. For a life of always having a boss."

Elby nodded. "But you have a Wharton MBA. What's standing in your way?"

"My father's dream, I think. Even if my mother had lived, my father would still have lost his dream because of me."

"There's more than one dream," Elby said.

"I don't think that's true. If you end a parent's dream, can you still live yours?"

Elby moved a step closer. "This is America. The next generation lives out the dream."

George shrugged. "I look around, and I see a lot of people's faces telling me they've lost their dream. Some pretend they've found another one. But it seems like camouflage to me."

"Are you saying that working for one of the world's best consulting firms on leading policy issues isn't your dream?"

George took a deep breath. "It sure doesn't feel like my dream. My father's given me a good example of how not to live. After his baseball dream vanished, he's been giving in to something that I don't ever want to give in to. A sense of failure."

Elby studied George as he walked past her toward the door. "I'd like to help if I can," she said. "Will you stay in touch?"

"Yeah," George said. "But only if you give me a hug."

❖

GEORGE WAITED UNTIL THE Thursday before Labor Day to start at JAM. A client needed a pro forma financial analysis performed for a proposed airport facility, and George was tapped to provide a supporting role on the project. Project managers and principals constantly changed the assumptions on which the projections were based, and George's bosses badgered him for periodic updates. He slaved away through the long weekend until the following Friday.

On the first Tuesday in November, Walter Mondale's campaign demonstrated the value of honesty: he told voters that he intended to raise taxes and lost forty-nine states. George arrived at work an hour late on election day, so that he could tell anyone who asked that he'd voted earlier that morning.

Over the next few months, the Prudhoe Bay project, on which George worked during the summer of 1983, became active. There were endless permutations on the financial projections, and the computer model he'd helped develop was reworked with new assumptions. The winter of 1985 was abnormally cold, and George surmised that the cold wave had revived interest in natural gas exploration. The work was tedious.

In school, there was always something to look forward to: Thanksgiving break, winter break, spring break, summer break. School was also where George set many of his own rules, doing what he wanted by and large when he wanted.

Most nights before taking off his suit, George studied himself in a full-length bedroom mirror. Confining clothes. Confining building. Confining job. He pictured his father wearing the same clean room garb as the other Woo Labs employees. He remembered his old prison uniform. He pictured his gray suit being worn by the other fifteen thousand workers in the Chase Manhattan Bank building. He imagined foreman Henry Pepper barking instructions at his father. He remembered how JAM principals and project managers told him what tasks to work on and the deadlines for completing each of those tasks.

Invariably, George backed away from that mirror. The gaze of his censorious eyes carried an unbearable weight. After months of this ritual, George sat down at his desk and turned his attention to the framed picture of his mother holding his infant sister in her arms.

"Guidance, Mom!" he called. "Some help down here!"

He remembered how his high school girlfriend Shannon had held him that afternoon at Little Wappinger's Creek after he'd been told by the school principal that he'd have to cut his hair before giving the valedictory address. Someone who loved him was holding him. Someone he trusted. Even Buddy was alive then.

George dug out a pen and a few sheets of paper:

> We know not from where it comes
> Or to where it goes
> The wild wind of blind chance,
> Suddenly a tempest blows
> Upsetting ordered circumstance;
> And when rude death rides that wind of woes
> To snatch a loved one from this living dance
> Life becomes shadowed, empty, and unpinned,
> Christ! bitter is the wind.

APRIL 3, 1985, WAS just two days before Good Friday. At 9:15 a.m., along with hordes of other commuters, George exited the Lexington Avenue subway at the Wall Street stop. He proceeded through the walkway that led to the Chase Manhattan Bank building. Along the way, he dropped a dollar bill into a hat next to a man holding an "I Was Exposed to Agent Orange in Nam" cardboard sign.

When George arrived at his desk, he saw a message taped to his chair ordering him to report to Mr. Ziegler's office. He traipsed to the managing principal's corner office. Mr. Ziegler was on the telephone with a client. An elderly man was shining the managing principal's shoes. Mr. Ziegler motioned George inside his spacious office and pointed to the couch. That's where George sat for the next ten minutes until Mr. Ziegler hung up the phone.

"George!" he said. "You need a shoe shine. Tommy here will fix you up. I'm going to stick my head in a meeting down the hall. I'll be right back."

Fifteen minutes later, well after Tommy had finished shining George's shoes, Mr. Ziegler reappeared.

"Something's come up," he said. "We've just landed a major new Pacific Rim client and we need your financial expertise. Most of the work will be done out of our Los Angeles office. So, we're sending you to LA. They've got an office waiting for you. The firm has a few furnished apartments out there, so you'll have a nice place to sleep. The sooner you can get out there, the better. Okay?"

George's eyes focused on Mr. Ziegler's red and blue suspenders. "Excuse me," George responded. "I'm digesting what you just said. Are you *transferring* me to JAM's LA office?"

"It's not a transfer. It's a temporary assignment. It's vital to the firm."

"How long do you plan to keep me in LA?"

"Between twelve and eighteen months. Remember, we'll provide you a place to live. I've stayed at one of the apartments. It's very convenient to the office. And the building has plenty of amenities. Also…"

George stopped listening to the sales pitch. The longer Mr. Ziegler's muffled voice rang in George's head, the angrier he got. Soon the managing principal stopped speaking.

"I can't do it," George declared. "I took a job in New York. If I'd wanted to live in LA, I'd have taken a job there. You're talking over a year. That's just too long. I'm sorry, but you'll have to get someone else for this assignment."

Mr. Ziegler stood up. "George, you don't understand. All the plans are in place. We bid the job figuring we'd use your skills. You have an office and apartment waiting in LA. It's all set." Mr. Ziegler paused, evaluating George's stony expression. "Having you out there is vital to the firm."

"I'm sorry. I'm not going. I just can't. My father's here. You'll have to get someone else."

"You know," Mr. Ziegler said, "when the firm makes plans for its junior consultants, it expects its *junior* consultants to carry them out. We expect you to take this assignment."

"Really?"

"George, I'm not asking you. I'm telling you. You're going to LA. It's part of the job. You're well paid."

George circled around the coffee table, stopping in front of Mr. Ziegler. "Nope." George's eyes narrowed. "I'm not going."

"What?" Mr. Ziegler asked, raising his hand.

"You heard me. Go find someone else. I quit."

George spun around on his freshly polished shoes. He walked to his office, picked up his jacket, and left the building. On the way back to the subway, he handed the disabled Vietnam veteran a five-dollar bill.

❖

IT WAS STILL MORNING when George returned to his apartment. He took off his suit, shirt, and tie, and laid down on the bed, facing the ceiling. Now that he'd made his statement to the corporate world, where did it leave him?

He jumped off the bed and went to his closet. Beneath the shoe boxes lay his mother's tattered white suitcase. He clicked the rusted gold knobs and opened it for the first time in over two years. Inside was the fifteen thousand dollars, still secured in two plastic bags. He closed the suitcase and fastened the knobs. Then he lugged it to the elevator outside his apartment door. Soon he was in a cab headed toward First Avenue. He told the cabbie where to stop and to wait while he went inside the office building. He rode the elevator to the Catholic Charities reception area and handed the suitcase to the receptionist.

"There's fifteen grand in there," George said. "You're doing God's work. Keep it."

The stunned receptionist opened the suitcase and smiled. Soon George was back in the cab heading toward his apartment. He got out, but hesitated before going inside his apartment building.

George kept his motorcycle garaged in a nearby lot. He walked there and started the bike. He began riding through the streets of Manhattan. In a matter of minutes he was cruising through Central Park, driving past the noontime cyclists and joggers. He made his way down Seventh Avenue, easing the bike into the left hand lane at the Lincoln Tunnel. Once the sky reappeared, George was in New Jersey. Before long, man and machine were heading south on the New Jersey Turnpike.

The melody to a punk rock song came into his mind. Words soon followed. George imagined himself stepping in front of a microphone.

"Out on an open road I still need to ride
To run from the day my mother and sister died."

He stopped for gas at the Molly Pitcher Service Center. By the time he'd filled the gas tank, it was midafternoon. Rain began to fall. He decided to call his father and made his way inside the service center. Soon his eyes settled on a row of public telephone booths. A bright light shone on them. The aluminum and glass enclosure began rocking back and forth. Then it exploded. A mystical figure wearing a cape appeared through the dust. Underdog stared at George, opened his lunch box, and offered George a peanut butter sandwich. The figure's radiant colors drew George closer to the shattered booth. He focused on Underdog's face. His angular jaw, gray sideburns, crow's feet, and forehead corrugations all seemed familiar. *Zap!* Underdog vanished.

George rubbed his eyes. Pivoting, he walked back outside into the oppressive gray haze. He jogged through the mist to one of the outdoor phone booths. There, he called his father.

"Hello," a woman's voice answered on the second ring.

"Oh, Annette. It's George."

"Hi, Mr. Bigshot."

"Can I speak with my father?"

"Sure."

"Hey," the elder Johnson said.

"Dad, I've got something to tell you."

"I'm listening. What is it?"

"I quit my job. They wanted me to move to Los Angeles, so I quit. I just left. Walked out."

"Jesus Christ! Where are you now?"

"In Central Jersey, on the bike. I'm gonna ride for a while."

"You okay?"

"I'm not so good right now." Young George paused before blurting out, "I'm sorry you're in a shitty job. And I'm sorry your wife and daughter died."

"You know what? You and me, we're always gonna be sad sometimes. We're always gonna have a void that's a part of us."

"I gotta go. I just wanted to let you know what's happened. Tell Mrs. B that I'm alright, okay?"

"Sure. Hey, Son?"

"Yeah."

"I love you. Don't forget that."

"I won't. And don't you forget how thankful I am for everything you've done."

"I won't."

"Love you, Dad."

A Conversation with Jim McDermott

Q: How long did it take you to write *Bitter Is the Wind* and what was the process like?

A: It was twenty-five years from the time I wrote the first words until I got a book contract. Before I started writing, I had conceived of the basic story line—a father-son relationship aided by a wise widow and dog. I also knew that I wanted to write about working-class life in small communities. I took a leave of absence from my first law firm for upward of a year, with the goal of completing a first draft by the time I went back to work. I met that goal. However, it wasn't a good first draft, but at least I had one. The first draft resembled a used car lot—containing a jumble of words—that was similar to the used car lot where I searched for old car parts when I was a teenager. From that point, I worked on and off for the next twenty-four years rewriting, and rewriting many times over, and editing and reediting it. In some respects, early drafts of my novel were like old cars that I tinkered with constantly. I had imaginary conversations with my characters for about a quarter century. I really got to know them pretty well. I find that they're still in my life, but not as present as they used to be.

Q: What prompted you to write *Bitter Is the Wind?*

A: I wanted to write about the constant pressures faced by the working class. I grew up in a small town, where I spent much of my youth plotting and relentlessly pursuing my escape. By my late twenties, I was a lawyer at a major law firm in Washington, DC. Instead of going to old places on a motorcycle or in a dilapidated old car, I went to new places in the first class cabin of airplanes. Instead of sleeping in campgrounds, or the back of my pick-up truck, or on people's couches, I slept in five star hotels and lived in a beautiful, urban apartment. Instead of interacting with unrefined and less educated people, I interacted with refined and highly educated people. I began to wonder why very few people in my new world came from the same working class background that I came from. In a certain sense, I knew I had achieved the American Dream, or was well on my way to achieving it. But I wondered about all the people I knew who remained in dead-end jobs living what I thought were dead-end lives. So I created some working class characters and set about searching for the American Dream—and for a way to tell a story addressing the questions I had been asking myself.

Q: Were there certain themes you wanted to explore?

A: Overall, I wanted to explore how you can open your world. And I wanted to explore the concept of power. I tried to infuse that concept throughout the entire story. The power to escape. The power to dream. The power to persevere. And, critically, what it feels like to be powerless.

Q: What led you to construct a plot in which a traffic accident claims the lives of the son's mother and sister and leaves the father and son alone?

A: Death is universal. I felt that I couldn't write a realistic story without death being a huge component. Those who have died affect your pursuit of the American Dream. Life in small towns can also be isolating. I wanted to explore what death leaves behind in a small town. Cemeteries are often prominent places in small towns. Cemeteries are wonderful places for imagining the lives led by the names on the tombstones. But what if your mother and sister die, and their tombstones are in the cemetery you regularly go by? Is the haunting memory too close?

Q: Parenthood plays an important role in your story, yet you wrote at least the first draft of the novel before you became a parent. Can you explain this?

A: Earlier generations always lay the foundation for later generations' pursuit of the American Dream. There is almost always parental sacrifice involved. Teenage parenthood is a big dream killer. In my story, the father's dreams are killed by his son who bears his same name. What happens when your very own flesh and blood prevents you from doing what you want to do? I saw this a lot when I was a kid—the act of creating a new life causes a slow death for those who created that life.

Q: Why did you interweave current events from the late 1960s through the mid-1980s into your novel?

A: Because I've always felt that people underestimate the role of current events in shaping people. The 1970s was a particularly undistinguished era in America. We had the Watergate scandal, President Nixon resigning in the face of certain impeachment, and Vice President Agnew leaving office after pleading to a crime. Then we finished the decade off with the sleazy gyrations of the disco era. Prominent leaders who are bad influences model behavior that can lead to bad decisions by ordinary people, at least in my view. If the leaders of your country are behaving immorally, why do you then have to behave morally?

Q: Why did you give your father an assembly line job but let his son work in high finance?

A: Because Main Street and Wall Street are powerful symbols. One place is where the powerless work, and the other place is where the powerful work. Over the years in writing and rewriting this story, I worked very hard at trying to make the father and son individual enough of characters to win readers' sympathies, yet representative enough to stimulate readers' intellects.

Q: Why did you choose a straightforward narrative storytelling approach, as opposed to some of the more fashionable stream-of-consciousness, diary/memoir, or other catchy modern approaches?

A: I've always preferred reading fiction that is beautifully written, yet understandable and readable. A well-written, straightforward narrative can be transforming and rewarding, yet accessible. Plus my degrees are in accounting and law, so I was trained in a more linear form of storytelling.

Q: How much of your novel is autobiographical?

A: I grew up in a small town. I worked on farms, at gas stations, and on an assembly line. I was never suspended from school or arrested. I did not deal drugs or lose my virginity in a trade for gas money. Also, thankfully, my mother is alive and well.

Q: Can you explain who Pete Statelman is, and why you dedicated your novel to him?

A: I met Pete about five years into my quarter century effort to get this novel published. For a couple of years in the 1990s, Pete was the night security clerk in my office building. I often worked late and, on my way out, I would see Pete reading great books of literature. So I struck up a conversation with him and we became friends. He worked for minimum wage, plus a 10 percent night shift premium. He was a highly educated and extremely well read guy about twenty years older than me, but he lived a pauper's and vagabond's life. He offered to take a look at my manuscript. Over the ensuing two decades, even after Pete had moved away, he wrote me long letters from various places in America critiquing my novel and offering advice on how to better structure and polish it. He helped me come up with the novel's title, along with the poem by the same name that appears in the novel. Pete seemed to innately know the story I was trying to tell, and he seemed to know how to pull it out of me and force me to shape it properly. Perhaps that's because Pete has his own mysterious story that remains shrouded in secrecy, at least from me.

Q: Are you currently working on another novel? If so, can you offer any details?

A: Yes, I have started another novel. Right now I don't want to say much about it. But it addresses income inequality and wealth disparity, which I think are critical social and cultural issues damaging not only the United States, but also harming many other countries around the world. People everywhere are increasingly living in an economically segregated world. Even fully developed western countries are becoming more like plutocracies, where the wealthy increasingly have all the power. So I hope to show how some modern-day lords think, feel, and act. I also want to reveal the fears and anxieties that reside within the rest of us. For some time now, I've been wondering why Occupy Wall Street fizzled after so much promise. Why isn't there any real class warfare going on in the world? Perhaps I secretly want to stoke one. A nonviolent one, of course.

Acknowledgments

RATEFUL ACKNOWLEDGMENT IS MADE to Pete Statelman for his keen storytelling insights and collaboration on the poem that ultimately gave this book its title, and to Adele Kimmel for permission to include her poem *The Warden's Resignation* and for her collaboration on the untitled poem in this book.

Over the quarter-century gestation period for this book, many people read and commented on earlier drafts. I particularly want to thank Karen Sonnergren, Ed Bungert, Don Pierce, Dick Marek, Ed Immergut, Annie LaHaie, and Steve Schlesser. I also want to thank my former law firm, Covington & Burling, which long ago granted me a nearly one-year sabbatical to compose the first draft.

And, finally, special thanks, gratitude, and love to my parents, my wife Karin, and my daughters Jessica and Elsa.